EVERYTHING MUST GO

ALSO BY CAMILLE PAGÁN

Don't Make Me Turn This Life Around

This Won't End Well

I'm Fine and Neither Are You

Woman Last Seen in Her Thirties

Forever Is the Worst Long Time

Life and Other Near-Death Experiences

The Art of Forgetting

EVERYTHING MUST GO

a novel

Camille Pagán

LAKE UNION
PUBLISHING

Published by Lake Union Publishing, Seattle

www.apub.com

ISBN-13: 9781542037426 (hardcover)
ISBN-10: 1542037425 (hardcover)

ISBN-13: 9781542037433 (paperback)
ISBN-10: 1542037433 (paperback)

Cover design and illustration by Liz Casal

Printed in the United States of America

First edition

In memory of Rachael Brönsink Stiles

ONE

Laine

In the end, the dog did us in; Josh and I might have stayed together if Belle hadn't died. She was nearly fifteen, which is about as long as a spaniel mix can live, and there was a constellation of cancer in her abdomen. The decision to put her down wasn't, really. It would've been cruel to try to keep her alive.

For weeks after that final vet visit, I burst into tears whenever I thought of her. I was standing at the stove, sobbing over a pan of fajita chicken—Belle's favorite—when Josh sidled up to me and said, "She's a dog, Laine. I know it isn't fair, but they don't live forever."

"Was, Josh," I sniffled. "She *was* a dog." Actually, she'd been something else entirely, a creature wise and otherworldly. To look into Belle's eyes was to gaze into the soul of the Universe itself and be seen—not that I would've described it that way to Josh, who'd loved Belle but thought it was weird to call your pet your best friend. I'd once thought so, too, but that was before I'd learned just how disappointing humans can be. A dog, on the other hand, never said terrible things you couldn't erase from your memory. "And of course I know that," I told him. "I just miss her."

I adopted Belle the year after I graduated from the University of Michigan. I'd decided to stay in Ann Arbor and had landed a job as an editorial assistant for a local magazine publisher. But after six months of employment, I'd deduced that I would never improve my command of the English language by fetching coffee for the perpetually hungover editor I'd been assigned to—and worse, the magazine's writers were making more than I was for much less work. I struck out as a freelance journalist and discovered that I'd been right about the money—and as a bonus, I no longer had to worry about having a pencil thrown at me when I accidentally put too much cream in a cup of dark roast.

Still, all of my college friends had left town, and I was lonely. On a whim, I went to the local animal shelter on my twenty-third birthday. When I spotted a black-and-white runt huddling in the corner of the pen in an attempt to steer clear of her livelier siblings, it was love at first sight.

Belle had immediately become my constant companion. She'd slept at my feet every night; her wet nose had been my alarm clock each morning. If Josh and I traveled, Belle almost always came with us, which admittedly limited the type of trips we'd taken (well, that and our anemic budget). When Josh had told me he still wasn't ready to try to have a baby last Christmas—even though he'd been saying "next year" for nearly half a decade and was aware that my eggs were *thisclose* to their expiration date—I'd reassured myself that the timing wasn't good for Belle, either, as it'd become increasingly difficult for her to get around. She needed me.

I'd just turned off the burner when it hit me: no one needed me anymore. And if I kept waiting around for Josh to decide he was ready to start a family, no one ever would.

I wasn't going to pressure him—not about something as significant as whether to repopulate the earth with his own genetic material. He either wanted to or he didn't. And given the economy pack of prophylactics in the drawer of his bedside table, it was safe to say that he did not.

I looked up at Josh. "I want a divorce."

The flicker of surprise in his expression was gone as fast as it had appeared. "No, you don't. That's just the grief talking."

This wasn't beyond the realm of possibility. Yes, I really wanted a baby—and I also knew, deep down, that perpetually putting it off was Josh's thinly veiled way of saying no. But was I willing to blow up our twelve-year marriage over that? What would our families say? Josh and I had spent nearly our entire adult lives together.

I stared at him, waiting to see if he'd at least ask if this was about us having kids.

Instead, he shook his head and said, "This is nuts, Laine. You don't actually want a divorce. I can tell by the look on your face."

I didn't know what my face looked like, but I was willing to bet that beyond my newfound wrinkles—which, like a brood of cicadas, had emerged suddenly and all at once—there was at least some sadness there. That January, Josh and I had gone to New York to meet my older sister Hadley's newborn twins, Asher and Ainsley. When Hadley had placed Ainsley in my arms, she'd been so tiny and perfect that I'd started to cry a little. Josh noticed and asked if I was okay. I assured him I was fine—just struck by the miracle of life in a way that I never had been before, even after the births of my youngest sister Piper's three kids. "I'm so looking forward to becoming a mother," I'd explained, gazing down at Ainsley's downy skin.

Josh hadn't responded, and at the time, I'd tried not to make a big deal of that. Afterward, I'd almost been able to let it go; Belle had just gotten diagnosed, and I'd been so busy trying to make her comfortable that there wasn't room for other concerns. Now I saw that his nonresponse had been the moment I realized—if only on a subconscious level—that the one thing I truly wanted for my future was the same thing he did not. And with Belle gone, there was nothing to distract me from that truth.

I met Josh's gaze, waiting for him to say he was at least willing to acknowledge what this was really about. Because he had to know. He just *had* to.

"Come on, Laine," he said. "We're about to have dinner." He was as lean as a greyhound and had a boyishness to him that made his frown seem almost petulant. Usually I thought it was cute, but now I kind of wanted to tell him to grow up. "And you know I'm in the middle of a launch."

Josh was always in the middle of launching something—a new consulting company; a partnership with some purported marketing genius; or most recently, yet another phone app that was going to be the one that finally made us wildly wealthy, never mind that I would have been thrilled with markedly middle class. He identified as an entrepreneur, and while this wasn't inaccurate, all that dreaming and scheming had yet to produce a business that made more money than it cost to run. In the beginning, I thought he was a visionary. In time, I began to have doubts—not about his brilliance but rather his ability to turn his visions into reality. Now, after a fourteen-year partnership, I'd come to believe that the four most frightening words in the English language were *I have an idea*.

I was not one to admit this, however. Because I loved Josh. He wasn't a mouth breather, didn't mind when I organized his underwear drawer, and was unflaggingly kind to waitstaff, which was to say he possessed many of the qualities I most desired in a partner. But really—I'd fallen in love with him because he believed in me; he saw possibilities for me where I did not, and his ideas for me actually seemed to work. For nearly a decade, one magazine after another had announced that it was again tightening its belt or, worse, folding. But late last year, it was Josh who suggested I harness my neat-freak tendencies and start a side business as a professional organizer. After just a few months, I was already making nearly as much organizing closets and cupboards part-time as I had working overtime as a writer. I loved the work, to say nothing of the instant gratification of a job well done and an immediate paycheck.

Most of all, though, Josh was really, *really* good with my family. My prickly father had adored him; my mother still did, as he always made her feel like the most important person in the room. He asked Hadley for advice, which was basically her love language. And whereas most men made Piper—who had praying mantis proportions and exaggerated facial features and had been a model since she was fourteen—feel like she was on display at the zoo, he acted like she was . . . well, normal. As a result, they were more friends than in-laws.

But if I had to pinpoint our problems (and I'd always tried awfully hard to avoid doing just that, as what good ever came from searching for trouble?), Josh and I were one of those couples whose conversations revolved almost entirely around our families and careers. Come to think of it, that was probably why we preferred to go to the movies for date night. And for the past year or so, we'd made love about as often as solar eclipses occurred. He swore it was because he was stressed about work. Now I couldn't help but wonder if that, too, was secretly related to his reticence to be a father.

"What's this about, Laine?" he said, rubbing his forehead.

Bad enough that his *launch* was the reason he seemed to think I shouldn't have brought up divorce. But if Josh couldn't see that my heart had been broken into a thousand paw-shaped pieces and that the only way to fix it was to tell me he wanted to try for a baby—today, and preferably right there on the kitchen floor before the fajitas triggered his reflux—

Well, then he and I had come to an end.

There was the issue of my not wanting to hurt him. Except he didn't look hurt. He was still standing there as calm as if I'd just informed him that I'd overcooked the chicken. I suppose I was, too, and now my eyes were dry.

"And if you weren't launching?" I said. "Then would you think it was a good time?" Experience told me that in about three to four months, his app, which was supposed to help people power nap, would have already gone the way of the mastodon. Of course, I wasn't really talking about coordinating our separation. But I couldn't bring myself to say, *This is about you, after a dozen years of marriage, not knowing the one thing that would make me say* never mind about getting a divorce.

It occurred to me that I was giving him an ultimatum of sorts, which wasn't like me. But I hadn't felt like myself since Belle had died three weeks ago. And I wasn't sure I ever would again.

"Laine," he said with a sigh, "you're missing the point."

"Isn't *that* the point?" I said, trying hard to keep my voice down; Josh and I didn't fight, and I certainly didn't want anything, even severing our marriage, to change that. "You and I aren't on the same page anymore. We want different things."

"That's crazy." His dark eyes narrowed. "But maybe I'm missing something. What exactly do you want?"

I stared at him, wondering if he'd failed to mention a recent head injury. Was he *actually* asking me to spell it out? When Josh had proposed all those years ago, I asked him what he saw for our future—after all, he loved talking about what was up ahead. He'd responded, "Well, Laine, we're going to be filthy rich and have a happy family." And the latter part of that declaration was exactly what I wanted to hear. I hadn't cared about a fluffy white dress and a magazine spread of a reception, or even swoon-worthy vows. No, I wanted a child. Being one of three myself, I knew that *more* usually meant less attention. Just a single small human to love me would do. They'd be the center of my universe, and naturally Josh's, too. That's what I'd wanted from my own mother; although she'd loved me and done her best, her focus had been not unlike wonky cellular service, in that getting through required you to stand in the exact right spot when the stars were aligned. But me? I'd get lots of things wrong, no doubt. My child, however, would always know that I was there for them.

"Just wait," Josh had said, gazing at me like he'd hand me the moon if I asked for it. "We'll be amazing parents one day."

But one day still had not come.

Now, if I confessed that the D-bomb I'd lobbed at him was actually a pre-paternity quiz, it was entirely possible he'd give in just to keep the peace. Because if Josh and I had anything in common, it was our aversion to hurting other people's feelings. And that was great when it came to, say, artfully declining an invitation to a multilevel marketing sales pitch disguised as a cocktail party. But this was our future child we were talking about, even if said child was still just a single cell in my body. And they didn't deserve to have a parent whose heart wasn't really in it.

So I took a deep breath, silently apologized for the half lie I was about to tell, and said, "I don't know what I want, but it isn't this."

TWO

Laine

Josh spent that evening acting like I'd been the one who'd suffered a concussion. "You're just upset about Belle," he kept muttering. "It'll pass."

And at first, I'd wondered if he was right. Still, I decided to sleep in the small second bedroom of our town house. I used it as an office, but we kept a futon in there for the houseguests who'd never actually materialized; Josh's family wasn't far from Ann Arbor, where we lived, and mine expected us to visit them in New York (probably because that's what we always did). I'd assumed that one day in the near future, it would become a nursery. I'd even painted the walls a delicate gray so that it would be easy to redecorate when we were ready. Best-laid plans and all that.

As it happened, sleeping on a lumpy mattress that smelled like wet dog—but *my* wet dog, which was at once comforting and heart-wrenching—only made my biological clock tick even louder. So when my phone lit up on my desk the following morning, I'd been in the middle of Googling all things fertility.

It was Hadley, so I declined the call to continue reading about how decidedly un-rosy my pregnancy prospects were. It was the end of May;

I would turn thirty-eight in July. Some of the medical websites I'd been browsing suggested I might still have time, since my mother'd had Piper at thirty-seven. But that had been her third child, and in a cruel twist of fate, it turned out that the more children a woman already had, the less trouble she typically had getting pregnant. And Hadley, who was forty but also luckier than me and loaded, had gone through fertility treatment for more than two years before finally giving birth to her twins.

Come to think of it, Hadley was probably the best person to talk to about this. Trouble was, I didn't actually *want* to tell her about Josh. Hadley and I hadn't been close as kids—she was always off running this student organization or doing that honors project, and then she graduated from high school early and took off for Yale, and that was that. I hadn't needed her back then. But as adults, we'd come to realize that being raised by the same parents at the same time was like being the last few to speak a dying language. Admittedly, Hadley and I were more alike than we were different, whereas Piper was, quite frankly, unlike anyone I'd ever met. Really, Hadley was my closest friend these days.

Yet she was nonetheless my sister—and a sister said things that most friends would not. The minute I admitted what I'd done, she was going to list all the reasons I was a fool. Worse, I wouldn't be able to tell her the truth about why I'd made that decision, because either she or Piper would call Josh and tell *him* that this was about me wanting to start a family immediately, and he would then acquiesce to impregnating me out of obligation. How odd that the thing I'd spent years longing for was now the very one I was trying to avoid.

I'd just put my phone on silent when Hadley's name appeared on the screen again. My sisters and I had a rule: if it was important, we'd call twice. I sighed and picked up. "Hey, Had. What's wrong?"

"You tell *me*," she said.

I hated when she did that—pulled out her freaky psychic ability to just know when something was upsetting me. She'd probably sensed a disturbance in the force the moment I dropped a grenade on my marriage last night and had been waiting for me to muster the courage to tell her about it.

"You're the one who called twice," I pointed out.

"True. It's about Mom."

It often was; Hadley was forever complaining about our mother. Unfortunately, most of her complaints were valid—and I'd made it my personal mission not to focus on our mother's shortcomings, as there was no reason for life to be any more unpleasant than it already was.

"Let me guess: either her favorite shade of lipstick has been discontinued or she's been buried beneath her belongings," I said. Our mother believed herself a collector of fine objects, but she was a hoarder by any other name. (You can see, then, why I had a thing about organizing.) When my father had been alive, he complained enough that she'd kept her stockpiling somewhat under control. But since he'd died four years earlier, the Brooklyn apartment where we'd grown up and she still lived had become uncomfortably packed.

"I wish," said Hadley. "Unfortunately, Bashir found her wandering through the aisles this morning."

Bashir ran the bodega down the street from my childhood home. We'd spent our adolescence lurking around there. Sometimes he'd give us free candy and tell us to get lost, but mostly he'd played the part of friendly uncle, showing us the right way to count out change or demanding the name of whoever had broken our hearts so he could have a word with them. "So?" I said. "Maybe she was hungry."

"She was buying cat food."

Phone still to my ear, I stood to stretch my legs, which were as stiff as sticks. Every day, my body presented new evidence of its rapid entropy. This didn't bode well for my uterus. "And?"

"And she hasn't had a cat since before Dad died."

"How do we know she hasn't adopted another one?" My mother was not a dog person, which was another reason I rarely made the trip from Ann Arbor. But she had yet to meet a feral feline she didn't want to call her own.

"Because I was just at the apartment last week." *Unlike you*—we both knew that was what she meant.

"I was just in town in January, Had," I reminded her. "I saw Mom plenty while I was there, and she seemed just fine." In fact, the visit had been unusually easy; Asher and Ainsley's arrival had put her in a nostalgic mood, and she told all kinds of stories about what the three of us had been like as babies. Apparently Hadley had walked and talked early, and Piper had come out looking like she belonged on a jar of baby food. And if my mother were to be believed, I'd bypassed first words and waited until I could clearly articulate an entire sentence to begin interacting with the rest of my family.

"Maybe she did, but she's not now. Do you know what Bashir told me? Mom was in her *nightgown*. I bet it was one of those lacy ones that she has no business wearing."

"Well, if I live to be seventy-two, I'm going to wear whatever the heck I want, too. Anyway, that's just like Mom. You know she thrives on attention."

"For the love, Lainey."

I snorted. There was nothing offensive about that nickname, except that whenever I heard it, I immediately became my fourteen-year-old self. And that self was markedly less tolerant of her older sister, who had long mistaken her for someone who needed a second mother. Granted, Hadley *had* often played the role out of necessity—forging my parents' signatures on permission slips and report cards that my mother had neglected, slipping me cash so I could get a hot lunch when I'd forgotten the one Hadley had packed for me, even taking me shopping for my first bra. Still. I was fast approaching forty. "I clearly don't get what you're trying to say, Had. Feel free to enlighten me."

Hadley let out a long sigh, which was followed by a wail from one of her twins in the background. "Mom's losing it, Laine. And we need to talk about what we're going to do about that." Another cry rang out, and a mix of envy and sadness began swirling inside of me. I knew infertility had been a struggle for my sister. But now that she was on the other side of it, I wondered how often she thought about how lucky she was.

"Leticia!" Hadley yelled directly into the receiver. "Can you please check on Ainsley!"

"That was my ear," I said, wincing. "But for the record, I really don't think Mom is 'losing it.'"

"You haven't noticed that she keeps forgetting the words for things?"

"We've talked about this before." Our mother had been more scatterbrained since our father had died, but it had yet to cause any major problems for her. "Being alone isn't great for clear thinking," I added. I knew this because I'd done a story on surprising causes of memory loss for a health website a few months earlier. In fact, that was probably why I'd been unable to pluck the term *garment box* from the recesses of my mind while shopping at the Container Store the week before. Josh had always worked out of coffee shops and shared office spaces; he claimed the hum of human activity was essential for his creativity. But Belle had been my sounding board and de facto colleague. Now it was just me, rattling around in a tiny office that suddenly seemed far too large. Evenings aside, my life as a divorcée wouldn't be all that different from my current existence, which seemed doubly depressing.

"Lonely? She's a social butterfly," said Hadley. "She's seeing her wine club and bridge buddies instead of spending all her time by herself. Regardless, something's wrong. The other day, she started talking about Dad like he was still alive."

"I do that with Belle." It was true: her urn was on a small table beside my desk, and more than once, I'd spoken to it just as I used to when she'd hang out on the futon while I typed away. At first, I was alarmed by my own behavior, but according to Google, this was a relatively normal way to deal with grief.

Still, hearing that my mother was having one-woman conversations made me feel guilty. I'd decided long ago not to bother trying to peer beneath her glossy facade. In my twenties, I'd once asked her if she resented my father, who was always hiding out in the small workshop he'd built on the back patio; when he was around, she practically had to do circus tricks to get his attention (and even then, he often rewarded her by grousing about how the house was a mess). The only time they ever seemed happy was when they were on their way to the cabin they rented in the Berkshires, which I cannot describe because we girls had never been invited—not once. At any rate, she'd looked at me like I'd just sprouted a second head. "Laine Francis, that's the most ridiculous thing I've ever heard. Your father and I have a wonderful marriage," she'd scoffed. "We're incredibly lucky." Going deep with her was a fool's errand.

Except now I wondered if maybe I should've tried harder anyway.

"Sure, Laine, but Belle's only been gone three weeks," said Hadley.

Maybe it was the fact that she remembered how long it had been and hadn't called Belle "the dog" like everyone else did, but my throat had gotten tight and I couldn't respond right away.

"Laine? You still there?"

I swallowed hard. "I'm here."

"What's coming up for you?" she asked in what I recognized as her coaching voice. Hadley had become a life coach because—well, because of course she had. Telling other people how to live was what she was born to do. I paused in a futile attempt to enjoy my last moment of peace for the foreseeable future. She believed all problems were fixable, and my marriage would be no exception. And yet now that we were on the phone, it felt dishonest not to tell her.

Also, maybe deep down I was hoping she would fix me.

"Um, nothing?" I said. "Except Josh and I are getting divorced, and before you ask why, I'm not ready to talk about it yet."

There was silence on the other end, which told me that she was just as stunned as I felt. Sure, I'd already told Josh. But admitting it to my sister made the decision feel . . . real.

She cleared her throat. "Wow. I knew something was up, but a *divorce*? You? Josh? Have you been brainwashed by a cult? Abducted by an alien and implanted with a microchip or three?"

The laugh I attempted came out like a snort. "Negative on both counts."

"Then what, Laine? You two are the happiest couple I know."

But I didn't want to be a happy couple anymore. I wanted to be a happy *family*. Except I was afraid to tell Hadley this. Josh had basically been a brother to Hadley since the day I'd brought him home to meet everyone, and Hadley didn't believe in keeping secrets from the people she loved. If I told her, she would for sure tell Josh.

"Where is this coming from, Laine? Did Josh *cheat* on you?"

"No."

"Hurt you?"

"Of course not."

"I didn't think so, but that's still a relief. So what is it, then? I mean, a separation is one thing. A little time away from each other is totally understandable. But a divorce? That's like cutting off your nose to spite your face. Josh is a part of our family."

"I didn't say you couldn't talk to him again."

"But he's not going to come home for Christmas. Or go on vacation with us," she said, even though we hadn't traveled together in several years. She continued, "He won't be a part of our family anymore, Lainey. Not the way he is now."

I squeezed my lids shut. She was right, of course. What was I even doing? "I know that. And that all sucks. But . . . well, I can't get into it. I'll tell you more when I'm ready."

"I'll be waiting," she said, not unkindly. "And when you're ready to process your emotions, you know I'm happy to help."

That was a hard pass from me. "Thanks, but I'm good."

"Listen, I don't want to tell you what to do."

This was often what my sister said right before she told me what to do.

Sure enough: "Why don't you come to New York for a little bit? Just to clear your head and get some perspective. It'll give us a chance to sit down together and talk about what we're going to do about Mom. No pressure, but I *could* use your help with her, even for a couple of days. The twins are nursing around the clock, and I've still got a full client load. And you know Piper's got her hands full with her kids and all of her shoots."

Most models fizzled out by their late teens, but Piper had defied the odds. Just the other day, I'd opened a magazine to look for a story I'd written, only to see my little sister staring back at me, draped in more jewelry than a sane person would ever actually wear at one time. Maybe it was because her career had launched her into adulthood early, but she'd gotten a head start on having kids, too. Her eldest, Rocco, was already ten; Jae was eight; and Kaia was five.

"I'm not asking you to move here," said Hadley. "Just, like, take a week to make sure Mom's not eating expired food and leaving her front door open for all of New York to pick through her things."

"A rummage sale isn't the worst idea. 'Everything must go!'" I managed to quip. Besides my mother's actual death, one of the things I dreaded most was having to deal with her belongings. Sure, I was a whiz at organizing. Still, she had so. Much. Stuff.

"Har har. Seriously, come visit! I'll pay for the plane ticket if you want—Topper and I are happy to cover the fare." Hadley's husband, Topper, was a young guy with old money and had a 10 percent stake in the city of Manhattan (only a slight exaggeration). "You don't have to drive now that . . . well, just let me know."

There was a new lump in my throat. I didn't have to drive now that Belle could no longer make the ten-hour trip with me.

"Hey, Laine?"

"Yeah?"

"I probably shouldn't tell you this, but I'll feel bad if I don't."

"Okay . . ." I waited for her to say something about Josh.

Instead, she said, "Ben's in town. I ran into him when I went to check on Mom last week. I just thought you should know, since you're coming to visit."

I nearly dropped the phone.

I'd describe Ben as my oldest friend, but the truth was, we hadn't been friends since the winter before I graduated from college. Yet the very mention of his name and what I'd been calling a scar revealed itself as a wound that had never fully healed.

"That's impossible," I scoffed. "He's in Australia. Maybe you saw someone else." Then my face flushed, because I only would have known he was on the other side of the continent if I was checking up on him on social media. (Which was, of course, exactly what I'd been doing.)

"Nope," said Hadley. "He's back. I talked to him for a minute."

I inhaled sharply, waiting for her to tell me what they'd spoken about.

"I really hope that isn't a reason for you not to see us."

"Ridiculous," I spat.

"Good, then you'll come," she said, and just like that, I saw that I'd been outmaneuvered. "I'll have Topper's assistant reach out to you about a flight. Can't wait for you to see how big the twins have gotten. They miss their auntie. And I do, too."

"Love you," I said.

"Love you more."

I sat there staring at the wall for a long time after we got off the phone. And instead of worrying about my mother's so-called declining mind, or the future of my marriage or the statistical probability that I could carry a baby, all I could think about was Ben and how much I did *not* want to run into him after sixteen years.

But also, how much I did.

THREE

Laine

I was six when Ben and his family moved in three doors down from the brownstone my parents owned. It was a hot summer morning, and I was on the stoop, waiting for Hadley and her friends to stop ignoring me and ask me to jump rope with them; Piper, who was still too small to be on her own, was inside with my mother.

Then their moving van pulled up and out climbed Reggie, Ben's father. Ben's older brother, Bobby, was trailing behind him. Ben's mother must have been there, too—she didn't disappear until a couple of years later—but I don't remember her now and can't even recall what she looked like anymore.

Then there was Ben. He was short and skinny, with close-cropped hair and warm brown skin. As Reggie fished keys out of his pocket and began up the stairs of the brownstone where they'd just purchased an apartment, Ben leaned against the wrought-iron fence like he didn't have a care in the world. When he spotted me, he smiled and waved. I glanced over my shoulder to see if he was waving at someone else, but Hadley and her friends were at the other end of the block and there was no one behind me. So I smiled and waved back.

I think he's about my age, I thought as he disappeared after Reggie into the brownstone. *But he'll probably want to play with Hadley.* Everyone always wanted to play with Hadley, who knew all the games and all the places to hang and all the kids in our neighborhood. But me? While I wasn't naturally shy, being Hadley's sister sometimes made me feel that way, and my closest friend, Tracy, had moved away that winter. So I spent most of my time finding ways to entertain myself. That usually meant cleaning up after everyone, since it was the best way to get my mother's attention without throwing a tantrum.

A few minutes later, Ben emerged from the apartment on his own. He looked around for a moment before ambling over to our stoop.

"Hi," he said. "My name's Ben. What's yours?"

"I'm Laine," I said. He was smaller than me but seemed more grown-up. Or maybe just self-assured in a way that I wasn't. "You moving in here?"

"Yep. What's it like?" I'd later learn that they'd moved from California; Reggie, who was an engineer, had been transferred for work.

"S'okay. I've never lived anywhere else." My mother's father had purchased a run-down brownstone back when our Brooklyn neighborhood, Carroll Gardens, was a working-class haven rather than the yuppie mecca it's since become. He'd spent years renovating the brownstone and turning it into a two-family home; my mother had inherited the whole building after her parents moved to Florida. We'd lived on the ground and garden floors, and my parents rented out the floor above us.

"Cool," he said. "Wanna be friends?"

Something told me he wasn't into My Little Pony or Care Bears and wasn't going to want to have a tea party with me, the way Tracy had. And I didn't care one bit. "Yeah," I said.

"Me, too. I better go back before my dad starts looking for me. But maybe we can play later."

Then he stuck out his hand. It was such a funny, adult thing to do that I burst into giggles, but I shook it all the same.

"Friends," he said, and when he looked at me, I got the weirdest feeling. Later I would recognize it as the feeling you get when someone sees you—really sees you. But I wouldn't fully understand just how rare that was until it was too late.

"Friends," I said.

And we were for fifteen years, until he told me I was a people pleaser who would rather please a manipulator than her oldest friend—and I made the mistake of trying to defend that manipulator.

Because she was my mother.

FOUR

Sally

Three girls. A gift—that's what my mother always said. She was one of three, and yet she had just me. It was a different time, she claimed. She and my father didn't have much, especially in the beginning; they didn't want me to ever know what it was like to own but a single dress, or to split two potatoes among five people and call it supper. I was the one to have a big family. I would've kept going, too, if Hank hadn't told me three was enough. So our apartment wasn't the Plaza. So what? I loved the sound of all those voices in one place. I miss them, my girls. New York's become too big for my taste. Piper is . . . where is it she and her gaggle live lately? That loft in Tribeca. No, no, she's over in Williamsburg now. Of course. Closer, if only as the crow flies. And it takes Hadley an hour to get here from the Upper East Side. It would be faster if she'd take the train like she used to. Better yet, she could move to Brooklyn Heights or Cobble Hill. Heaven knows she and Topper could afford to buy a whole block if they were so inclined.

But maybe it's better if Hadley's not here too often. She thinks something's wrong with me. She doesn't have to say it—I know. I know. I see her hawk eyes, the way she listens too closely when I speak.

Perhaps she's right. I did give Bashir more than he bargained for, though I didn't realize it until I caught him with his mouth hanging open. Like the things teens wear these days aren't far worse! Just yesterday, I saw two bottom cheeks peeking out of a pair of shorts, and that child couldn't have been older than fifteen.

Laine. I'll call Laine. My girl, my easy girl. You're not supposed to pick favorites, and, of course, I haven't, but it's nice to be able to speak to at least one of your daughters and not have her tell you—a fully grown woman who managed to raise three self-sufficient humans—how to live your life.

"Laine, dear? It's Mom."

"Hey, Mom." She sounded tired. She'll never admit it, but a mother always knows. "How are you?"

"I'm fine, just fine. I saw Shawna this morning." Bless her, I look a decade younger than I did when I walked into the salon. That woman has a way with color.

"I'm glad to hear that. What else have you been up to? Have you been to wine club lately?"

Have I? Just yesterday, wasn't it? Or no—last weekend.

"Mom? Are you there?"

"I'm here! Just thinking about the new Bordeaux we tried. Oh, and we had the most exquisite Rasteau."

"That sounds nice."

"It was! And you, love? How's Josh? And Belle?"

When she didn't respond, I knew I'd done something wrong. I just couldn't figure out what, exactly.

Then I remembered. "Oh, Lainey, I apologize—I forgot about your dog. She's been with you so long, and, well—this is just so sudden. I'm very sorry, dear. I am."

She sniffled, but then she said, "It's okay. I'm getting over it. Hey, Mom?"

"Yes, Lainey?"

"I need to talk to you about something."

Oh dear. Nothing good ever came after that sentence. "What is it, love?"

"It's about me and Josh."

But I was wrong—this was very good indeed! "You're expecting, aren't you? How wonderful!"

More silence. *Dear Sally Francis, could you stop shoving your foot in your trap for a change?* "I'm sorry, Lainey. I shouldn't have jumped to conclusions. I've just been so eager to be a grandmother."

Another sniffle. "You already have five grandchildren. And knowing Hadley and her bionic uterus, she's probably not done yet."

"Yes, well, I mean one of *your* children. You two would have such beautiful babies." With Laine's sturdy Ukrainian stock and Josh's fine Japanese features—oh, their children would just be gorgeous. So odd that, after all these years, they still hadn't had any. They never said they didn't want to. Maybe Laine, like Hadley, had been struggling to get pregnant.

"Yeah. I thought so, too." She paused. "But Josh and I are divorcing."

It took me a moment to process what she'd just said. "I'm sorry . . . what?"

"It's kind of a long story, but we want different things."

"Laine, my love, you're very smart, but what you want is hardly the most important thing in a marriage." I glanced over my shoulder at the kitchen table. A chill came over me when I realized what I was doing. Hank was always with me, of course. But he hadn't been *here* here for more than four years. And yet lately . . . well, no matter.

"Maybe so, Mom, but it's over for me and Josh. I'll tell you more later, but I just thought you should know."

At once, I felt very heavy, like I used to when the girls would pull on my arms and legs to get my attention when they were small. "Oh, Laine, we love Josh. And I know you do, too! Are you sure about this?"

She wasn't—otherwise, she would have answered me right away. I felt my heart swell; there was still hope.

"I don't want to talk about it quite yet," she said. "I just felt . . . like I should tell you."

"Thank you," I said. Laine wasn't a talker, not like Hadley, so when she told me something, it meant more somehow.

"Thanks. The real reason I called is because Hadley called me."

"I should hope so. We were just saying we don't see nearly enough of you."

"Yeah, she asked me to come visit. I'm thinking about it. But, Mom . . . are you doing okay?"

"What do you mean?"

"I mean Hadley says you've been forgetful lately."

Well, yes. But wasn't a woman allowed to have a moment from time to time? "You and I both know that your sister is always making a mountain out of a mudslide."

Laine coughed. "Molehill."

"Tomato, tomahto. But, darling, why *don't* you come visit? I could use some help around here."

"Really?"

"What do you mean, 'really'? I would never ask if I didn't mean it."

"It's just that you don't usually like anyone to . . . touch your stuff."

No, I didn't, and Laine had followed me around for nearly eighteen years sifting and sorting. However well intentioned, all that organizing meant my things often got broken, went missing, or were declared unnecessary. As if there were such a thing. Besides food, water, and heat, what is *necessary*, anyway? Then again, Laine did keep Hank off my back for all those years. "Mostly I need some help with my bills, love. There's a pile of them and they exhaust me. Also, I haven't been able to find the password for my online bank account."

"Mom. That's kind of a big deal. Did you tell Hadley? You know she'll be there in a heartbeat."

"I didn't ask for her help." Because she'd probably use it as evidence that I needed to be shipped off to an old-folks home. I'd sooner leave in a body bag. "I asked for yours." She was quiet on the other end of the line, so I said, "Hadley? Are you there?"

"It's Laine, Mom. And I'm here."

Oh dear. But I always did get them confused. "HaLaPi," Hank and I used to call the lot of them, and sometimes we'd just yell that out. Of course, it was almost always Laine who'd come running. And even now, she was being gentle with me, as was her way. She'd never shine a light on my flaws. "HaLaPi!" I said as cheerfully as I could.

She sighed, and I felt the tiniest bit of fear start to zip through my veins. I needed her. I needed her to come see that I was fine, truly I was. It was just that I could use a little help from someone who wouldn't judge me.

And Laine must have known that, because she said, "I'm flying in later this week."

FIVE

LAINE

Josh came rushing into the town house just as I was wheeling my suitcase to the front door. "Can we talk?" he said, slightly out of breath; he'd been at a ridiculously early breakfast meeting with an investor. Though his face was unlined and his hair was still thick and free of grays, he looked tired, and kind of down in the mouth. I probably did, too. Nearly a week had passed since I announced I wanted a divorce, and I think both of us had been waiting to see if this was a storm of a mood that would suddenly pass, leaving a rainbow in its place.

Instead, I kept dreaming about babies—Hadley's twins, my neighbor's adorable toddler, infants that didn't exist but felt all too real in my dreams. And when I opened my eyes in the morning, I felt the same sense of absolute certainty about my decision to end our marriage. The trouble was, that certainty waned as the day went on. Just the night before, I'd thought about crawling into bed with Josh and calling the whole thing off. It was a good thing I was getting out of town for a while. Like Hadley said, I needed perspective; a chance to think without Josh being there all the time, influencing my decisions.

"Um, I guess? My Uber will be here any minute now," I said. Topper's assistant had emailed me with flight options within an hour of my getting off the phone with Hadley. After some debate, I'd decided to swallow my pride and accept their generosity because I couldn't stand the idea of spending ten hours in a car without Belle or Josh to keep me company.

He shoved his hands in his pockets. There was a latte trail down the front of his rumpled button-down, and I resisted the urge to tell him to hand it to me so I could go spot-treat it. "Sure you don't want me to drive you to the airport?" he asked.

"No, it's okay," I told him. The car service cost thirty dollars that I would have preferred to put in the savings account I'd earmarked for our future family life—the one we'd never have. But Josh seemed so unconvinced that I actually wanted to divorce that I'd started to wonder if he was onto something, and I was eager not to be in a confined space with him for even half an hour, lest I really lose my resolve. After all, I'd already announced my plan to my sisters and my mother. I couldn't take that back now. . .

Could I?

"Then I'll make it quick," he said. He was staring at me with puppy-dog eyes, which didn't bode well. "The thing is, Laine, I don't want to get divorced. What am I going to do without you?"

At once, I understood how faulty my reasoning had been. Belle was gone, but someone *did* need me: my husband.

And how. While the man could code in his sleep and do complex equations faster than I could figure out how much to tip a waiter, he was markedly less adept at handling everyday life. For example, his idea of cooking involved microwaving leftover takeout, and more than once, he'd walked around an entire day with his sweatpants on backward. (When I'd pointed this out to him, he'd admitted that something *had* seemed off about the fit.) Who would pay the bills, stock the fridge, and remind him to take his vitamins? Leaving him would be like abandoning a calf in front of a wolf den.

As my gaze moved from Josh's spiky black hair to the warmth of his dark eyes to the perpetual half grin of his thin lips, a wave of sadness came crashing over me. I adored him. He needed me. Why wasn't that enough?

It was almost like he was reading my thoughts, because he leaned forward and said, "I love you. Last I checked, you love me, too. Has that changed?"

"No," I said, shaking my head morosely. Josh and I had met not long after I'd adopted Belle. Like me, he'd attended the University of Michigan, although he'd been a year ahead of me. And like me, he'd decided to stay in town after graduation. I'd left Belle at the "dog parking" spot outside a café for all of a minute to order a coffee, and she'd barked her head off in protest until he'd strolled up and scratched behind her ears. And I'd immediately thought: *That's a man I could build a life with.*

Now here we were, nearly a decade and a half later. It pained me to think that for all of Josh's big plans, aside from Belle's absence, our daily existence now was almost exactly like it had been then.

He'd begun to pace. The man hunched like he was forever trying to catch wind of what an Oompa Loompa was saying, but somehow it was incredibly charming on him. Why couldn't he make this easy and say the one thing I'd been dying to hear? "You have to give me a chance to make this right, Laine," he said. "Actually, you know what?"

I didn't, and the glimmer in his eyes—which looked an awful lot like the one he got when he had one of his million-dollar ideas—was slightly alarming.

"I'll make an appointment with a marriage therapist," he said, nodding with satisfaction. "That's exactly what I'll do."

A zing of excitement zipped through me. Maybe a therapist would help him come around to the idea of having a family without me needing to push him.

Then reality set in, and with it, the quicksand of pessimism. I knew Josh better than he knew himself. And while I was sure he *intended* to make an appointment, he would immediately get distracted by work, and before long, he wouldn't even remember telling me that he was going to do that. Maybe he would have to learn how to tiptoe past the wolves on his own.

"Sure," I said, not meeting his gaze.

"You'll see, Laine. Haven't the past twelve years been good? Remember our honeymoon?"

Recalling the quaint bed-and-breakfast where we'd stayed in Old San Juan didn't lift my mood. We'd barely left our room except to get food, and even then, we'd run right back to bed. Where had that passion, that ease, gone?

"Remember when we first moved in here, the way Belle ran around out back like she was a puppy?" he said. The town house was beige and bland, but we'd chosen it because it was pet friendly and had a small yard—we'd get a bigger one when we had kids, we'd agreed.

Now my gloom was threatening to pull me right under. How had I not seen it earlier? Josh and I talked about children the way people who never bought a single lottery ticket discussed what they'd do once they won.

I blinked back sudden tears. "Obviously."

He'd stopped pacing and was looking at me intently. "And remember when my dad died, how you were there for me? Then I was able to do the same for you six months later?" Neither of us had been close to our fathers, and as we discovered, that can cause a very particular kind of pain. We'd spent hours rehashing memories and futilely wishing these two men—one a Japanese immigrant, the other a fourth-generation New Yorker—would have been less short-tempered and more present in our lives. Josh had vowed to be a better father than his own had been. What'd happened to that promise?

"Josh, I do. I remember all of that. But . . ." I wasn't going to guide him across the divide, but I'd at least shine a light in the right direction. "Where do you see us in ten years? Five, even?"

"I see us healthy and wealthy, living in a much bigger home that we actually own," he said immediately. Then he winced as he glanced around, like the very sight of our place—which was small, sure, but tidy and filled with the items we'd chosen for it—brought him shame. "I'll have started a new company, obviously. Maybe we'll get another dog."

I turned to the wall because if I kept looking at him, I'd either start sobbing or throw my suitcase at him. Another *dog*? Was he kidding right now?

A terrible thought occurred to me just then.

Josh was a wonderful person . . . who also happened to be deeply detached from the reality of here and now. And I could not deny that I'd enabled him to be that way, and I didn't know how not to do that anymore. Which meant he was never going to change—at least not while I was in the picture. And as such, we would not be having a child together, because he would never, ever be ready.

Through the window, I saw that a black sedan had pulled up in front of our town house. "That's me," I said.

"Let's keep talking about this—we'll figure it out," he said with so much confidence that I almost believed him. "Send my best to Mom." He was an only child who'd always called his own mother, Irene, by her first name, but mine had been *Mom* to him since the first time I brought him to New York. There was just something about my family, Josh remarked early on, that made him feel like he belonged.

"I will," I said.

"Hey, Laine?"

"Yeah?"

"I love you." His face got all screwed up then, and I almost told him I hadn't meant any of it. We were compassionate, intelligent human beings who'd vowed to stay together till death did us part! Surely, we could work through this whole baby situation.

But then I remembered that he hadn't mentioned kids once during the course of our conversation.

"I love you, too," I said quietly. "I'll see you in a week."

~

"This isn't weird at all. Right, girl?" I whispered.

The small ceramic urn I'd just taken out of my carry-on did not respond.

I was aware that it wasn't a great look, but I couldn't stand to leave Michigan without Belle—what was left of her, at least. Of course, even when Belle was alive, she wouldn't make a joke and lighten the mood when Hadley said something that ticked off Piper. Nor had she been the one to help me sort through the junk mail my mother had accumulated and empty her fridge of food that had expired six months earlier. That had always been Josh's job. And although it had been my choice to go without him, that decision had triggered a deep sort of loneliness that I hadn't felt since Belle died.

And so, in an arguably misguided attempt to feel just a little less alone, I was about to put my dog's ashy remains through the airport security scanner. Sometimes you had to do what you had to do.

"Excuse me!" I said to the woman who was looking at a computer screen filled with X-ray images of luggage. "I just want to give you a heads-up that there are . . . um, remains in this bin," I said, pointing to the gray container on the conveyer belt. "The one with the tiny vaselike-looking thing. I've sealed it with tape and placed it in a plastic bag." *Sorry, Belle,* I added silently as I glanced at the urn.

"We may have to open and examine it," said the agent, barely glancing in my general direction.

"If you do, you're going to get the ashes of a dead person all over everyone else's suitcases," I said sharply. I felt as shocked as the agent now looked, and not just because I'd just admitted aloud that I thought of my dog as a person. At any other time, I would've nicely asked her to be extra careful, but apparently initiating a divorce had strengthened my spine. As someone who had a long history of going above and beyond for others at her own expense, this was probably not the worst development. "You can call your supervisor if there are any issues," I added in a slightly less righteous tone.

Two minutes later, Belle was back in my bag. I glanced inside the carry-on one more time to make sure she was secure, but it only served to remind me how different this trip was going to be.

My eyes began to blur with tears, so I ducked into the bathroom. Once I was in a stall, I let myself sit there and cry for a little while—my flight was still an hour out—and when that was over, washed my hands and splashed water on my face and hoped no one would notice my swollen eyes.

Piper called just as I was approaching the gate. It took me a while to find my phone in my bag. When I picked up, I instantly regretted it.

"Gah, Lainey, why didn't you tell me you were coming in this weekend?" she said by way of a greeting.

I threw myself down in one of the seats near the podium. *There's still time to change your plans,* I reminded myself. "I knew Hadley would tell you," I told her. "And I'm going to be in town for a full week. We'll have plenty of time to talk about this."

"Well, good, but Rocco is going to be at Levi's when you get in, and he'll be disappointed," she said, and I could just see her pouting on the other line. Piper had divorced Levi, Rocco's dad, soon after giving birth to Rocco; she hadn't married Jae and Kaia's father, Silas, and unlike her and Levi, they were on good terms. Before I could ask about her younger two, she added, "Don't worry, Jae and Kaia are both with me for the weekend."

"Great. I can't wait to see everyone," I said with as much enthusiasm as I could muster. I was excited to hang out with my nephews and niece, but I still felt depleted from the emotional roller coaster of the past week—and preemptively exhausted from dealing with Piper. She was charming and gorgeous and had this way of making everything and everyone around her sparkle a little brighter. And sometimes it took an incredible amount of energy to orbit her sun.

"Well . . ." she said, and I waited for her to say something about Josh. "I'm ruining the surprise, but we got a *puppy*!" she exclaimed. "She's this adorable little Morkipoo. Her name is Alexis von Wigglebottom, but we call her Lexi."

"A Morkipoo? As in half poodle?" I said. Belle had been viciously attacked by a toy poodle dog at a dog park a few years earlier. I knew there were no bad dogs, only bad owners—but the damage to our psyches had already been done. Since then, we had crossed the street whenever we saw a small dog with tight curls.

"Only a third, actually. I know you like bigger dogs . . ."

No, I liked one particular medium-size dog who was now dead. Piper, oblivious to my pain, plowed ahead. "But HRH is so adorable that I just *know* you'll want the number for my breeder after you meet her."

I somehow doubted that. "What does 'HRH' mean?"

"Her Royal Highness!"

I was officially uninterested in meeting this purebred rat.

"Anyways!" said Piper. "Now that I know you're going to be in town, I want to have everyone over for dinner tonight. What time will you and Josh be in?"

So *that's* why she didn't ask. "Hadley didn't tell you?" I asked.

"Tell me *what*?"

I took a deep breath and assured myself that it didn't matter if I informed her now or tomorrow or next year. "Josh and I are getting divorced."

"Stop."

"No, I'm serious."

"That's nuts, Laine," she said with obvious irritation. "Also, hello? I'm your *sister*. When were you planning on telling me this?"

"It's only been a week, Piper. I'm kind of processing." I cringed because this sounded like something Hadley would say.

"A *week*! Are you kidding me?"

I kind of wished I was. "I'm not."

"Oh my gosh. You left him, didn't you? *Why?* Josh is the best."

You take him, then, I thought.

"Oh, poor Joshy," she said dolefully. "He's probably so heartbroken. What's this about? Did you meet someone?"

"Yeah, right," I scoffed.

"Fair. Laine, this is like the dumbest thing you've ever done, and you gave up the best city in the world to live in some Podunk town."

I didn't even bother trying to make my case, as I'd already done so—repeatedly. Ann Arbor wasn't a perfect place, as there really was no such thing. But it was small without being claustrophobically so, charming without being twee, and compared to New York, the people were just so *nice.*

Also, it had been six hundred miles from Ben's home base, and when I was trying to figure out where to live after college, that detail had been paramount. As an added bonus, my mother had acted like I was moving to Siberia, which felt like proof that Ben was wrong—I *wasn't* most preoccupied with what she wanted. Not all of the time, at least.

"Listen, you and I have to have a *serious* talk. But first, dinner at my place tonight. Bring Mom?"

"Okay," I said, even though I felt the opposite of okay. I was glad Piper was loyal to Josh, but was I chopped liver?

"Good. I'm going to call Josh right now. Yes, that's exactly what I'm going to do," she said in a voice that told me she was really talking to herself. "Okay, Laine, I'll see you later on. *Mwah* and more soon!"

"Oh, me? I'm fine," I said to the phone, as Piper had already hung up. "Thank you so much for asking."

SIX

Laine

For many, New York is a new beginning—a fresh start, a different identity, a better future. But as my cab sped down the Brooklyn-Queens Expressway, Manhattan's skyline glittering to the west, all I could see was my past.

Ben and I were the only kids our age on our block, and unlike the rest of the pack of elementary schoolers who roamed our neighborhood, he was uninterested in declaring Hadley his leader. Still, we were an unlikely duo. Whereas I was constantly worried about screwing up—and worse, someone finding out I did so—Ben delighted in doing what he wasn't supposed to. He was a freewheeling B to my type A, and nothing made him laugh harder than telling our teacher that I'd eaten his homework or informing our classmates that I was out sick because I'd gone swimming in the Gowanus Canal, which was practically a sewer. But when no one was listening, I would match him quip for quip. Like so many other kids of our generation, we were really into yo-mama jokes for a while: *Yo mama's so ugly, she threw a boomerang and it wouldn't come back to her. Whatchu looking at? Yo mama!*

Then Ben's mom took off when he was nine, and suddenly those jokes weren't funny anymore.

Up until then, our friendship had been all fun and games. But a week or two after his mother left a note saying she wanted something different for her life, I'd come over to get him and found him curled up under his bed, weeping. I'd waited for him to stop, but he kept crying and crying, so eventually I called to him. He'd yelled at me to go away. I wouldn't, though. I sat there until he was willing to take my hand, and after a while, he crawled out and let me give him a tissue.

"You won't tell anyone?" he sniffled, not meeting my eye.

"Never," I vowed. "Only ever us."

He still didn't look up, but he smiled a little. "Only ever us."

That was when our friendship became a safe place, where secrets could be shared and promises didn't even have to be spoken aloud in order to be kept.

Ben loathed his place—the apartment reminded him of his mom, even years after she'd been gone—and with me just three doors down, he didn't really have to spend much time there. I don't know that my mother was happy to have him at our place so much as she barely noticed; what was one more body watching TV on the sofa, or another serving of mac 'n' cheese, which Hadley had made, anyway? We stayed out of her hair, and she knew I'd clean up afterward.

Ben's dad didn't push him to come home. Instead, Reggie started showing up wherever Ben was. He'd sit on the stoop with my mother while Ben and I played on the sidewalk, and even though we were mostly free-range kids, sometimes they'd trail behind us on the way over to Carroll Park, or every once in a while walk all the way over to Prospect Park with us. Sometimes I overheard them talking, and it was usually about Ben and if he was doing all right—the implication being that he wasn't. *He's fine,* I wanted to say. *Can't you see? He has me.* And for reasons I didn't understand, even back then, I was enough for him.

Ben and I stayed as thick as thieves in middle school, though there was a period of time where we tried to be sneaky about it because everyone thought we were dating and that made both of us gag. He got into a magnet high school while I went to the one near our neighborhood, which made it easier to sidestep other people's opinions. Most days we'd meet at Carroll Park after the last bell, and head out on whatever adventure we'd decided on before ending up at my place to do our homework and have dinner, only to head back out and roam the city until my curfew.

Ben started high school nearly as scrawny as he'd been in elementary school, but he filled up and out by his junior year. It wasn't long before my girlfriends, and even my sisters, started referring to him as "hot." I knew he was objectively attractive, but he was also . . . Ben, the kid who sometimes snorted when he laughed and looked like a baby bunny when he cried. He may have been exceptionally easy on the eyes, but he was my best friend. And as my mother had remarked offhand—although more than once—nothing ruined friendship faster than romance.

Our senior year of high school, I got into the University of Michigan, where I'd applied after seeing its picturesque brochure. He was accepted at the University of Pennsylvania, where he intended to major in finance; for someone who didn't believe in studying, his grades had always been stellar, and he figured he'd go make a couple million quickly and retire early.

I guess I didn't really understand that we were leaving each other—or at least I didn't accept what that would mean in practical terms—until the night after graduation. We were on my back patio, sharing a wine cooler that we'd stolen from his dad, which we'd poured into plastic cups, and he'd turned to me. It was dark, but my mother had strung twinkle lights along the fence, and they made his eyes shine bright. "Laine?" he said.

As I looked at him, something strange in me stirred, something that hadn't been there before. Except the way he was staring back at me made me think it wasn't new for him; it was just the first time I'd noticed it. And to be honest, that terrified me. I loved what we had. I didn't want to ruin it.

"Only ever us," he said quietly.

I swallowed hard and forced myself not to look away. "Only ever us," I said.

Then the moment passed, and we went back to being Laine and Ben. At least, that's what I told myself.

But three and a half years later, we would have a fight that would end our friendship for good. And eventually I would come to see that it hadn't just been that fight.

No, the night after graduation set the end in motion.

~

Growing up in New York, change was the one true constant. I'd blink and a favorite shop was a glass-walled condo; I'd return from a brief vacation to discover a neighborhood fixture had decamped to Vermont or Arizona or some other place that was said to offer much more for far less. But as the cab pulled off the expressway and entered Carroll Gardens, I was reminded of how much this pocket of Brooklyn still looked like the city of my youth. Redbrick brownstones and cars parked bumper to bumper. Shopkeepers spraying down the sidewalks while children played and yelled and outran their parents. People—everywhere people. I was at once comforted and overwhelmed. It was just one week. Hadn't I gotten through countless other trips to see my family without running into Ben? Admittedly, he hadn't been in New York then; like me, he'd managed to land everywhere but the city. But even if I saw him now, I'd simply be cordial and go on my merry way. No big discussions, no arguments that only made things worse. Just . . . goodbye.

Again.

In retrospect, my decision to stay in Ann Arbor after graduation had been largely fueled by my desire to avoid Ben—and maybe my mother, too. At the time, however, I told myself that I simply wanted to live in a greener, less expensive place that had a slower pace—and all of that *was* true, even if it wasn't the real reason I became a townie, as the longtime permanent residents referred to themselves.

I didn't come home for the holidays that first year after college, since Belle was a puppy and needed so much attention. (That was my story and I was sticking to it.) Then I met Josh, and his very presence felt like a shield of sorts, which made it easier to head back to the city for special occasions. I knew through social media that Ben had moved to California soon after college—he'd actually hated finance and went to get his culinary degree at the Culinary Institute of America, right in the heart of Napa County, then moved to San Francisco. And like me, he rarely returned to New York. A particularly ill-advised bout of browsing revealed that he'd gotten married to a stunning woman named Celeste in his early thirties, but they'd since divorced. And if the photos he posted were to be believed, it appeared he'd left California after their divorce and had been bouncing around working as a private chef for the kind of people who owned three homes and spent almost no time in any of them.

Except now he was back in Brooklyn. I almost wished Hadley hadn't told me, so I could focus my entire attention on getting through the week quickly, then launch headfirst into my new life as a potential parent. Granted, the particulars of said life remained murky. From what I'd gathered online, getting pregnant was complicated and nerve-racking. Temperatures to monitor, hormones to check, ultrasounds, and more: Could I really go through that on my own? And that wasn't even the more involved and expensive procedures, like egg retrieval and storage, which I might very well need.

Then there was the other half of the problem. The fact that I hadn't been able to muster up the courage to type "how to find a sperm donor" into the search bar didn't bode well for my ability to actually get pregnant. Well, not without Josh. My ob-gyn's next available pre-fertility appointment was in September, but I had a list of ob-gyns who took my health insurance, and I intended to call them right away to see if *someone* could tell me what I needed to do to get my body ready for a baby.

But first, to see my mother and determine just how hyperbolic Hadley was being about her mental faculties.

The cab pulled up in front of my mother's brownstone. I paid the fare, grabbed my suitcase from the trunk, and headed straight for the door. Though I was here to help my mother, I almost wished I'd asked Hadley if I could stay with her; she and Topper had a Park Avenue penthouse, and the guest rooms—there were two—were spacious and welcoming and, of course, miles from one particular Carroll Gardens apartment I was trying to steer clear of.

Even as I climbed the stairs of my childhood home, my eyes had landed on the building three doors to the left. Same brown cement facade and well-tended stoop; same wrought-iron flower boxes—today brimming with purple and yellow pansies. My pulse quickened as I realized just how not ready I was to face Ben. After all, what would I say? *I never did confront my mother, but that's only because it would've broken her heart, and one broken heart is more than enough for the Francis women. Also, I'm really not a people pleaser anymore. I just left my husband, and not a single person I know is happy about that, including me.* I shook my head, trying to knock these thoughts loose. Yes, Ben was in town, but there was little chance he'd moved back in with Reggie. He'd probably just been visiting when Hadley ran into him.

My mother had never changed the locks all these years, and I still had my old key. But I rang the doorbell anyway because I didn't want to surprise her. I was beginning to wonder if she was even home when she finally buzzed me in.

A long hallway separated my mother's apartment from the stairs leading to the upstairs apartment, which she rented out. All sorts of people had tap-danced above our heads over the years: families and couples and singles and roommates, and once, terrifyingly, a buttoned-up accountant who moonlighted as a clown. But for the better part of the last decade, Roger and Rohit had lived there. Hadley, Piper, and I took comfort in this—not only was the couple unflaggingly punctual in paying the rent, they were handy and had probably saved my mother thousands in home repair bills.

When I got to her door, she was standing there in a silk bathrobe and a matching hair wrap.

"Mom?" I said, remembering what Hadley had said about the nightgown she'd worn to Bashir's. "Did you just get out of the shower?"

"No, dear," she said, touching the wrap. "Why?"

I gestured to her getup.

"I'm comfortable like this. And I wasn't expecting visitors."

"You remembered I was coming, right?" I said gently.

She tilted her chin indignantly. "Of course, Laine. You're not a visitor. This is your home." Then she smiled and opened her arms to me.

As I embraced her, she smelled like gardenias and coffee, just like she always did. Her eyes were moist when she let me go.

"Why are you crying?"

She smiled again and dabbed the corner of her lids with her wrist. "It's just been so long since I've seen you."

Guilt washed over me. It had only been five months, but I wasn't exactly vying for daughter of the year—especially compared to Hadley, but even Piper. Maybe I should have found a place to board Belle so I could have visited more often.

No, said a voice from deep within me. If anything, I wish I'd spent more time with Belle—not less. My mother was the one who followed her around like she was a toddler in a store full of blown glass, constantly fretting that Belle—who was nothing if not well behaved—was going to topple her tchotchkes. What I should have done was tell my mother the truth: the way she treated my dog hurt my feelings.

Well, I thought wistfully, *it's too late for that.*

So I said, "I know. I'm sorry. But I'm here now."

Her face lit up. "Yes, you are, my girl, and that means everything to me. Come on in."

~

I don't know what I was expecting, but the apartment wasn't in any worse shape than it had been the last time I'd been in town. In the living room, the wall of bookshelves was still crammed full of books—like me and Hadley, my father had been a reader. In front of the books, my mother had shoved various glass and ceramic figures, picture frames, and an assortment of random items, including but not limited to a wine cork, a pair of nail clippers, and a bottle of prescription-strength ibuprofen that had expired in the late nineties. Sure, my mother had left a towel on a chair, and I spotted the corpses of several houseplants, some unopened boxes in the corner, and a plate with a piece of half-eaten toast on top of the piano. This was the way she lived. It made me want to immediately start putting things where they belonged, but I saw no sign of a declining mind.

"Not too bad," I said to myself.

"Don't judge me, Laine," said my mother, flopping down on the sofa. She draped her arm over her forehead and paused before peering at me. "Your sister already does that enough for all three of you."

"Hadley means well," I said, because she *had* been doing most of the heavy lifting over the past year or seven.

"Meaning well and doing well are two different things, aren't they?" said my mother.

I smiled at her. Her gray eyes were bright, and she seemed to me nearly as sharp as she'd always been. And the way she'd always been was . . . a bit forgetful. When we were young, it wasn't a surprise if she didn't show up for a field trip she'd agreed to chaperone or put two sandwiches in my lunch box and two apples in Hadley's (and that was when she remembered to actually pack them at all). She was loving but absent, even when she was right in front of me, and over the years, I'd learned to find what she didn't offer from other people. And when the one person who'd given me most of what I needed left my life, I'd adopted Belle, then married Josh.

The apartment was long and narrow, with the living room, kitchen, and dining room on the first floor, and three small bedrooms on the garden level. I wandered through the dining room into the kitchen. There was a moldy baguette on the counter beside a toaster that barely functioned but which my mother refused to replace. The floor, too, was in desperate need of mopping. Nothing that an hour of elbow grease wouldn't fix—yet it was clutter, not grime, that had always been my mother's Achilles' heel. "Mom," I called, "don't you still have Iwona in to clean?"

"She stopped coming," my mother called back.

A shriveled orange sat in the middle of a matte white bowl on the counter. Except for a canister of coffee, the fridge was nearly empty, too—Hadley had tossed all the out-of-date food, but no one had replaced it. No wonder my mother was as frail as a baby bird. She was running on caffeine and fumes.

"Mom," I said, walking back to the living room, "your cupboards are completely bare. I can order you groceries if you don't want to go out."

She quickly hoisted herself up into a fully seated position. "I'll have you know that I have plenty to eat."

I eyed her skeptically. "Oh yeah? Medium roast is enough to sustain you?"

"Laine, love, I like to go out for meals. I always have. Or at least I have since Hank's been gone."

It was strange to me that she'd called my father by his first name—he was always *your father* when she spoke of him—but before I could mention it, she continued.

"I go to Georgie's for bagels and Zaytoon's for shawarma and Bar Tabac when I want a good steak and a nice glass of wine. There's simply no sense in stocking up when it's just me."

"No, I guess there's not," I allowed. "So, what happened with Iwona?" My mother's housekeeper had come in weekly for as long as I could remember.

She looked strangely surprised. "What's that?"

"Iwona," I repeated. "Why doesn't she come in to clean for you anymore?"

"Oh!" she said, standing from the sofa suddenly. "Iwona. Iwona. Yes, Iwona. Well, the thing is . . ."

Her eyes darted around, almost like she felt guilty. After a moment, she said, "It's just that apparently my checks to her bounced."

I startled. "Are you out of *money*?"

"I should hope not," she said with a frown.

That made two of us. But at least it was just her checking account. Both my parents had been raised by parents who'd survived the Great Depression and had passed on their aversion to debt; my father, in particular, had been a careful saver. Odds were, my mother wasn't transferring cash over regularly like she was supposed to. Fortunately, that was a fixable problem, and those were the best kind. I glanced at my watch. "I hate to change the subject, but we really need to get going if we're going to make it to Piper's on time."

"Piper's?"

So Piper had forgotten to invite her. Typical. "She wants us to come over for dinner tonight. Hadley and company will be there, too."

"Well, that sounds lovely!" she said, starting for the door.

"Mom, you'd better get changed."

She glanced down at her robe. "Oh, right. Yes. I'll go put on a dress." Then she looked at me. "All of my girls in one place. What a treat."

I pushed my lips into a smile, trying to mirror her enthusiasm. It wasn't that I didn't want to see my sisters. It was just that Hadley would try to probe my psyche under the guise of conversation, offering me one unwanted nugget of marital advice after another, while Piper would probably sic her dreadful little dog on me and make thoughtless remarks about Belle and then get upset if I so much as hinted that I was hurt. Then my mother would ask me to smooth things over with everyone . . . which is exactly what I would end up doing.

Because as much as I wanted to claim that I'd changed, Ben was still right.

When push came to shove, the only member of my family I was willing to disappoint was myself.

SEVEN

Laine

"Oh dear, Laine, there's no hurry," said my mother as I directed her around a pile of dog poop that had been left in the middle of the sidewalk. Stupid human—it would have taken mere seconds to clean up that mess.

"Sorry, Mom," I said, slowing my stride. You can take the woman out of New York, but you never take New York out of her pace. Or judging from my mother's moseying, at least not until she's in her seventies. "I didn't mean to rush you. It's just that we're already half an hour late." And I hated being late. It reminded me of the worst parts of my childhood. Missing the bus to summer camp. Showing up for birthday parties after the candles had long been blown out. Overhearing my friend Selena's mom tell her that she'd asked my mother to arrive an hour earlier than she actually expected her. These, and so many other instances, were why I set all clocks four minutes early.

"Since when has Piper once worried about being tardy?" scoffed my mother. Her arm was linked in mine, and she pulled me closer. "She won't care. But if you do, love, skip the bouquet next time." As much as I despised being late, I also hated arriving at someone's house empty-handed. After parking, we'd stopped at a corner grocer a few minutes earlier to grab some flowers.

"It doesn't matter—we're here now," I told her. Piper's apartment building was a big glass-and-steel number that extended far into the sky, casting a shadow on the street below it. The doorman ushered us in and dialed Piper.

"So fancy," said my mother in a stage whisper as the doorman directed us into the elevator, then hit the button for the seventh floor.

"You know Piper," I said as we began to rise. "She's always liked nice things."

"Maybe she should have married Silas," chirped my mother, referring to Kaia and Jae's father. "He's rich and very nice. And then all of my girls would be happily married, just like your father and me," she added.

I nodded in response, even though I didn't agree. Even four years after my father's death, she was still trying to sell the story of their perfect marriage? I supposed it was her right, but I'd married Josh in part because he *wasn't* like my father, who was forever muttering about how things—including but not limited to his apartment, his wife, and even sometimes me and my sisters—weren't the way he wanted them to be. Josh may have been absentminded, and sometimes absent, but he was content with his life.

Well, that made one of us. He and I probably *did* seem happily married, to everyone else, but I couldn't help but think of our union as the marital equivalent of a lovely house located directly above a sinkhole. At least Topper and Hadley were a good, if unlikely, fit. In spite of his old-man nickname, Topper was nearly a decade younger than her. His primary objective appeared to be to enjoy life, whereas Hadley had emerged from the womb with a to-do list in hand. When they started dating six years ago, we'd all thought Hadley was getting her midlife crisis out of the way early. After all, Topper had been a twenty-seven-year-old blue blood who'd attended all the best schools because some far-back family member had founded most of them. His business card literally read "Philanthropist." But he'd been wild about Hadley. And in hindsight, we should have known she'd never have bothered dating him if he, too, weren't part of her plan.

Then it hit me. My mother must have forgotten that I'd told her Josh and I were divorcing. But before I could remind her, the elevator deposited us on Piper's floor.

"Auntie Laine!" said Kaia, flinging open the door to their apartment. She was wearing a tutu and a cape, and her black curls formed a halo around her head.

"Hiya, kiddo," I said, scooping her up in my arms. "I've missed you."

"I missed you, too! Where's Uncle Joshy?"

"Um." Was this the time to tell them we were getting divorced? What if I changed my mind? "He's in Ann Arbor. He had to work."

"Awww," she pouted. "Auntie Laine? Mama says Belle died. Did she get run over?"

"Yes, she died," I said, hoping that saying this out loud wouldn't turn on the waterworks. "But she didn't get run over."

"What happened? Did someone poison her? Or kidnap her? Mama says bad people take dogs and make you pay big money to get them back."

Man, New York kids—I forgot how quickly they grew up. But then I smiled to myself, because it had just occurred to me that if all went well, I'd be raising my future child in Ann Arbor, where they'd have room to run and play and good public schools and wouldn't learn about extortion in kindergarten.

"She was really old, and sometimes when you're really old, you get really sick," I said.

Kaia's brown eyes widened. "Is that going to happen to Grammy?"

I felt a sudden pang. "I sure hope not."

"Whew!" she said. She hopped out of my arms. "You're sad, but you'll feel happy after you meet Lexi! Come on," she said, motioning for me to follow her.

"Be right there. Let me say hi to your mom and aunt first," I called as she headed into the boys' bedroom.

"Hey, you!" Piper squealed. Except for the bedrooms and bathrooms, her apartment was one big open space, and she was leaning against the kitchen island, waiting for me to come to her.

"Hey, Piper," I said, walking over. She felt especially bony as I hugged her, or maybe I'd just forgotten how slender she was. "Here," I said, handing her the flowers. "I brought these for you."

"Ooh! Thank you," she said, sniffing them. Her straight chestnut hair was even longer than usual, and she was that rare non-French woman who looked amazing with bangs.

My eyes darted to where she'd just set the flowers on the counter. "Do you want me to put them in water?" The daisies would droop within the hour, but mostly it was the sight of them splayed out among the appetizers that made me twitchy—there was a place for everything, and those were *not* in their place.

"No, I'll do it in a few," she said before taking a sip of her wine. "Go say hi to Had."

"Over here!" Hadley waved at me from the sofa, where she was nursing one of the twins. Her light brown hair was piled in a messy bun on top of her head, and except for a swipe of lip gloss, her face was bare. She looked tired but happy, like a subtly persuasive commercial for motherhood.

"Hey, Had," I said, plopping down at the opposite end. "Kisses from afar."

"I'll be done in just a second." Answering the question I hadn't yet asked, she added, "Topper's in Kaia's room putting Asher down."

"That's good of him," I said, and I meant it. Our father hadn't exactly been a hands-on parent. He'd put in long hours at the water treatment facility where he was a supervisor, and in his spare time, he'd made models of things we had no interest in—cars, rockets, sailboats.

"I mean, it's also his job," said Hadley. "He knows I can't do this alone."

I nearly winced. If Hadley couldn't handle parenting on her own—yes, she had twins, but she was also superwoman—how on earth was I going to pull this baby thing off? Granted, Piper was a single mom, but both Levi and Silas had 50 percent custody. This would be 100 percent on me.

"Gorgeous? I can't do it." Topper had just come out of the bedroom. His eyes were bloodshot, and for once, he looked older than Hadley. "He just will *not* go to sleep."

Asher wasn't crying, and maybe that was why Hadley glanced at me and smirked so subtly that, had I not spent the first sixteen years of my life sharing a room with her, I would never have caught it. Swiftly and with such certainty that it looked like a dance sequence, she pulled down her shirt, stood, and handed Ainsley to me. "Would you mind? Anyway, the two of you should get to know each other."

"Not at all," I said, looking down at a drowsy, rosy-cheeked Ainsley. She was so . . . lovely. Something deep in me got all tight and painful then, and I couldn't even coo at her right away. By the time I got my voice back, she was asleep.

"Auntie!" Jae was just outside the bedroom he shared with Rocco. "Come meet HRH Lexi!"

"We're waiting for you!" called Kaia.

"That's so sweet of you," I told them, "but Ainsley just fell asleep. Give me a minute or two?" Or twenty, I thought, peering at her. If I felt this level of affection for my niece, I could only imagine how I'd feel about my own child.

There was a sharp bark and Ainsley stirred in my arms. "Shhh," I said, bouncing from heel to heel.

"*Such* a cutie," said Piper, coming up next to me. She touched Ainsley's head softly. "I wouldn't mind another baby or two."

I obviously wouldn't have minded one myself, but mostly I was thinking: *Another two?* I supposed if I could pop out several kids and still have a concave, stretch-mark-free stomach, maybe I'd want to birth a basketball team, too. Still, hadn't she learned anything from our childhood? Less was more. Then again, Piper had never had a problem grabbing the spotlight, so this had probably never occurred to her.

All at once, I realized I hadn't heard a peep from my mother since we'd walked in. "Uh, you guys? Where's Mom?" I said, glancing around. I was pretty sure she was fine, but her comment about me being happily married *was* a bit concerning, and I hadn't paid attention to whether she'd followed me into the apartment. For all I knew, she'd gotten back on the elevator, wandered out onto the street, and was now chatting it up with a bunch of twentysomethings.

"I'm right here!" my mother announced from behind me, and I nearly startled Ainsley awake.

"Mom, you scared me," I said, but I realized I sounded like I was chiding her. In a softer tone, I added, "I hadn't seen you since we got here, and I thought . . ."

"Oh, Laine," she said, squeezing my shoulder lightly. "You thought I went missing, didn't you? I was just in the bathroom. But you are so sweet to worry about me. Thank you."

"Sorry," I whispered. Hadley was right; she was more forgetful than usual—but she also seemed to be more appreciative of me, and wasn't that what I wanted? Anyway, she definitely wasn't a flight risk.

"Ladies! A toast!" Piper announced. She'd managed to carry four champagne flutes over at once. She held one out to me, but I shook my head; I didn't like wine, but more importantly, I wasn't ready to put the baby down.

Piper lifted her glass. "To Laine coming to visit."

"To Laine," said Hadley, who had come back in the room. She stole a glance at me before raising her glass. "Cheers!"

"Cheers," I said quietly, hoping Ainsley wouldn't rouse.

"Indeed! And to my family," said my mother. "All in the same place at one time." Then she smiled at me. "Well, almost all of us. It's really not the same without Josh."

No, it wasn't. As they clinked glasses and took sips of their champagne, I blinked back fresh tears and wondered whether, if the baby in my arms were mine, that would be enough to justify removing Josh from the family that loved him so.

EIGHT

Laine

The rest of the night went more or less as I'd predicted. Hadley had cornered me in the kitchen to inquire why I hadn't considered meeting with a coach or therapist before making a decision as major as divorce. Then Piper inserted herself into the mix to snap a selfie of the three of us, which she'd immediately texted to Josh. Sure, they'd always gotten along great, but I had a strong suspicion she was going to do everything in her power to try to get us back together—beginning with making him feel like nothing had changed. And instead of trying to sugarcoat that, as I normally would have, I said this to her.

"Chill, Lainey. Nothing *has* changed yet," she said, making a peace sign with one hand and taking a shot of herself with the other. "Don't worry, this one's for Insta."

"Speaking of which, I'm just not convinced you really want this," Hadley said to me.

"I do," I said, but even I could tell my voice lacked conviction. Truth be told, I wished Josh was there right now to distract my sisters.

"Why, exactly, do you think she's doing this?" Piper asked Hadley. Whoever said multitasking was a myth had never witnessed my younger sister choosing a photo filter while deep in conversation. "There isn't even anything *wrong* with their marriage."

"Oh, believe me, I know," said Hadley.

"Hello? I'm right here," I said.

"Maybe Josh doesn't want to stay married, either," said Topper, who'd wandered over. He'd fallen asleep on the sofa, right in the middle of dinner, but had since awoken and was searching for scotch.

"He wants to stay married," said Piper.

I jerked my head back. "And how do you know that?"

"Because, *duh,* Lainey," she said matter-of-factly. "But also, I called him."

"And what did he say?" I asked cautiously.

"That you've lost your mind." She shot me a Cheshire smile. "Kidding. He said he was baffled."

"That makes two of us," said Hadley.

I was really glad I hadn't told them why I was leaving him. I would—eventually. Maybe even after I was already pregnant. It was a shame I couldn't confide in them now, because the two of them could probably tell me more than any doctor about what it was really like to try to have a baby.

"Don't worry," Piper said to Hadley. "If this was really happening, she'd be melting down. Remember how bad I was when Levi and I split?"

"As if I could forget," said Hadley. "You dropped into the double digits—I practically had to force-feed you. And then it took another two months for you to stop crying." She gave me the once-over before turning back to Piper. "But that's not really Laine's style. I'm not sure how, but she's going to surprise us with this one."

I highly doubted that and was almost glad that Lexi chose that moment to appear at my feet. "Pet her, Laine!" said Piper, picking up the little yipper. "Come on, she's so soft."

"No, thank you," I said as Piper shoved her in my face.

"You don't want to pet this cute little face?" Lexi was lunging at me now, and I lifted a hand to shield myself, only to be rewarded with a set of tiny fangs taking to my palm like it was a steak.

"Ow," I said, yanking my hand away, which made my blood splatter directly onto Piper's cream rug. "Oh no," I said, immediately glancing around for a towel.

"It's not a big deal, Laine," said Piper, but she was frowning at Lexi. "Naughty puppy. Now Auntie Laine isn't going to like you."

"I like her just fine," I lied, reaching for some paper towels. I knew for a fact that Piper had imported that rug from Morocco, and I wasn't going to let the blood stain it. I quickly wrapped my hand so I wouldn't keep making a mess, then located a dish towel and some detergent. "Just give me a minute," I said.

In fact, it had taken nearly ten to clean the spot, and Piper had kept sighing deeply like she was somehow disappointed that I was helping her. Still, we hadn't ended up actually having an argument, and not because Josh was there to buffer or because I'd had to smooth things over. That was as close to a victory as I could ask. Really, if I had it my way, I'd head back to Michigan the very next morning, heart warm with mostly pleasant memories. End on a high note and whatnot.

But now it was nearly eleven, and my mother and I were finally back at the apartment. "I'm fried," I said to my mother, who was wandering around the living room, apparently hunting for something. She appeared to be wide awake. "Do you mind if I head to bed?"

"Course not, love," she said, riffling through a pile of papers that had been left on an accent table.

"Which bedroom should I take?" I should have asked her this the moment I arrived, as it was entirely possible I was going to have to sleep on the sofa. Not that it would have mattered, but I guess I wasn't so different from Hadley in that I wanted to know what the plan was.

"Why, your and Hadley's bedroom. Where else would you stay?" she said, looking at me curiously.

"Last time I was here, that room had been turned into a closet," I reminded her. "I'm guessing you haven't redecorated since then."

"Oh, that's right," she said, setting the stack of papers down. "I barely go in there. Try Piper's room, then." Piper had been a terrible sleeper as a baby, so my mother had put her in my room and moved me into Hadley's. Eventually Piper started sleeping through the night, but she threw a fit when my mother tried to switch us back. Hadley didn't care about sharing space with me—she was never home, anyway—so that was that until we all moved out.

"Okay," I said, because I hoped it would be. I walked over and kissed her cheek. "Let me know if you need anything, all right?"

She smiled at me. "Isn't that my line?"

I smiled back at her. And here Hadley had been making it sound like my mother was in the throes of dementia. I was glad I'd come to visit, because it had given me the opportunity to see for myself that, as usual, Hadley was overthinking it. *So much for managing her mind,* I thought as I headed down the stairs with my suitcase.

But maybe she's worried about what happened to Nana, argued another voice in me. My mother's mother had been diagnosed with Parkinson's disease in her early seventies. And though we hadn't seen her all that much, since she was living in Florida, it was obvious that it'd had an impact on her cognition in the end. Parkinson's wasn't supposed to have a strong genetic component (I'd done a story on it for a wellness website a few years back, in part because I wanted to find out if I was at risk for getting it). Yet I wouldn't have blamed Hadley if she was worried about how our family's health history would affect our mother, or even the three of us. Now that I was ready to have a baby myself, it was probably a good idea to start thinking about things like that. I really hoped I could get in to see a doctor soon.

I let myself into Piper's old room. My mother had turned it into a graveyard for broken and unwanted furniture, but the twin bed was free of clutter. And while she hadn't put the sheets on—no surprise there—she had left them in a pile at the end of the bed. I set the urn on a corner of Piper's old dresser and peeled off my clothes, then changed into pajamas and padded down the hall to the bathroom.

I was nearly there when I stopped and listened for my mother. I could still hear her knocking around upstairs, so I turned around and stuck my head inside her bedroom.

It was as tidy as the rest of the house, which is to say not very. There were shelves stacked with Depression glass that she'd inherited from her parents, and a mound of clothing on an armchair. In one corner, she'd shoved several large plastic bins full of something; I wasn't eager to find out what. But again, it was no worse than when I'd been here in the winter.

My lids were heavy, and my brain was operating at sloth speed, so I headed to the bathroom to wash up quickly. Then I made the bed and got in.

I hadn't slept well since Belle died. Every time I crawled under the covers, all I could think about was how she wasn't there to warm my feet. But tonight, it wasn't Belle I thought of when I closed my eyes.

Ben and I now had *not* been friends for longer than we had been inseparable. Belle had made it easier not to think about that. Now with her gone, too, it was hard not to reflect on the hole Ben had left in my life.

It wasn't like I hadn't tried to make friends after Ben. I'd joined book clubs and went to coffee with other writers and befriended the wives of Josh's entrepreneur buddies. But I'd never found another person who could finish my sentences. Or one who wanted to split every spicy dish on the menu with me. And I never ceased to be surprised at what a chore it was to have to give someone the backstory to a current story in order to make them understand what the heck you were talking about. I'd never had to do that with Ben—because he'd been there the whole time.

I was still ruminating when I heard a loud thud, which was followed by the sound of a door closing. My eyes flew open.

I supposed it could have been Roger and Rohit—except I knew that the front door to the brownstone, which was made of thick old oak and had leaded windows, was nearly silent. No, it was almost certainly the door to my mother's apartment. Except who was coming and going at this time of night?

I leapt out of bed. "Mom?" I called as I climbed the stairs to the main floor. "Is that you?"

She didn't answer.

I hadn't thought to pack a bathrobe and I wasn't wearing a bra, so I grabbed one of the throws from the sofa and wrapped it around my shoulders. Then I fished my mother's keys, which were buried under chewing gum and coupons, out of the bowl next to the front door and let myself outside. "Mom?" I called from the stoop.

"Over here," called a young guy stumbling down the street with a few friends.

"You wish, boozer," I called back, but then I blushed. One day back in the city and I was hollering at strangers.

I glanced around, but there was no sign of my mother. Bashir's bodega was still lit up—he'd always done a brisk business at night—but I realized I'd have to actually get dressed to head over there. Anyway, I hadn't checked the back patio yet.

My mother wasn't there, either, and I was starting to get alarmed. I'd just walked into the kitchen when I heard noises coming from overhead.

She wouldn't have gone to the apartment upstairs . . . would she? As much as I wanted this night to be over, I knew I had to check.

I padded up the stairs, which were strewn with dusty tumbleweeds. I wasn't expecting a floor you could serve steak off of, but it was unlike Roger and Rohit not to vacuum. Stranger still, their door was cracked open.

"Hello?" I called.

"Hmm?" said a voice.

It didn't sound like my mother, which is probably why it took several seconds for me to realize that it actually was her.

"Mom?" I was officially confused. "Is everything okay?"

"Who's there?"

Panic was setting in, but I didn't want to throw open the door to someone else's apartment. "It's me? Laine?"

"You girls should be in bed!"

"Mom?" I was starting to freak out. "Are you in there with Roger and Rohit? Can I speak with them?"

"Who?"

"Your tenants? Are they on vacation?"

"I don't know." Her words were strained, and nothing about this seemed right. I was going to have to break my own ethical code and let myself into a place where I hadn't been invited. But hopefully Rohit and Roger would understand, even if *I* didn't understand why they'd have my mother over at this time of night.

I pushed the door open. Then I gasped.

The apartment was empty—well, it was free of furniture. But there were piles of newspapers and what looked like bills and packing slips all over the floor. Worse, cardboard boxes were stacked all over the living room and kitchen. My mother was sitting in the middle of a pile of them, peering down into a half-opened box.

"Mom," I said slowly, "*what* is happening? When did Roger and Rohit move out? Did they leave some of their boxes behind?"

"Who?" she said again.

Pain shot from my stem to my stern as she finally looked up at me. Her eyes were glassy and confused—just like my grandmother's had been when the worst of her disease set in.

"Hey, Mom," I said, pushing some boxes out of the way so I could sit down beside her. "Why are you up here?"

"This is my home," she whispered.

My mother's family had lived upstairs when she was a girl; she only moved into the downstairs apartment after she married my father. "I know that," I said softly, and now I was on the verge of tears. "But you didn't tell us that your tenants moved out."

"I'm sorry."

"Don't be. It's okay." *Hold it together, Laine,* I commanded myself, even as another voice in me said, *This is even worse than it seems.* "Where did all this stuff come from?"

"I was just trying to clean up my apartment."

"Okay. That's good," I said, but as I glanced around, I knew I was just rationalizing. No wonder her place hadn't been as bad as I'd been expecting—judging by the number of boxes she'd hauled upstairs, she'd probably spent the past several weeks cleaning. And yet none of this made the situation any better. Hadley was right: something was seriously wrong with our mother.

"Listen, we should really get you to bed," I said.

"I am tired," she said softly as I helped her to her feet.

"Of course you are." Meanwhile, it was my turn to be wide awake. "It's nearly midnight. Do you have the key to this apartment?" I asked as I guided her toward the door.

"Why . . . I have no idea," she said, reaching into her pockets. "I don't think so."

I decided to leave the dead bolt unlocked for the time being and pulled the door closed behind us. "It's okay," I told her as we slowly descended the stairs. "It's all going to be okay. We'll come back tomorrow morning and deal with this."

At once, she seemed lucid again, as if my very presence had broken the spell she'd been under. And yet this didn't make me feel better. "Oh, Laine," she said, squeezing my arm. "You really are the best."

"It's the least I can do," I told her, because it was true. My poor mother, alone day in and day out. I could have called her more often. I could have visited every two to three months. She would've learned to put up with Belle, or I could have left Belle with Josh if need be. Now, on the cusp of hopefully having a baby, I saw the opportunity I'd missed during that childless, commitment-free time.

As I helped my mother get in bed, then turned off the light and closed the door behind me, I couldn't help but reflect on Ben's role in all of this. It was enough to curdle the nostalgia I'd been having earlier. If only he'd kept his accusations to himself, maybe it wouldn't have taken me so long to realize he'd been wrong, or at least misguided. My mother's instructing me to keep our relationship platonic wasn't an attempt to manipulate me; she loved me and wanted to protect me.

And lo and behold, she'd been spot-on: love *had* ruined everything. My friendship with Ben, yes. But it had also pushed me away from New York. And in doing so, I'd squandered my chance to take advantage of my mother's last good years.

NINE

Sally

Humans aren't meant to have so much stuff. I know this. I do. I know. My mother told me herself not to get too attached to my things—after all, she said, you can't take them with you.

But this is my home, isn't it? Can't I do what I like? Haven't I earned at least that?

Now Laine was peeking at me as she picked at her breakfast, probably searching for signs that last night was more than a one-off. I knew I should have locked that place up, sealed it tight. It's just that it's so hard to sleep and then I wander up there . . .

And then I don't know what happens.

That's the part that scares me.

"Mom."

I knew what she was going to say next. Well, bless her for not insisting we discuss it yesterday evening. After years of being a night owl, I find that I'm far sharper in the morning these days.

"Do you want to talk about the upstairs apartment?"

"What's to talk about?" I didn't mean to sound the way I did, so snappish. "I'm sorry. I brought some things up there, is all."

"I know, and that was smart of you. But when exactly did Roger and Rohit move out?"

"This spring. Or maybe it was late winter. A while ago." The exact timing escaped me.

"Why didn't you tell us?"

"I thought I did." Or at least I don't remember *not* telling them.

"So they moved out and you didn't find another tenant?"

"I was going to. In fact, I was going to ask you to help me with that while you're here."

Laine nodded and took another sip of her coffee. "That makes sense."

Yes, yes, it did, and I was glad she thought so, too. The way she'd been peering at me not minutes earlier made me think that she was going to have me sent away to the place where old people go. The infirmary. No, the nursery. Not that, either. The . . .

Nursing home. The very thought of it made me shudder. My mother's moaning and crying had rung in my ears like gunfire each time I left her. What if that happened to me?

What if it was already happening?

No, I thought, shaking my head. *No, Sally Francis, you have a choice here. You give in to that kind of thinking and you're already a goner. You fight to stay among the living.* I just needed to exercise my brain. Wasn't that it? Maybe I would go for a long walk. That was supposed to be good for sharp thinking. I could do a crossword puzzle. Though it always left me puzzled. But I could try. Maybe I could even call Iwona and practice my Polish. Learn a foreign language. Wasn't that what one of those health stories Laine wrote said to do? I'd have to see if I could find the clipping in my files. I used to collect all her articles. But I wasn't about to ask her now.

"You okay?" Laine's hand was on my arm.

I spilled the beans before I could think not to. "Just thinking about something unpleasant."

She smiled at me, looking like the spitting image of herself as a young girl. She was so pretty, with her dark wavy hair and big brown eyes. Why she carried herself like someone far less attractive was anyone's guess. "You are very lovely, my dear Laine. You should really try to take advantage of that."

"You're sweet, Mom."

"I'm honest." No one has ever accused me of being sweet. *Selfish.* That's what Hank said to me. Only once, when I'd asked him to put down those damn models of his and take me out dancing. Or to dinner. Something that didn't involve going all the way to northern New York just to have a little bit of romance. But you can't take words back. Once they're out of your mouth, they take on a life of their own.

"I do have another question."

"Anything." Because Laine wouldn't judge me. Wasn't that what I had been telling myself? That had never been her way; no reason to think it was about to change now.

"When did you start boxing up your apartment?"

Had I done that? I didn't think I had. "I'm not sure, exactly."

"But you decided to store the boxes in Roger—er, the upstairs apartment."

I nodded, because that part, at least, was right.

"Why there, instead of, I don't know, Piper's bedroom?"

There was no easy answer for this. Why did a person do anything? Hadley had made some comments about my boxes, about how they were multiplying like barn animals. So I took one little package upstairs to make things look tidier. One package, up we went. Then another. And maybe another. I suppose I hadn't been paying enough attention to just how many I'd let stack up. But I was going to go through them all, and soon. That had always been the plan.

But the papers. So many papers. Decades' worth of bills and art projects and report cards and tax documents, all gathering dust in Piper's room. I'd needed space to sort through them all, and the upstairs apartment offered the perfect solution. Because I couldn't just throw them out without a second glance. Nor could I leave them for the girls to sort through after I was gone. My journals were in there, somewhere. And sure enough—I found most of them. Those familiar memories; that bittersweet time in my life. I'd loved to write, if only for myself. I didn't want to forget a thing about how love had found me in the most unexpected place. Now I couldn't even manage to write more than a sentence or two at a time without losing my train of thought. How I missed all that.

"Mom." Laine broke through my thoughts. "It's okay, we can figure it out later. But I do think it would be a good idea for us to go upstairs again before I leave, just to get an idea of how many boxes you have and where we can put them, so you can get another tenant in there. We can do it together, okay? So it's not too overwhelming."

We. The very word made my heart swell. This was why a woman had children: to go through this life and know that she was never truly alone. "I'd love that. Do you have time?"

"Of course, Mom. I'm here all week, remember?"

I clapped my hands together with delight, and she shot me a big smile. "You're welcome to stay here as long as you'd like, Laine. You and Josh can move in with me if you want! Lord knows I have the space."

She immediately stopped smiling and had started poking at her croissant like a tiny bird. Strange. Piper was the one I'd had to convince to eat.

"Darling, are you and Josh doing okay these days? I know work has been up and down for both of you."

She didn't respond.

"Oh, Laine, love, know that I'm not criticizing you. I just want to make sure you're . . ." I could not seem to locate the word I was searching for and was forced to improvise. "That you're going to be able to support a family. I assume you're almost ready for that."

I'd offended her. I could tell. Sometimes the truth was the hardest thing to hear, and I was having a difficult time keeping it bottled up lately. Just the other day, I'd told my friend Mary that yellow just wasn't her color. I shouldn't have jabbered like that, obviously, but judging from her reaction, you'd think I'd just informed her that her beloved son was the second coming of Ted Bundy. Everyone says they want the truth. If that were actually true, people wouldn't take such measures to avoid it.

"I'm fine, Mom," she said. "I've started working as an organizer—remember?"

I hadn't until she said that.

"I'm between jobs right now, but it's been going really well," she continued. "That's why I can't move to Brooklyn. My clients are in Michigan. Anyway, I want to raise my child in Ann Arbor." She covered her mouth, like she'd said something wrong. But what could be wrong about that? I'd been waiting for years for her to say she was ready to have a family of her own.

"I understand, and I'm so happy to hear you talking about children," I said, patting her hand. How silly of me to think she would move back. Besides, I didn't need her to babysit me. I just needed to get things in order so the girls could see that I was fine. "Love, would you mind if I spent an hour or so upstairs before you join me? I just want to go sort through a few things." Laine wouldn't judge me. She never had. But I did want to try to make it look less . . . overwhelming, let's say, before she started poking around.

"Of course not." She squeezed my fingers, which I took as a sign that all was well. "I was thinking about taking a walk, anyway—I want to see how the neighborhood has held up. Then I'm going to have lunch with Piper and Hadley. We'll have some time before this afternoon, and maybe we can look again tomorrow afternoon after brunch when we go to Hadley and Topper's."

"Perfect." I didn't recall making plans to go all the way to the Upper East Side, but it was fine. At least Laine would be with me.

"Perfect." She leaned in toward me. "Don't worry, Mom. Going through everything will be fun."

Would it, though? Because ten minutes later, I was staring at the upstairs apartment and wondering how I'd ever let it come to this. If only I'd kept things tidy in my own place. If only I'd asked Laine to come more often and help me like she used to, rather than waiting for us to tackle it all at once. Now the place was in disarray, and it was entirely possible that once Laine realized what I'd really done, she'd side with Hadley and have me locked up. I'd have to work hard to convince her otherwise.

Oh, Sally, dear girl, silly old fool, I thought as I took in the piles of papers and stacks of boxes. *Humans aren't meant to have so much stuff!*

TEN

Laine

I wanted to believe my mother was fine. She'd been clear-eyed and lucid that morning, and our conversation had been going swimmingly right up until I asked her about Roger and Rohit moving out. Then she'd begun shaking her head and muttering, almost like she was having an entire conversation with herself. She'd come back to me just as quickly, but it was too late—I knew it'd been more than a senior moment. And when I added that to her confusion and scared doe eyes from when I found her in the upstairs apartment, I was forced to admit that Hadley was right, as usual. My mother was not okay—and the three of us were going to have to do something about it before it got even worse.

I'd always done my best thinking while walking Belle. So as soon as my mother went upstairs, I headed out. Now, as I speed walked through the neighborhood in the direction opposite Reggie's place, my heart hurt—literally hurt, like someone was sitting on my chest. My mother had always said she'd sooner jump off the Brooklyn Bridge than go to a nursing home. But she was only going to get worse from here; what else could we possibly do?

I'd already gone a few blocks when I realized that I didn't actually want to think through this on my own, and I couldn't exactly chat with

Belle's urn in the middle of broad daylight. So when I hit Smith Street, I reached into my bag and pulled out my phone. I could've waved my tattered white flag by calling Hadley, but I wasn't ready. Not yet. Without thinking about what I was doing, I called Josh instead.

He picked up on the first ring. "Laine? You okay?" He sounded surprised, and no wonder—I rarely called him unless something was wrong.

"Um, not really?"

The low hum of conversation in the background told me he was in a coffee shop. "Is it about us?"

I almost said, *It depends on whether you made an appointment with a therapist,* but caught myself. "No."

"Your sisters?"

"It's Mom," I said. "She asked me for help, which should've been my first clue something was off—she never does that."

He laughed lightly. "Really? Because I can. She had you running errands all over the tristate area when we were there in January. And who can forget the great bread incident of 2012?" My mother had sent me on a never-ending mission for the perfect loaf of challah. She used to bake it herself when we were children, but somewhere along the way, she'd decided deriding other people's bread was more delicious.

I started to smile, but then I remembered why I was calling him, and hot tears began forming behind my eyes. "Remember how I told you Hadley said she's losing it? Well, uh . . ." I ducked under an awning to get out of the foot traffic. That's when I realized I was next to Georgie's, the bakery my mother had been talking about. Except, judging from the dirty windows and interior and the cobwebs over the counter, she hadn't been buying bagels there for some time. Were it not for everything else that had happened in the past twelve hours, that wouldn't have been a big deal. But now the sight of the empty building seemed devastating. "I found Mom in the upstairs apartment last night after we got back from Piper's house. It was nearly midnight, and she'd wandered up there. Roger and Rohit moved out, and she's been bringing stuff up there."

"Huh. What kind of stuff?"

"She's been boxing up her apartment, apparently, and trying to organize everything upstairs. I'm going to go help her sort through it later today. And that part is good, as far as I'm concerned. It was the way she was acting when I found her that worries me. She looked . . . confused." Like she had dementia, though I couldn't bring myself to say it. "I feel awful, Josh. I've totally dropped the ball on her over the past year, especially while Belle was sick." The last few months of Belle's life were a blur of vet visits and cleaning up her accidents and trying to make just a few more memories while we still had the chance. Aside from that and work, I'd barely had the energy to put on pants—which was why I sometimes didn't bother. Calling my mother regularly had disappeared from my to-do list. But that had been a choice on my part. I saw that now.

"Oh man. That's really upsetting," muttered Josh. "But you can't blame yourself."

I did, though. That was the thing.

"Laine? You there?"

God bless this city—you could cry your face off in broad daylight, and not a single person gave you a second glance. I swallowed hard and wiped my eyes. "I'm here. I'm just overwhelmed."

"Want me to drive out there?" he asked.

"No," I quickly said. Gah—why had I called him? He was going to think that I wanted to stay married. And maybe I secretly did. After all, why else would I reach out to him? "I just wanted to talk to you before I talked to Piper and Hadley."

"Seriously, Laine, I can come. You know they're less likely to bulldoze you if I'm around," he said gently.

This was true. Four years ago, they'd wanted us all to go to the Florida Keys together, and when I said Josh and I couldn't afford it but wouldn't allow Hadley and Topper to pay for us as they'd offered, both of my sisters had acted like we'd just declared a feud. As Josh explained, we *did* want to see them, but we also weren't comfortable being anyone's charity case. We'd ended up going to a place at the Jersey Shore that had turned out to be a roach motel, and I'd apologized to everyone for nearly six months. Still, Josh had been the one to keep that battle from turning into a war.

"No, I'm okay for now. I'll be home in a week anyway."

"Good, because I just referred you to someone looking for an organizer."

"Really? Who?"

"Melinda! She said she needs help with the whole house."

"Wow, thank you. That would be amazing if it worked out," I said. So far, I'd only done single rooms—closets, kitchens, garages, that sort of thing. An entire house could be a game changer. Moreover, Melinda was the wife of Ravi Mahadik, who'd been one of Josh's closest friends since college. Ravi had started a flatbread pizza company, which was so successful that he used the profits to create a Greek yogurt line that had promptly been acquired by a massive food conglomerate. He and Melinda lived in a house that had to have at least twenty rooms.

"Of course," said Josh.

He really was a good guy. It wasn't just that he was great with my family. Who else would buy me a lemon cake on my birthday (unlike my mother, who had never been able to remember that I really didn't like chocolate)? Who would kill spiders for me and make small talk with the neighbors as I stealthily disappeared inside? Maybe my sisters were right about this being a mistake.

There was a silence, but that wasn't abnormal for us. Finally, Josh said, "Hey, hang in there, okay? I'm here if you need me."

"Thanks," I said, feeling weepy all over again. "That means a lot to me."

"Sure. I love you," he said quietly.

"You, too," I said, and in that moment, I did more than ever. Forget my being needed by someone else; Josh was there for me when I needed *him*. If that was not a partner in the truest sense of the word, then what was? Besides, what if I couldn't even get pregnant? Then I would've destroyed our perfectly good life for nothing.

I'd just wiped my eyes and stuck my phone back in my bag when I heard a voice. "Laine?"

Goose bumps scampered up my arms. *Not here,* I thought. *Not now.*

But this was happening here. Now. Because as much as I wanted to hightail it in the opposite direction, I couldn't possibly pretend that the voice I'd just heard wasn't one I knew nearly as well as my own.

And, of course, it belonged to Ben.

ELEVEN

Laine

When I spun around, he was standing there smiling at me. His skin was several shades darker—probably all that time Down Under—and there were fine lines around the corners of his eyes that hadn't been there the last time I'd seen him, which only served to remind me of how long that had been. His pale blue linen shirt was rumpled, but in the tasteful, intentional way that didn't make me want to attack it with an iron, and his hands were in the pockets of his shorts like we were in the middle of a casual conversation.

Meanwhile, I was dressed in yesterday's T-shirt and my nose was a faucet. And had I even brushed my hair or checked to see if my mascara had racooned me? Granted, Ben had seen me at my worst plenty of times. But this wasn't the second first impression I wanted to be making. Not after the way we'd left things.

Shame and sorrow enveloped me as our fight came rushing back.

It was winter break of our senior year of college, and just like so many other nights, Ben had stopped by after dinner. He helped me do the dishes, and then we ended up in my bedroom. Since Hadley and I shared a room, my parents had never been weird about me having him in there—someone was always coming or going, and anyway, it was just Ben, who was practically the sixth member of the Francis family.

But Hadley was in Vail with the guy she was dating at the time, and Piper was in Europe for a shoot, and my parents were somewhere else—most likely my father was tinkering with something in his workshop while my mother was out with friends. So the apartment was unusually quiet, and Ben and I were lying on my bed side by side, listening to music. He asked me if I wanted to switch the CD. I did, but before I could add that I would take care of it, he leaned over me just as I was about to sit up, and suddenly our faces were two inches apart.

I remember that I could smell him. He always smelled really good—not like cologne, which I'd never liked; more like fresh spring air and the faintest hint of soap. One of us drew in our breath sharply, and I couldn't tell if it had been him or me. *I want to kiss him,* I realized.

And before I could give it another thought, his lips were on mine.

Warmth spread through me like wildfire as our mouths parted. I'd dated several guys by that point, and even the decent ones hadn't made me feel like *this*; my entire body was buzzing, and I had half a mind to devour him.

But as Ben and I broke apart seconds later, my desire was immediately replaced with panic. The attraction I'd picked up on at our graduation party had never disappeared, but it had simmered just below the surface, making it easier to ignore. Still, my mother had warned me. Several times, in fact—back in high school one night when she'd seen him with his arm slung over my shoulder, and more recently the previous summer, after Ben had left our house around midnight. "He's not the one, Laine," she'd said that last time, "so don't ruin your friendship by getting involved with him." I'd blushed and told her she was being ridiculous, but I couldn't help but take her words to heart. After all, she was my mother, and she knew me inside and out. And my parents hadn't been friends before they began dating. Though they weren't exactly blissfully married, they were happy enough not to split up, whereas most of my friends' parents were divorced. My mother obviously knew what she was talking about.

What had Ben and I just done?

"Um, hi," he said, grinning at me from the end of my bed.

I couldn't smile back. In fact, it hurt to even look at him, because I knew—the way you just *know* when you've been best friends with someone that long—that what I was going to say next was going to cause him pain. And yet my mother's words had already been etched into my mind, and maybe even my heart. "We can't do this," I mumbled.

He pulled back a little farther from me. "Says who?"

"Says me. If we get involved, it'll wreck our friendship." After all, college couples almost never ended up married; everyone knew that. And after we broke up, it would be impossible to revert back to the way we'd been before we got physical. So if I had to choose between scratching this itch—no matter how long it had been present—and keeping things as they were, I was going to choose the latter every time.

"Come on, Laine," he said. He wasn't smiling anymore. "I know you better than anyone. You don't really think that."

I did. At least I was trying to, while there was still time to avoid disaster. "Wouldn't you rather stay friends than date?"

"Why do we have to choose?" He propped himself up on his elbows and examined me. "Laine, I know you wanted to kiss me, so I'm not going to apologize for kissing you."

I didn't deny this. But I didn't say anything else, either.

"Who's in your head right now?" He narrowed his eyes. "This is about your mom, isn't it?"

I had no idea how he knew that, but I wasn't surprised. Like he'd said, he knew me better than anyone. "No," I said softly, but as his dark eyes reminded me, there was no use lying to him. "Yes."

"What did she say?" He sounded angry. But he never got angry—that wasn't his way—and I was already thinking to myself, *See? Mom was right. Just the hint of a conversation about love and we're already fighting.*

"Nothing. Just . . ."

"What, Laine? If you're going to let your mom make decisions for you, you at least owe it to me to tell me what she decided."

"That's not what this is." I sounded unconvinced, even to myself. "She just pointed out that love and friendship don't mix."

"Oh, because your parents are the gold standard," he said, arching an eyebrow.

"That's mean."

"I'm sorry, but it's true. You know I like your mom and dad, but they're pretty much roommates who tolerate each other. Don't you think they'd be doing better if they were actually friends?"

"Ouch," I said as tears pricked my eyes. I wanted to remark that at least my parents still spoke—unlike his, who hadn't been in touch in more than a decade—but I bit my tongue.

He reached out and touched my leg. His fingers were electric on my skin. I didn't pull away. "I'm sorry, Laine. But seriously, who cares what your mom thinks?"

"I do," I said quietly. I cared more about what she thought than almost anybody—because she was my *mother*. As she herself had remarked many times, I "got" her in a way that Hadley and Piper didn't, and when she complimented me, it often felt like the sun on my skin on a cool day. I wanted to please her, and I wasn't about to apologize for that. And—not that I'd ever say this to Ben—I had to wonder if he couldn't understand that because his own mother had been out of the picture for so long.

"Well, you're twenty-one years old. Don't you think it's time to let your mom stop manipulating you and make your own decisions?"

"That's mean, and this *is* me making my own decision," I said, even as my mental wheels were frantically turning. *Was* my mom being manipulative? This was turning into a terrible argument. How did I keep it from getting worse?

But it was too late. He stood and crossed his arms. "You act different around your family. Especially her. And I don't like it."

What a dumb thing to say, I thought. If I acted differently, it was because I had to. Ben didn't need me to clean his kitchen, for example, and Selena didn't need me to referee her younger siblings' fights . . . because I wasn't related to them. "Everyone acts different around their family." I glanced at the door, which was cracked open, praying that neither of my parents was nearby to hear him say this. "Let's change the subject, please."

"No, Laine. I'm not changing the subject. And no, not everyone. You."

"How?" I challenged.

"You do whatever they want!" he said with exasperation.

"I do not," I said, but my cheeks were flushing because I knew it was a lie. "And I don't see how we can be friends if you don't like who I am around my family."

"Oh, come on, Laine. I didn't say I don't *like* you. I said I don't like the way you *act* with them. Sally knows you're a people pleaser, and she takes advantage of that. The question is, what the hell does she have against me?" He took a step back, almost like he'd been hit. "Unless this is about me being Black."

"Are you serious?" I said. I wasn't being rhetorical. Ben and I had been friends for fifteen years. When, during that entire time, had she ever treated him differently or less than? I couldn't think of a single instance. And yet I immediately found myself rationalizing: She and Reggie were always friendly, and wasn't that proof she wasn't racist? She never unknowingly stuck her foot in her mouth the way I'd heard some of my other friends' parents do. Heck, one of her closest friends, Mary, was Jamaican!

But every one of these defenses suggested that she needed defending.

"It's all fun and games until it's about your daughter dating," he added, his voice barely audible.

"I cannot believe you'd say that about my mother," I whisper-hissed.

"And I can't believe she put me in the position to have to consider it."

I stared at him, trying to square his accusation with the mother I knew and loved. What if he was right—then what? He knew I'd never go up to her and say, *Hey, Mom, any chance you're a racist and don't realize it?* And even if he was wrong, the idea was already in my head; how was I ever going to get it out?

I wasn't.

"You know what? We're done here." I stood and started for the door.

"Oh, come on, Laine," he said, his tone instantly more forgiving. "Forget I said that."

I froze and stared at him. Forget? Who was he kidding? I would've given anything to hit a rewind button and go back to the minute before we kissed, but there was no undoing what had happened. My mother had been right: romance *had* ruined everything. "I'm never going to be able to erase that from my memory," I said, reaching for the doorknob.

"Where are you even going? This is *your* house."

"Away from you." I flung the door open. "This," I said, pointing between us, "*was* a mistake, and our conversation is proof."

He crossed his arms over his chest. "So you'd rather make your mom happy than yourself."

I didn't know why, but he wanted a fight. Well, too bad: I was *not* going to justify that with a response. "I'm leaving, Ben," I said over my shoulder.

"If you go, I'm not coming after you," he said.

I could barely bring myself to turn and look at him, because I somehow knew it would be the last time for a long time. And yet he'd crossed a line—a big one—in bringing my mom into this. If he really thought she was racist, why had he waited until just now to say that?

"And why would you even want to? You don't like who I am when I'm around my mother, and, PS, you think she has a problem with the color of your skin. I hope to God that's not true, but even if it is, she's *my mother*, Ben. I can't turn my back on her." Tears stung my eyes as I shook my head. "So, yeah—I guess this is goodbye."

~

That had been sixteen years ago, but the pain was still so fresh in my mind that it could've been yesterday. How could he possibly smile at me after that?

"Hello to you, too," he said pleasantly.

"Um. Hi." My tongue felt like sandpaper. "What are you doing in town?"

"Um." He arched an eyebrow. "I live here?"

"You're . . . staying with your dad again?"

"Long story, but no. I live at his place now."

My pulse quickened. That was going to make things even more complicated.

He continued, "Dad's over in Jersey, right down the street from Bobby. New York's no country for old men," he added with a twisted smile.

"Ugh, I'm sorry." I sounded too familiar for someone who wasn't anymore, and I quickly glanced away. Carroll Park was just across the street. Ben and I had once snuck a bottle of Reggie's whiskey onto the play structure, where we'd had our very first drink. And how many games of hide-and-seek and tag had we played there with Bobby and our friend Selena? How many impassioned conversations had we had beneath those very trees, about life and our futures and the people we planned to be?

All that friendship wiped away with one terrible, unfixable argument.

But now Ben was leaning against the side of the bakery like nothing had happened. Then again, he'd always had a way about him that put other people at ease. Our fifth-grade teacher had spent almost an entire year calling him Bobby, and instead of correcting her, Ben just played along. Because that was the kind of guy he was . . . at least up until a point.

"Then you're not in—" The word *Australia* was about to come shooting out of my mouth, revealing that I knew exactly where he'd been last. "California," I supplied, since that's where he'd been talking about heading before our argument.

"Not for five years now," he said. "After Celeste and I split—uh, she was my wife—I had to get out of San Fran. Been all kinds of places since then, but guess I'm a New Yorker again. At least for the time being."

For the time being? And what exactly had happened between him and Celeste? I had questions, lots of them. None of which I would be asking.

"Hey, how's your mom? Guessing you're in town to see her?" The way he said this made it sound like he knew my father had passed. "Hadley called me after your dad died," he added.

Damn it—how was he still reading my mind after all these years? "She never told me that," I said, making a mental note to have a word with my sister. "But why do you care how my mom's doing?"

"Come on, Laine. Don't be like that."

"I'm not being like anything," I said. "But I'm not going to pretend like you didn't basically tell me you thought she was the worst, then acted like I'd dropped off the face of the earth." *I needed you,* I added mentally. *I needed you to meet my dog, and comfort me when my dad died, and to know what was going on with my life.*

He frowned. "You're the one who said goodbye, Laine."

Oh no. I was *not* rehashing that. Especially not today, but not ever. "Let's not go there and say we did."

Now he was regarding me with amusement. "Some things never change, huh?"

I turned away briefly. Just like that kiss, this conversation was a mistake.

"And now look at us," he continued. "A couple of almost-middle-aged people."

"Fun," I deadpanned.

He broke into a grin, and even though I hadn't been trying to make him smile, I couldn't help but crack a smile myself.

"Well, lucky I decided to go get a coffee at this exact moment. Otherwise I might not've run into you," he said.

I hated that hearing him say he was happy to run into me filled me with a painful kind of joy. "You'd have seen me at some point, given that I'm staying three houses down," I said.

He tilted his head curiously. "Last time I checked, there were eight million other people living in this city. Remember when we were convinced old Mrs. Collins had died and that her apartment was haunted?" he said. "Then two years later we saw her wheeling her cart through Prospect Park?"

In spite of myself, I had to laugh as I remembered how Ben and I had both screamed and run in the opposite direction when she'd called our names.

Now Ben was laughing, too. His laugh was low and deep and had always made me feel like I was the most interesting person in the world. No one else had ever made me feel that way, but my delight immediately morphed into sadness.

"So, you doing okay?" said Ben after he stopped laughing. "Still the longest-suffering member of the famous Francis sisters? What else is new?"

I wanted to tell him everything—about Belle's death, my impending divorce, and why that had come about. Even the situation with my mom. All of it.

Except that wasn't who Ben and I were anymore. It wasn't who we'd ever be again. As friendly as he was being, the reality was that if either of us actually wanted to be friends again, we would have called, or emailed, or reached out in any other way that didn't involve a chance encounter.

"Listen, I've gotta go," I said as evenly as I could.

"Sorry. I didn't mean to pry," he said. I'd hurt him; I could tell from the way he was squinting.

Don't try to fix it, I ordered myself. *You don't owe him anything.* "It's fine," I said. "Send my best to your dad."

"Okay," he said. "I'll do that."

"Okay," I said, but I was still standing there dumbly. *One foot in front of the other, Laine,* I reminded myself. *Couldn't be easier.* "Bye," I said, and before he could see me cringe at how stiff and stupid I sounded, I set off toward the apartment.

I'd counted out eight steps when he yelled, "Lainey!"

Lainey. How dare he.

But in spite of myself, I spun around. He was in the same place, hands shoved in his pockets, except his face was kind of twisted up. If I didn't know better, I'd say he looked regretful. "What is it?" I said.

He shrugged, but I knew that shrug. It was the opposite of *I don't care*. "It was really good to see you," he said.

Yes, but it was also terribly painful. So painful that I almost wished I hadn't bumped into him in front of a vacant bagel shop. This was why people in recovery didn't have the occasional drink; it only made it harder to stay on the wagon.

"You, too," I said. Then I took off for my mother's before I could give in to the temptation to turn back around and see if Ben was still standing there, watching me walk away once again.

TWELVE

LAINE

When I got back to the brownstone, I headed to the top floor, assuming my mother was already up there like she said she was going to be—not that I actually expected her to be doing much of anything without my help. But the place was empty, save all that mess, and I'm sorry to say I was relieved about that. I couldn't stop seeing Ben's face, which was really a composite of younger him and older him. And I needed to get him out of my head before I interacted with my mother.

After our blowup, I'd had to twist myself into knots to keep thinking good thoughts about her. Every time she gave me advice—even if it was just to grab a sweater before I headed out—I found myself wondering if she was manipulating me. And I couldn't help but take a magnifying glass to every situation that involved anyone of a different race. I couldn't find evidence that Ben was right—but that was probably owing to my own blind spot, I reasoned, since I understood that it was impossible that she wasn't unintentionally racist at least some of the time.

Although I didn't quite realize it at the time, staying in Ann Arbor after graduation must have been another way to avoid second-guessing everything she said and did, not to mention my responses to her.

Time and distance did what they do so well, and eventually my anxiety eased, mostly resurfacing at pivotal moments. When I first brought Josh home, and she whispered loudly, so everyone could hear, "He's a keeper, Laine!" my immediate reaction was to question whether she somehow felt more warmly toward Asian men, and why she couldn't summon that same warmth toward Ben.

By that point, it didn't matter; our relationship was nonexistent. She'd asked why Ben hadn't come to my college graduation party, and when I'd told her we'd had a falling-out, she'd nodded knowingly and never brought it up again. Oddly, that hurt even more than her pressing for details. *Don't you care?* I wanted to shout. *You spent years welcoming him into your home. You knew he was more important to me than anyone. How can you act like he never existed?*

I didn't say any of that, though. Because after having my heart broken by Ben, the last thing I needed was another fight.

As much as I wanted to start cleaning the upstairs apartment right away—if anything could soothe me, it was bringing order to chaos—I knew I needed to make sure she hadn't wandered into the neighborhood in a negligee. But when I let myself into her apartment, I found her dozing on an armchair in the living room. Relieved, I left her there and quietly headed back upstairs.

I'll never know if it was nature or nurture or both, but I'd always had a proclivity to organize. I can still remember waking early as a young child, long before anyone else in my house had stirred, and going from room to room to clean. I can't recall what I did, exactly—probably put the shoes in the foyer, maybe placed the dirty dishes in the sink and put the toys in the toy box. But I can still see my mother's bleary-eyed expression changing into delight when she wandered into the living room. "What an angel you are," she said to me. Piper was fussing in her arms, but she put her in the rocker anyway. Hadley had just emerged from our bedroom, and my mother ignored her, too, as she hugged me. "You're so good, Lainey," she said, kissing the top of my head. "I hope you know that." I was not well spoken like Hadley. I was not irresistible like Piper. But in that moment, I was the center of her attention. And that was even better.

I didn't know why I craved my mother's attention; maybe it was the same reason some children who were rarely allowed to have sugar were inclined to secretly hoard candy under their beds. But once I learned how to get it, it was the party trick I used over and over—scrubbing the brownstone from top to bottom while they were in the Berkshires, locating my mother's purse after she'd spent an hour searching, straightening Piper's room for her so she and my mother wouldn't fight. I never resented a minute of it; there was something inherently comforting knowing that however messy the outside world was, everything between our four walls could be just right, at least for a little while.

Maybe that was why the sight of the boxes and papers all over the upstairs apartment—which looked even more plentiful in the full light of day—didn't intimidate me. Unlike the contents of my childhood home, these were not the things my mother cared about. Otherwise she never would have boxed them all up. This would be easy.

The first step of organizing is to survey the situation in its entirety to determine what, precisely, you're dealing with; only then can you formulate a plan and begin to actually deal with it. And so I walked among the piles, taking it all in. *What an odd variety,* I thought to myself. There were a few larger boxes, though they didn't have handles. In fact, now that I was really looking, most of the boxes were various sizes, but few larger than a shoebox. Maybe Bashir had given them to her—he often handed out liquor boxes to people who were moving. But no; unlike those boxes, with their splashy labels and strange sizes, these were almost entirely basic brown cardboard, the kind most companies used for shipping. And as I looked closer, that's exactly what these were; every single one of them had an address sticker affixed to the front and had been mailed to one Sally Francis.

I picked up a box to examine it. I hesitated for a moment—my mother had always been big on privacy—then reassured myself that she'd already given me permission to help her. I began to pull the tape off the top, which is when I realized that unless my mother was a whiz at packing tape, which I highly doubted, the box had never even been opened. Beneath the cardboard flaps was a sea of pale pink tissue paper. I fished around for a second before retrieving a tall bottle with pink letters. "Liquid Face-lift," read the label. Odd. My mother had a professed aversion to aging, yes, but why had she not bothered to take out this product and use it?

A quick shake told me the box contained more stuff, so I reached into it again and pulled out a wrinkle-blasting peel, and beneath that, a box full of silicone pads that were supposed to prevent crow's-feet from forming, though the woman on the front of the package looked like she was recovering in a burn unit. A receipt confirmed that my mother had been the one to make the purchase . . . which had been *$175*? For three items?

I pulled another box off the top of a stack. This one had been opened, at least, but it contained a handheld tool that purported to slice and dice even the toughest foods. Except, my mother barely cooked. Why had she purchased this? Was it a gift that she'd forgotten to give? Topper did like to cook; maybe it had been for him.

But as I glanced around, it was like I was staring at one of those 3-D posters and my vision had just now adjusted. Now the shape of this situation was crystal clear: every last box in the apartment was an item that had been shipped to her. And a good number of them, maybe even half, had never even been opened, let alone used.

I tore through them, tossing them aside instead of arranging them as I normally would've. Every package made my heart sink deeper in my chest. There were hundreds of dollars' worth of items; thousands, if I were doing honest math. Many of the household products were from a single supplier, a multilevel marketing company that the *Washington*

Post had recently featured in a scathing exposé. I'd heard Ravi and Josh talking about it, as one of their B-school classmates was high up the food chain at the company, and the story had been something of a scandal in their circle. But the majority of the items were random. Gaudy earrings that I couldn't imagine my mother wearing, purchased from a home shopping network. Some incredibly small newborn onesies, which I assumed she'd bought around the time the twins were born—until I saw that they'd been ordered just a few weeks earlier. A product that purported to make dingy old grout look brand-new again. Thin, velvet-covered hangers that were supposed to save space and prevent creases in clothing. This last product I could get behind. But how could my mother have purchased it without bothering to open it?

There were still a dozen or so boxes left when I gave up. I couldn't do it—I just could not do it. Because every single package was further proof that something was wrong with my mother. Really, something was wrong with *me*. Hadley had clearly told me our mother was not well. Even before I'd discovered the thousands of dollars of purchases she neither wanted nor needed, she'd been dropping bread crumbs for me for months—a missed word here, a lost thought there, forgetting something, like my last birthday, that she wouldn't have even a few years earlier. And all the while, I had been insisting that it was nothing but loneliness and everyday aging.

I sat in the middle of the living room, too overwhelmed to stand or even cry. As I looked around, I knew in my heart that all this stuff wasn't just more work for me and Hadley and Piper.

It was the beginning of the end.

THIRTEEN

Laine

When I went back downstairs, my mother was still on the armchair, but she was awake. I must've still looked upset, because she immediately asked me if everything was okay.

You tell me, Mom, I thought, though I was a little relieved, too, that she'd picked up on my emotional state. If I'd been younger, I would've taken this as a sign she cared. Now I was viewing it as evidence of her lucidity—and the more of that I could find, the better. "Fine," I lied. "I was a little surprised by the boxes upstairs, though. Did you buy all those things?"

"Oh, Laine," she said, waving a hand dismissively. "First Hadley, now you? Can't I spend my own money the way I want to?"

"Of course you can," I said quickly. "I was just curious."

"It's just a few things."

If by *a few* she meant several dozen, sure.

"Okay," I said. It didn't *feel* okay, but I wasn't going to sit and argue with her. I needed to talk to my sisters, to see if maybe—just maybe—I was overreacting or overthinking this. Speaking of which, I had four minutes to get out the door if I was going to be on time. "I've got to go meet Piper and Hadley soon," I told my mother. "Are you sure you'll be okay here by yourself?"

She smiled brightly. "Haven't I been by myself for years now?"

"Yes," I said, unable to ignore the guilt that her comment triggered in me. "You have." She'd also spent some of that time turning the upstairs apartment into a warehouse for expensive tchotchkes. But she wasn't a toddler, I reminded myself; I couldn't tote her everywhere with me. Besides, I needed to talk to my sisters without her around.

"You're a good one, Laine Francis," she said as I bent to kiss her cheek. "Don't you forget that."

"I won't," I said softly.

But I wasn't the one who needed to be reminded not to forget.

~

My sisters and I had agreed to meet at a restaurant off of Central Park—and by *we*, I mean Hadley had told us that's where we'd be gathering. The host informed us that there was a wait, so we gave her a cell phone number to call us when our table was ready, then grabbed coffee and donuts from a street vendor and headed into the park.

"Laine, what's wrong?" said Hadley as we made our way down the winding trail. Usually we had to push through a throng of tourists, especially near the park's entrance. But except for the occasional jogger whizzing past us, we were practically alone today.

I took a sip of my coffee, which was bitter and burnt. Then I sighed and said, "You were right."

"About which part?" retorted Hadley with a grin.

Over Hadley's head, Piper rolled her eyes at me, but I couldn't even smile.

"Mom," I said. We'd just passed under a low bridge, and there was a wooden bench up ahead on the path. "Why don't we sit?"

Piper, who was dressed in the drab athletic clothes that she often wore in an attempt to blend in, took one end of the bench; Hadley, who was wearing a boho-style caftan that I knew for a fact cost as much as one of the many magazine checks I was waiting on, took the other. I plopped down between them.

"So you've seen it for yourself now," said Hadley.

"Yeah," I said miserably. "It's bad."

"What happened?" asked Piper.

"Where do I even start?" As awful as I felt about not listening to Hadley, I felt worse about what I was about to tell her and Piper. I took a deep breath. "So, Mom's been buying a bunch of stuff from God only knows where, and she's not even opening most of it. She's just hauling it all upstairs. I found her up there last night looking totally confused."

"Wait, what about Roger and Rohit?" said Piper.

"Apparently they moved out months ago and she never thought to mention it. And that's not even the bad part. You guys . . ." My voice caught. Back at the apartment, I'd tried to tell myself it was okay. But now, here with my sisters, there was no sugarcoating the bitter truth. "She was totally out of it. It was horrible."

"I knew it," said Hadley, but for once, she didn't sound happy about being right. "I called her around nine a week or two ago, and I swear she didn't know who I was right away. Then she tried to act like it was fine. I let it slide, and I shouldn't have."

"Crap. What was in the boxes?" asked Piper.

"Cosmetics and grout cleaners and cooking tools and . . ." I shook my head. "Basically, a ton of junk she doesn't need and maybe doesn't even want, given that she's leaving it boxed up. It's awful, but that's not all. She's losing her mind, you guys. Or at least her memory. Hadley, I'm sorry I didn't listen to you. Piper, I owe you an apology, too. We could have addressed this sooner if I'd been here. I think I didn't want to see it because, deep down, I knew how awful this was going to be."

My sisters' arms were around me before I'd even realized that I'd started to cry.

"It's okay," said Piper, stroking my hair.

"Don't worry, Laine," said Hadley, pulling me close. "I knew you'd understand when you saw it for yourself. I'm just sorry I wasn't wrong."

"That's the first time you've ever said that," I said, sniffling, and she elbowed me lightly. "Seriously, though, she's only seventy-two. That's so young to have dementia."

"Maybe it's Parkinson's, like Nana Meyers had," said Piper.

"I'd considered that, too," I admitted.

"I don't know for sure, but I've been looking into this, and it really doesn't seem like she has any other symptoms," said Hadley, frowning. "Either way, we need to get her to a neurologist. I should've made her see someone months ago."

"*I* should have," I said. "You'd just had the twins—you didn't need one more thing to deal with." I could've found a way to help my family without abandoning Belle. Why hadn't I at least tried? "I've been slacking, and I'm sorry."

Piper's face crumpled. "Is this going to happen to us? I mean, first Nana Meyers, now Mom. What are the odds?"

Summer had arrived early, and it was nearly eighty out, but a chill ran up my spine. Yes, I didn't want to pass on some unknown condition to my hypothetical child. But there was another issue, and it was just as weighty. Piper had her three kids to care for her when she was old and gray. Hadley had her twins, not to mention a younger husband and money enough to buy whatever help they needed. Me?

I had no one.

No wonder my biological clock had turned into a gong.

"What do we do now?" I asked. "We can't force her into a nursing home. We'd have to jump through all kinds of legal hoops to do it, and even then—well, we all know she thinks it's a live burial."

"What else are we going to do? There's really no other solution." But even as she said this, Hadley's eyes homed in on me.

"No way, Hadley," I said, because I knew exactly what she was thinking. "I can't. I'm not moving back." *Because I want to get pregnant and have a child, and New York City is the last place I want to raise them.* The myriad inconveniences of raising a child in the city began parading through my mind: Having to schlep a stroller up and down the subway stairs. Preschool that cost as much as college tuition. Walking six blocks just to find a small patch of grass to let the baby play on. I'd face plenty of hurdles raising a child in Michigan—but they wouldn't be nearly as bad as those I'd encounter here.

"Why not? If you're serious about getting divorced . . ." she said.

"Then this could be your fresh start," said Piper, finishing her sentence.

"What happened to you two wanting me and Josh to make things work?" I said.

"Well, that's not out of the question. And if you do make up, I know he'll move here for you," said Hadley, and I didn't bother telling her that Josh was more likely to get struck by a stray comet than move here; as much as he liked the buzz of other people, he claimed the cost of living was insulting. "And now that Roger and Rohit are gone, you could take the upstairs apartment. I bet we could work it out to where you're barely paying rent—maybe an early inheritance kind of thing. And there's a second bedroom, so you could keep writing from home."

"But my organizing business is just getting going," I said. And I needed that money now more than ever; our health insurance was terrible, and based on what I'd found while researching single parenting, raising a child cost a cool $233,000—and that was if everything went right. "I'm between clients right now, but I have another lead—a big one," I said, thinking of Ravi and Melinda's palatial home.

"New York would be a *way* better place to make bank. I know so many people who need to hire someone," said Piper. "I'd be happy to help you." Her enthusiasm must have been contagious, because I'd started to smile. Piper would help *me*? I didn't hate the sound of that.

"And wouldn't it be amazing if we were all living in the same place?" said Hadley. She hugged me again. "You'd be able to see the kids more. And us! This could be a blessing in disguise."

I nodded, but instead of imagining my nieces and nephews, I was thinking of Ben. Even though our run-in had been awkward and had stirred up some old feelings I would've preferred to keep buried, at least a small part of me was curious about the possibility of living three doors down from the man formerly known as my best friend. I doubted we'd ever be as close as we used to again; too many years had passed, and too many un-take-backable words had been exchanged. Yet he'd been happy to see me, and I had to admit that seeing him had made me feel . . . younger somehow, and beneath my angst, sort of warm and fuzzy. What if—just what if—there was some way for us to be friends again?

Except there was one massive problem about moving back—and it rendered any thoughts about Ben inconsequential. How could I possibly care for a child and my mother at the same time?

"I don't know," I said. "I don't want to become Mom's minder. It would ruin our relationship."

"Or it could make it stronger," said Hadley. "It just depends on the intention you set."

"Spoken like someone who doesn't want the job," I said.

"I can't *have* the job," said Hadley. "Our nanny just quit."

"Leticia?" said Piper, just as I said, "Why?"

"She found a family that will pay her more *and* rent an apartment for her. She didn't even give notice," said Hadley with a sigh. "We'll find someone else—at least, I hope we will—but now I have no childcare and a full-time client load. Laine . . ."

She didn't have to finish. I knew. I was the one who was childless, and now dog-less, and who could work from anywhere.

Who owed it to her sisters to pick up some of the slack.

Guilt enveloped me as I thought about how little I'd done to help my family over the past decade, let alone the past year.

"For the sake of argument, let's say I move here," I said. "I'll need to work; I won't be able to be there with Mom twenty-four seven. So doesn't it make more sense to hire someone to help her? A home health aide or something?"

"Yeah, right. She'll never go for that," said Hadley. "You know that. Even if that weren't ridiculously expensive, she's too private to allow someone to stay with her. Anyway, it sounds like what she most needs is someone to be there overnight. We could set some kind of alarm so you knew if she wandered outside or upstairs."

I could *almost* imagine raising a baby in the upstairs apartment. There was a second bedroom, and the place was bright and clean and had built-in shelving that would go a long way to keeping things uncluttered. But then I pictured my mother barging through the door moments after I'd gotten my baby to sleep, and then having to help her *and* my wailing infant.

"I love living in Ann Arbor," I said quietly. I wasn't ready to tell them about wanting a child—not when it would seem like more evidence that I was making a mistake in divorcing Josh. "You both know that."

"Come on, Laine. What could possibly make you think that's better than the best city in the whole world?" said Piper, gesturing to the skyline, which was shining over the park's treetops.

Her comment reminded me of a trip my mother and I had taken to Bloomingdale's. I remember it because it was a rare excursion we'd taken on our own. "Just think, each person you see has an entire life, filled with experiences and thoughts and people you'll never know about," she had remarked as we were going up the escalator. I couldn't have been older than ten or eleven at the time, and I remember her comment making my head hurt. Every person browsing handbags or trying to sidestep the overly aggressive perfume sprayers—all with a completely different story! Even now, it broke my brain to think about it. It wasn't like I'd chosen to move to a town of twelve residents in the middle of farmland. Still, Ann Arbor was certainly more manageable than New York.

It was also nowhere near Ben.

And now my sisters were staring at me with such hope—and yes, love—that I couldn't bring myself to tell them the truth: their request had put me in an impossible position.

"I'll think about it," I said, but when they threw their arms around me again, I knew what they'd actually heard was *yes*.

FOURTEEN

Laine

As a child, I didn't cradle baby dolls in my arms or draw pictures of the family I imagined having one day. Nor did I attempt to parent Piper, who was three years younger than me—not the way that Hadley did, proudly pushing her around the neighborhood in a stroller and, in doing so, earning herself the nickname of Little Mama. For me, motherhood, much like adulthood, was a proverbial bridge I'd consider crossing if and when it materialized. Looking back, I suspect I got that from my own mother, who mostly took life as it came at her.

I can still remember the day I realized I wanted a child. I was in my midtwenties and I had taken Belle to the arboretum. I preferred not to run unless I was being chased, but she desperately needed the exercise, so I'd purchased a pair of jogging shoes and learned to mostly keep up with her. On this particular morning, I'd let her pull me down the winding dirt path all the way to the river. We'd just reached the water when I saw a man and a woman holding the hands of a small boy. "One, two—" They swung him into the air on "three," making him squeal with delight, which made them laugh and look at each other like they'd just discovered gravity. I knelt beside Belle, who was happily panting, and watched the trio do this again, and again, and again.

Unlike Josh, whom I'd been dating for a year or two at that point, I didn't want big things for my life. And sometimes I'd worried about that. Why *didn't* I care about being rich, when it clearly made everything easier? Shouldn't I want a fabulous career, a taste of fame, or an opportunity to do something that would change the world for the better? Or what about health? I could have been stronger, thinner, more energetic. I could have tried to be prettier or better dressed or at least charming. It seemed to me that I should've been attempting to becoming *more,* like most everyone around me seemed to be.

But when I watched that family, desire—so potent that it bordered on primal—finally emerged. Suddenly I knew what I wanted for my life, and it was the beautiful, mundane joy of being a parent. And after Josh and I got married and I casually mentioned being ready for a baby the first time, then the second, then the eighth—and he responded, just as casually each time, that he hoped for a baby, too, but he still wasn't quite ready—I told myself, *When you really want something, you're willing to wait for it. Be patient.*

What I didn't know then was that every time you defer your dream, it grows a bit weaker, a little less urgent, until one day you've all but forgotten it's there. Really, if Belle hadn't died, I wonder if anything about my life would've changed. I didn't have what I really desired. But things were easy, and you can almost mistake that for happiness.

I felt wretched as I rode the subway home after brunch with my sisters. I did want to help them, and, of course, my mother. There was no way she wasn't aware that something was wrong, and even if she'd never admit it, that had to be terrifying for her. But doing the right thing—and I was pretty sure moving back was right—meant putting my dream on hold yet again. And this late in the game, that was akin to abandoning it.

When I got home, my mother wanted me to go grocery shopping with her, and I agreed, thinking it would be a good trial run for us becoming roommates. Our excursion turned into a two-hour trip; she sauntered down every aisle, considering all of her options, only to fill her cart with less than a dozen items. Then it was dinnertime, so after dropping the groceries off, we'd walked over to a little French place a few blocks away. There, she'd talked my ear off about her friend Mary and her wine club and how she and my father had met—they'd been set up at a dance by a couple of friends and hadn't particularly liked each other at first. But her favorite Supremes song had come on, and he'd whisked her to the dance floor, and the rest, as she said, was history. She'd told this story plenty over the years, and she'd always looked so happy when she recounted it. This time, though, I had to plaster a smile on my face, because it occurred to me that they hadn't really liked each other after that night.

"The place is a mess, Sally," he'd often mutter under his breath as he read the paper.

"Would you prefer I spend hours scrubbing in a shapeless house-dress?" she'd respond, reminding him that however messy our apartment may have been, she was not—her hair and makeup were just so, she was wearing a stylish outfit, and looked almost exactly as she had before birthing three live humans.

"Both, please," he'd practically growl, and she'd laugh like he was hilarious.

But soon after, she'd disappear into their bedroom or go out to meet a friend, not to return for hours at a time. Sometimes I wondered if she ever thought about leaving us behind, like Ben's mom had. Reggie was a lot chattier, and frankly nicer than my dad, and yet Ben's mother had still left. What was to say my own wouldn't have enough of my father—and yes, us—one day?

I always made sure to clean the apartment a little more than usual after my parents had one of these exchanges.

In spite of my less-than-happy recollection about my parents, dining with my mother had been really nice. It had been ages since she and I had sat and talked like that—just the two of us, without Josh or my sisters or anyone else there to join in. She didn't have a memory slip all night, either, and this only affirmed my suspicion about her needing to be around people. What if my presence made all the difference in how the next part of her life unfolded?

But as I tried to picture what this life would look like if I were a bigger part of it, I kept seeing myself trying to jiggle an infant on my hip while running up and down the stairs to help my mother. I was again struck by the impossibility of caring for my elderly parent while trying to have a baby. It didn't matter how much money I had, how carefully I structured my calendar, or whether I brought in an aide or a nanny (or both) to help. Heck, even if I decided to remain married to Josh and have him move to New York with me, it still wouldn't make enough of a difference. There was no way to be the parent I wanted to be while also attempting to be there for my mother as she faded away. Which meant I had a decision to make.

~

The next morning, my mother was showering when Josh's photo lit up on my phone. It was a shot I'd taken of him and Belle on the beach in Lake Michigan just a year earlier. It seemed so long ago that it might as well have been ten.

I thought about letting it go to voicemail. But divorce or no divorce, I owed it to Josh to tell him I was considering moving to New York to live with my mother. However, I needed to make sure that she didn't catch wind of that—not before I'd spoken to my sisters, and yes, my husband—and she'd probably come traipsing out of the bathroom at any moment. I couldn't go on the back patio, because the bathroom window was right there and you could hear everything through it. So I put on sunglasses and a hat and went out to sit on the stoop.

"Hey," I said.

"Laine?" He sounded kind of panicky. "Are you in the middle of something?"

"Nope. The real question is, aren't you?" It was Saturday, but Josh didn't observe weekends, even when he was between launches. I used to tell myself that it was just what he was doing to get his projects off the ground, but in time, I'd come to see that he had the same aversion to downtime that I had to clutter.

"No," he said. "Piper called me yesterday."

I frowned. "Is she your divorce hotline or something?"

"No," he said, drawing the word out like I was slow. "She's my sister-in-law, Laine. And you know we're friends. She's been giving me some great marketing ideas for the app. But she also told me you're talking about moving back to help with Mom. Is that true?"

Couldn't Piper wait for me to share my own news, even if it wasn't actually news yet? "Well, I guess you already know, then. And yeah, I'm considering it."

"That's the second weird, split-second decision you've made in less than a month. Are you sure you're okay?"

Actually, I hadn't made up my mind yet, and I could feel myself getting irritated. I took a deep breath, then another. "I still have a lot to think through," I said as calmly as I was able.

"What about our place, Laine? What about your business?"

"It's my mom, Josh. I have to at least entertain the possibility of helping her."

"Well, we could move your mom here."

My mother was a lifelong New Yorker who had once asked me if restaurants were open after eight in Ann Arbor; even though she'd visited a handful of times, she seemed convinced it was the sticks.

But wait, I thought suddenly. *The real question is, why are* you *thinking about this as though moving back in with Josh is an option?*

"Josh, do you really think you and I should be making 'we' decisions right now?"

"Lainey!" My mother had just opened the door. "I've been looking for you. Who're you talking to?"

I stood and turned to face her. That's when I realized she was wearing a silk negligee.

"Mom, I think you should go inside and put some clothes on, okay?" I said, trying to direct her toward the foyer.

"Don't change the subject!" she said, stepping onto the stoop. "Who are you chatting with? You've got a big frown on your face."

"It's Josh, Mom." I sighed. "Josh," I said into the receiver, "as you can probably tell, my mother just came outside." I added in a whisper, "She's wearing her nightgown."

"Yikes," he said as my mother took the phone from my hands.

"Joshy! How are you? Tell me everything," she said, leaning against the stoop's wrought-iron handrail casually. She looked almost like a teenager. Except I somehow suspected that even a teen would have thought to throw on, say, a bra, if not a robe.

"Oh yes," she twittered to Josh, either not registering or not caring that the passersby were gawking at her. Maybe I could cry in public without being paid any attention to, but a seventy-two-year-old self-made lingerie model did not go unnoticed.

"Mom, it's time to say goodbye," I told her, putting my hand on her back to guide her inside. But when I reached for the doorknob, the door didn't budge—because my mother had removed the rock I'd used to prop the door open, and the lock had done what locks are supposed to do.

"Crap," I muttered. Unless my mother had stashed her house keys in a cavity, she clearly didn't have them on her. But it was my fault for relying on the rock—even as a young child, I'd known you didn't leave the apartment without keys on you.

"That's right. Oh yes, I will," said my mother to Josh, who was clearly humoring her. "Absolutely. Hope to see you soon. Love you, dear boy. Bye!" She handed the phone to me. "Well, what is it? You still look like someone killed your dog."

I winced, but she didn't notice. "The thing is, Mom, neither of us have keys."

"And?"

"And that means we're locked out."

"Oh, that's no problem," she said with a wave of her hand. Before I could ask her how that could possibly be so, she was already moseying down the block in her bare feet and negligee. A construction worker hanging scaffolding on a brownstone across the street whistled, and my mother turned and gave him a glowing smile and her best pageant wave.

I was too alarmed to be mortified. My mother had always loved the spotlight, but this was not that. And at once, I realized that whether I lived with her or not, caring for her was going to be a roller coaster—and we'd barely just begun the ride.

"Where are you going?" I called, beginning down the stairs. But my stomach sank when I realized I knew exactly where she was headed.

She was already at the door. "Reggie has a key," she announced, pressing the doorbell for his apartment.

"What?" I was confused. She and Reggie had been friendly when Ben and I were young, but I'd gotten the impression they'd mostly done that for our benefit; by the time we were old enough to walk ourselves to the park, they'd gone back to being cordial, only occasionally stopping to chat with each other.

"Mom, Reggie doesn't live there anymore," I said, coming up behind her. "Ben does."

"What?" Her face fell. "But I just spoke with him."

My pulse quickened. It was far too early in the day for her to be drifting back to nowhere land. "No, Mom. He's—"

Before I could continue, Ben was in the doorway. In spite of myself, I smiled, and he smiled back. Then I remembered that my mother was more than halfway to naked.

If my mother's state registered, he didn't show it. "Well, two Francises at one time! This is a pleasant surprise." He met my eye. "Or did you change your last name? I don't know if I ever asked you that."

Of course he hadn't. I wasn't married the last time we'd spoken at length. "I didn't," I said quietly. "And I'm sorry to bother you. It's just that—"

"Hello, Ben! We're locked out!" my mother announced. "And I wanted to see if your father still had a key."

"My father?" said Ben, arching an eyebrow. "He's been living in New Jersey for almost a year now. You hadn't heard?"

"Oh," said my mother. Then her face brightened. "That's right. Do you think you might have it? I think he kept it on a hook in the cupboard."

Ben and I glanced at each other. "I don't know, but why don't you two come in and I'll see if I can find it?"

"Such a gentleman!" I cringed as she put her hand on his arm, but his face didn't change. He was a damned good actor.

As she leaned in toward him like they were old friends, it was all I could do not to throw her over my shoulder and run out the door. Who cared if we didn't have a key? Anywhere was better than here. "Thank you, dear Ben. It's so nice to see you after all this time."

Kill me now, I thought. I had no idea if their paths had ever crossed after he and I stopped talking. But there was no reason to believe that he didn't still think the same things about her that he had then. And yet here she was, clad in a nightgown, making demands.

"It's nothing, Mrs. Francis."

"Please call me Sally. Haven't I been telling you that since you were a boy?"

This was true—even if her version of parenting meant turning on the TV and maybe tossing us a snack before heading off to do whatever she was going to do, I'd never seen her be anything but kind to him.

That, maybe more than anything else, was why his accusation stung so badly. "You sure have, Sally," he said.

She beamed again. "That's better. It's been far too long since I've seen you, you know."

"I do," he said, still smiling at her benevolently as we headed into the foyer. Was he faking it, or had he softened to her?

Ben's apartment was on the first floor. He opened the door for my mother, who sauntered in like she owned the place. He paused and looked at me. "You are aware that your mother's dressed like a Victoria's Secret model?" he whispered.

"Yes," I whispered back. "I didn't want to get into this earlier, but we think she might have dementia."

"Damn. I'm sorry, Lainey."

"It's fine," I said softly. Maybe it was the whispering, or the sincerity in his voice, but I suddenly felt woozy with déjà vu; it almost felt like we'd turned the clock back two decades and were back to being Ben and Laine again. *If only that were possible,* I thought.

"It's not," he said, then gestured for me to follow him. "But come on in."

My mother's apartment had barely changed in several decades, so I guess I was expecting Ben's place to look like it had when we were kids. But the walls, which had once been blue, were now a bright white. This made the weathered marble fireplace, which I'd barely noticed as a child, the focal point of the living room. Gone were the overstuffed velour couches; instead, a pair of pale gray Scandinavian-inspired sofas flanked a glass coffee table, where a selection of books had been artfully stacked. The built-in bookshelves were still full, but now everything was just so—paperbacks with paperbacks, fiction separated from photo collections, the occasional matte white vase or paperweight between different groupings.

Should I acknowledge that it had changed? Say nothing? I didn't want to start up a whole big conversation, but I didn't want to be rude, either. "You've done a lot," I finally said as I stood awkwardly in the middle of the living room.

"Yeah," said Ben, glancing around. "I couldn't pass up the opportunity to buy this place from my dad, but it was too . . ."

Sad. It was too sad to keep it the way it had been when his mom was there . . . and after she wasn't.

"I get it," I said. "It looks great."

"Thanks." He nodded, then looked at my mother, who was standing in the hallway. "Um, Sally, where did you say that key was?"

"The key?" She wasn't wearing that glassy expression that she'd had when I found her upstairs, but she'd clearly forgotten why we were at Ben's.

Buckle up, buttercup, I thought to myself. My father had always said that when we complained, meaning, *You think this is bad? It's about to get so much worse.*

"The key to your apartment?" Ben said gently to my mother. "You said my dad had one here?"

"The key, yes," she said, nodding. "In the kitchen cupboard. The one closest to the fridge."

"Thanks," he said.

I was dying to know how he'd updated the kitchen, but he hadn't gestured for us to join him, so I watched him disappear behind the old oak door separating the room from the rest of the house. Then I turned back to my mother, who was sitting on a wooden accent chair with her legs twisted around each other, one foot tucked behind her ankle. On the one hand, I was more than three decades her junior and could barely cross one leg over the other. On the other, couldn't she have thought to wear some sort of support garment?

Mostly, though, I was thinking about how I was possibly going to handle this on a regular basis. Both Hadley and Piper had been exhausted during most of their pregnancies. Was I going to have the physical energy to bound around after my mother, to say nothing of the mental fortitude that it would require?

"And there we have it," said Ben as he walked back into the living room, dangling the key from his fingers. His eyes met mine, and I saw that despite his cool demeanor, he was as surprised as I felt.

"Thank you," I said as he handed the key to me. "I had no idea your father gave my mother a key to our place, but Sally always has a few tricks up her sleeve. Don't you, Sally?" I said, but when I looked at the chair where she'd been, she was gone. "Mom?" I waited, but she didn't respond, so I called again, "Mom, where are you?"

"She just wandered into the hallway," said Ben. He smiled at me, and for a split second, I felt myself warm.

Then I remembered why this was weird.

"Don't do that," I said in a low voice.

"Do what?" he asked calmly.

It was one thing for him to pretend everything was fine with my mother. But with me? That was insulting. "Act like nothing happened," I said, staring at him. "I appreciate that you're being nice to my mom, especially since—well, you know what we talked about. But you don't have to be nice to me."

He didn't say anything for a moment, but he didn't look away, either. Finally, he said, "I'm sorry, Laine. I thought about reaching out to you a million times."

I had, too, and had never once acted on that impulse. And still, I asked him, "Then why didn't you?"

He shrugged. "I guess I figured you didn't want to hear from me."

I did, I thought. *More than almost anything.* I'd made friends in Ann Arbor, of course. But—and I knew this was stupid, but all the same—often I'd be having coffee with one of them, and we'd be in the middle of the conversation, and I'd think about Ben.

And how I wished whomever I was with were him.

My mother's voice pierced the silence. "Laine! Are you coming? I'm in the foyer!"

I looked at Ben. "Well, that's me. Thanks for the key."

He ran a hand over his head. "Laine, I'd really like to catch up. Can we please find a time to meet while you're in town? Even just for, like, fifteen minutes for coffee or something?"

He was a big part of the reason I'd steered clear of New York the past sixteen years and, in doing so, missed an opportunity to spend time with my mother. Seeing him would probably make me start looking for signs that she had ulterior motives, even though I was supposed to be supporting her. For that reason alone, getting together was a terrible idea.

And yet I heard myself say, "I'd like that. When?"

FIFTEEN

Laine

After returning from Ben's, I'd called Hadley and Piper in a mild panic—though what I didn't tell them was that a good deal of that turmoil was owing to my conversation with Ben, and the fact that we'd agreed to meet for coffee in two days, which was the earliest his work schedule and my plans with my family weren't in conflict. Hadley had immediately calmed me down by putting things into perspective; as far as incidents went, she said, that one wasn't nearly as bad as when my mother did a peep show at Bashir's.

Even so, she'd proposed having our mother over to her place for brunch the next day so we could start warming her to the idea of getting help, and Piper and I had readily agreed. Something had to change, and soon.

The rest of the day had been blessedly uneventful, and my mother had even tucked in early. She was in good spirits the following morning, too, and spent the subway ride to the Upper East Side telling me all about the grandchildren her friend Mary never got to see. How lucky she was, she said, that her own grandchildren were all in the same city as her.

As she prattled on, a related drama was playing out in my mind. Here I'd been thinking that New York was the worst place to raise a child. But if my mother didn't have much time left—good, lucid time, at least—didn't I *want* to be here at the start of my child's life so she could know them? And what about Piper and Hadley? It wasn't like they'd be free childcare, but wouldn't it be easier to have them around as I raised a baby?

I was still thinking about this when we arrived at Hadley's. She and Topper lived on one of the top floors, and the elevator let out directly into her apartment. The doors had just opened when Josh galloped past, whinnying as Kaia, who was on his back, ordered him to giddyap.

I nearly stumbled backward. This was supposed to be my week to think about our divorce—without him. Why was he here?

"Josh?!" I said when I finally found my voice. "What are you doing?"

"Neighhhhh," he whinnied from the other room. "I'm being a horse. And hi, Laine!"

"Josh!" said my mother, making a beeline for the family room, where he was prancing in circles.

I glanced at Hadley, who was jiggling Asher on her hip. "Did you know he was coming?"

She shook her head. "Nope. I'm as surprised as you are. I almost called you when he got here, but I figured you'd find out soon enough."

"Not so fast," I said to Piper, who'd been standing beside Hadley but had started to slink in the other direction. "This was your doing, wasn't it?"

She froze and opened her already enormous eyes even wider. "Well, yes. He's always been a part of our family—"

"Twelve years," I said.

"Fifteen, technically," she said.

"Fourteen and a half," I said evenly, when I actually wanted to throttle her. "Piper," I said, "I'm here to have some time *away* from Josh. I'm trying to clear my head."

Piper glanced toward the family room. “I get that, Laine. But we’re about to have a big talk about Mom, and the fact is, the two of you *are* still married. It’s not like you’re on bad terms or anything, and it didn’t seem right not to have him here. Like it or not, he’s a part of our family.”

Piper had crossed plenty of lines in her day, but I’d never known her to overstep like this. I didn’t feel angry anymore, though. No, now I could feel a sob gurgling up from deep within me. Leopards didn’t change their spots, but I guess I thought my sister would, because I felt devastated that she didn’t even think to ask me what *I* wanted and needed.

I didn’t say anything, which Piper immediately misread. “See!” she declared. “I knew you’d understand when you had a chance to think it through.”

Josh had unlatched Kaia from his back to hug my mother, but now he was walking over to where we were standing. He smiled shyly when he reached me. “Hey, Laine. I hope you don’t mind, but after your call yesterday, I didn’t want you to have to deal.”

It was a lovely overture—and one he normally wouldn’t have made, especially not in the middle of a launch. During the worst flu of my life two years earlier, I’d had to ask him to stay home in case I passed out on my way to the bathroom. He’d not taken Belle to the vet with me once over the past year—not even for that last terrible visit—because he’d been too busy working, though he claimed he wanted to give us time to be together. I had to admit, he really did seem to be trying to change.

But that didn’t mean he’d warmed to parenthood, I reminded myself.

“Then I talked to Piper and, well, I got in the car and took off,” he added.

The sobby sensation was gone, but I was still off-kilter. “You drove?” I managed. He hated driving, especially long distances, and never got behind the wheel in the city. I have to admit I was a little impressed.

"Yep. I'm parked in one of those hundred-dollar-a-day lots, but that's still cheaper than a last-minute flight."

My mother, hand in hand with Kaia, walked over and put her free arm around Josh. "Isn't it wonderful? All of my family in one place," she said, beaming up at him. "And not because of a birth or death, but just because! What an absolute treat!"

No, no one had died, but telling her that we thought something was wrong with her would be nearly as bad. When I looked over at Hadley, she appeared to be at a loss for words, and was stroking Asher's head in a way that I recognized as anything but absentminded. After a moment, she said, "Hey, Laine? Can you help me in the kitchen?"

"Absolutely," I said, eyeing Josh, who'd just started tossing a Nerf football back and forth with Jae.

Hadley had a long galley-style kitchen with a butler's pantry off the side. She passed Asher to Topper, then dragged me into the pantry. I had to hand it to her—the tiny room was a work of art, with clear canisters lined up in rows on the shelves and baskets full of paper towels and cleaning supplies arranged neatly on the floor.

"We can't possibly bring it up now," I whispered.

"We *have* to," she said. "That's why Josh is here, after all."

"You heard her! All of us together 'just because,'" I said, making air quotes around the words. "This is going to crush her."

"Laine," said Hadley firmly, "the longer we wait, the worst this is going to get."

"So you're suggesting we go line up in the living room and deliver our verdict?"

"Not at all," she said, shaking her head. "You and Josh should pull her aside and tell her. Then, when she's ready to talk about it, we'll all be right here."

I pulled my head back in disbelief. "Me and Josh? Why?"

"You're her favorite."

I snorted. "Her favorite? Yeah, right."

"It doesn't matter if you think it's true or not. Everyone else knows it," she said. "She thinks I'm too bossy and still treats Piper like she's a child. You're the only one she listens to. And with Josh there, she won't make a scene."

I didn't like this plan one bit, but I'd rather execute it than turn my conversation with Hadley into an argument. "Fine," I said. "I'll go get her and Josh, then drop the ax."

"Thank you," she said with such appreciation that I almost forgot that this was a terrible idea.

~

Josh and I asked my mother to speak with us privately in the living room. "Are you about to give me good news?" she said eagerly after I told her there was something we wanted to discuss, and my stomach immediately sank because she thought we were going to tell her we were expecting. Just as bad, Josh didn't seem to pick up on what she was implying, and I had to work hard not to start down the rabbit hole of rumination about whether he'd ever even wanted kids, or if he'd just told me that because it was what I wanted to hear.

Instead, I explained that all of us had begun to notice she was slightly more forgetful than usual, and that we were worried about how she was leaving the house half-dressed. "I'm a grown woman, Laine," she responded, but her voice lacked conviction. "I can wear whatever I want."

Then she got angry when I mentioned seeing a neurologist. "There's nothing wrong with me," she muttered, wringing her hands in her lap. "You think I'm turning into my mother, but I'm not."

"I don't think that at all, Mom. Nana Meyers had Parkinson's, right? There's no sign you have anything like that. But you're seventy-two. It's the right time to get a checkup." I'd been attempting to reassure her, but every word only seemed to make her more upset.

Josh had been the one to soothe her. Irene saw a neurologist every year, he told her, just to make sure everything was working. It was a perfectly normal thing to do. "Think of it like data collection," he said, putting his hand on her back. "Until we get some information, we really can't make any decisions. We're still in phase one, if you think about it."

She was still twisting her hands, but she nodded in agreement, then thanked him.

And just like that, I saw that Piper had been right to invite him. He'd known just what to do; he'd made everything easier. Maybe it was time for me to rethink his offer to bring my mother to Ann Arbor.

Or for him to move here with us.

Moments later, Hadley poked her head into the room, and I told her to get Piper so we could all talk.

Now my mother was sitting beside me on the sofa, and Hadley had just handed her a mug of coffee. Piper took one of the two velvet armchairs across from the sofa, and Josh was in the other. It struck me that Topper hadn't joined us, even though he and Hadley had been married nearly as long as Josh and I had. Then again, I reminded myself, he didn't have the same kind of relationship with my mother that Josh had.

"Oh my," said my mother, looking around the room. "I just . . . didn't see this coming. You all being here means you think it's serious."

"No," I fibbed. "It's only a doctor's visit. We'll start there and figure out next steps after."

"Well . . ." said Hadley, taking a seat on the other side of my mother. "Did you three talk about living arrangements?"

My mother's head shot up. "Living arrangements? What do you mean?"

"You need help, Mom," said Piper. "Someone to keep an eye on you."

"Like a child?" she said. I could only remember a handful of times my mother had gotten really angry with us as children, and her cloudy expression warned that she was on the verge of going there again. "If you're talking about a nursing home, I'll let you know that I'll walk into the Gowanus before that happens. I won't do it."

"That's not what we're talking about," I said. *Not yet,* I added silently.

"Mom, there *is* one possibility the four of us have been talking about . . ." Hadley began.

I stared at my sister over my mother's head. *I haven't said yes yet!* I thought with irritation.

Hadley either didn't see me or chose to ignore me. "And that's having Laine come live with you. *Not* as a babysitter," she said pointedly. "Just so she could help you when you needed it."

"Laine?" said my mother. She placed her hand on mine. "Are you really willing to move to New York? I know how much you and Josh love Ann Arbor."

Now Josh and I looked at each other. She couldn't seem to remember we were getting divorced—and who could blame her? He was here, with me, and we were acting like we always did.

"Mom," I said carefully, "I don't know if Josh would be moving in with me. We're separated, remember?"

Her face twisted up. "Oh," she said after a moment. "That's right. So you need your own space. Well," she said, brightening suddenly, "you could take the upstairs apartment, Laine! I'd be happy to rent it to you for far below market value. Maybe I can even figure out some way to let you use it for free."

Hadley was smiling at me now. I knew that smile; it meant she thought everything was settled. "Topper and I have talked, and since Mom uses the rental income to pay for property taxes, and Laine, you're . . . transitioning," she said tactfully, "we're willing to chip in for your rent to make sure that this isn't a financial difficulty for you or Mom."

So I would be a nearly thirty-eight-year-old woman being subsidized by her sister. I wanted to feel grateful—I really did. After all, this would make it easier to afford to have a child, and it wouldn't be forever.

But I don't want to, I thought.

This isn't about what you want, argued another voice within me. *This is about doing what's right.*

All eyes were on me now, and I could feel heat rising to my face. Hadley and Piper were all but on the edge of their seats, eager to hear me say I'd ease their burden. And Josh—well, I couldn't exactly blurt out the real reason I couldn't help my mother, because then he'd have to admit, right there in front of everyone, that he really didn't want to do this whole dad thing—except he wouldn't actually do that. Instead, he'd say, "Laine, it's okay—I'm finally ready!" Because if I knew one thing, it was how important it was for him to be a good guy, especially when it came to my family. He wouldn't realize he'd made the right choice for the wrong reason until it was already too late.

I wondered if I was about to make that same mistake, too.

Then I turned to my mother, who looked incredibly childlike as she awaited the decision that we—*I*—was about to make on her behalf. And it hit me: here I was thinking about how best to serve a child that was wholly hypothetical.

But my mother? She was real. She needed me *now*. And hadn't I just admitted that this wouldn't be forever? I could live with her for six months, a year; maybe eighteen months tops. After all, it took nine months to gestate a child, and that wasn't including however long it would take to actually get pregnant. While I was lining up my future, I'd give her a chance to enjoy the present.

I swallowed hard and plastered a smile on my face. "Okay," I announced. "I'll do it. I'll move back."

SIXTEEN

Sally

My Laine, coming to live with me! How wonderful, how very lucky. I wasn't one of those mothers who expected her children to stay in the nest forever. I urged my girls to be independent, the way my mother had with me. But I suppose I thought that Laine would eventually return to New York; if not following college, then after sowing some of her wild oats in the Midwest. After all, this is where the rest of us are. Yet she never did. But now she and Josh are willing to take the upstairs apartment, lend me a hand. My heart could burst just thinking of it.

It almost makes up for the fact that my own daughters know what's happening to me. They didn't have to say what comes next; I know all too well that I could go right into a home. I'll need to work harder at this. Think before I speak. Maybe a note beside the front door to check what I'm wearing. A few safeguards. And Laine . . . well, she won't make such a big deal when she sees me slipping. She'll help me along so they don't have to put me away quite so fast.

Except, she seems upset. Not at me—she gave me a teary hug at . . . Hadley's. Piper's? Persian rug. Oil painting. Yes, Hadley's. Said she wanted to do this, was excited to spend more time with me. But her shoulders were stiff as she stole glances at Josh as he wove through traffic to get us back to Brooklyn.

Now, Josh, he sounded like his same old easygoing self as he told me all about his new business, whatever that is. Laine, though—her words were curt. Clipped. Especially when she was speaking to him. It might have been the least pleasant ride I've ever been on, and Piper once threw up three times on the train on the way to see Hank's cousin in Connecticut.

Well, all couples have their moments. Certainly Hank and I had our troubles. I still don't know exactly what we did to get past them, except to keep going. That's what the vows say, don't they? Through good times and bad. Then death did us part, and that's when the guilt really set in. I'd owed him more than I'd given him. And he'd owed me more, too. No one tells you how fast it all flies by. Well, I suppose they do, but by the time you realize it's a cliché for a reason, you've already missed the moment. And yet there is joy there, even if it doesn't go as planned. A shared history. A life. Children.

A *baby*. Of course. That's probably what Laine is thinking about. Both of her sisters have beautiful families of their own, and I see the way she looks longingly at Asher and Ainsley. She's ready; I can tell.

Oh, I thought suddenly. But Josh never talked about being a father. And of all the things he mentioned when we were in the living room discussing their move to New York, he didn't once say anything about children. Was that what this was about?

Before long, we were home, and Josh dropped me and Laine off in front of the apartment while he went to park. Once we were inside, I sat on the sofa and patted the spot beside me. "Laine, love, come sit."

She kicked off her sneakers and walked over. She was trying to put on a brave face; I could tell.

"What is it?" I said as she sank into the sofa. Sometimes she would lean against me, let me stroke her hair. Not today. But I took her hand all the same. "It's about a baby, isn't it?"

She looked so startled, you'd think I'd just summoned the ghost of her father. "How did you know that?"

"A mother has her ways, dear. Now, what's going on?"

She shook her head miserably. The last time I saw her face drop like that was at Hank's memorial service. "It's nothing."

Well, we both knew that wasn't true. So I waited for her to continue.

"Okay, it's something," she said, leaning back against the cushions. "The truth is, Mom, Belle's death made me realize that I'm only getting older. That if I want to have a baby, I need to get moving on it."

"The dog died?" I said, but I immediately caught my gaffe. "I mean, of course I remember she died. That can be hard on a person, very hard. Remember when Pebbles passed?" I'd loved that cat, the silly old scamp. All orange cats are of the devil—that's what my mother used to say, and Pebbles was certainly not the exception to her rule. Every spring, he'd spend several weeks yodeling to be let out at the crack of dawn, even though we'd had him fixed. And I never could figure out why he had a thing about doing his business all over Hank's model sets. It's a wonder Hank didn't drop him in an alley on the other side of Brooklyn. But that cat was one of the best friends I ever had. It was a shame that animals didn't live longer.

"I know," said Laine, and that's when I realized I'd not kept my thoughts in my head.

I laughed at myself because what was the alternative—go pull an Ophelia in the bathtub? *Get thee to a nunnery, Sally Francis,* I thought, and thankfully, this time, the thought stayed whence it came. "I didn't mean to change the subject, love. Tell me more about wanting a baby."

"It's fine," she said, except she was staring at the bookshelves. Ah, that's where my reading glasses were; I'd been looking for those.

"Laine. I've known you thirty-seven years and ten months, not counting all that time you spent swimming around my womb, making me fat and miserable."

I saw the surprise, then, mixed with her pain.

"You thought I'd forgotten how old you were?" I suddenly wanted to weep. I'd scared her with those packages. At once, it came rushing back to me—the credit card Hadley had hidden, how I'd stashed the computer somewhere I was least likely to find it, to try to keep myself from buying things I didn't need when loneliness set in, or whatever spell it was that came over me. It hadn't worked, and maybe that was the worst part of all. "Oh, love. I'm not gone yet. I'm still in the game."

She gave me a small smile. "I know, Mom. And yes, I want a baby. But Josh . . ."

"He doesn't," I said, squeezing her hand. "That's why you're divorcing him."

Now she looked truly stunned. I was, too—I hadn't remembered that until just that moment.

"Please don't mention it to him," she said, glancing at the front door. "I don't want him to say yes just so I won't divorce him."

Oh, my poor girl. "Laine, love, you know it's okay to ask for what you want, don't you? You should tell him you want a child."

There was such terrible pain in her eyes as she looked at me. How had I not seen it earlier? "I have asked him, Mom. I've asked so many times that I don't want to ask anymore. He knows, and he's decided to overlook my request. So I'm going to come live with you. And though Josh may not know it yet, he's staying in Michigan. I'm sorry—I know how much you and everyone love him. I feel terrible."

"You mustn't." I let go of her hand and put my arm around her. I felt her head on my shoulder. Her sigh was heavy, but there was some contentment there, too. My daughter. Since the day she'd emerged, wide-eyed and observant and eager to please, she'd had a wonderful smell to her. Not a perfume or a food or a shampoo, but just this clean sort of scent, like a sunny spring day. It was one of the many things that made her uniquely her. I inhaled deeply, let myself enjoy her presence. After a moment, I added softly, "I want you to make the decisions that are best for you—not anyone else. That's all I've ever wanted for you. I hope you know that."

SEVENTEEN

Laine

"There," I said to Josh, patting my hands together. "Now you have a place to sleep."

My mother was napping, and Josh and I had spent the past hour reorganizing the room I'd once shared with Hadley. It had taken twenty minutes just to clear a path to the bed—my mother had amassed decades' worth of clothing, most of which was now thrown haphazardly in boxes or piled atop our old bedroom set. Maybe I was still raw from our unexpected heart-to-heart about my wanting a baby, but I hadn't expected cleaning the bedroom to be quite so emotional. Here was the brown terry-cloth bathrobe I used to "borrow" from my mom as a kid, even though it made me trip over my own feet; there was the denim dress that she'd worn to my college graduation. It wasn't that she hadn't thrown any of it away. It was that I knew that when the time came, I wasn't sure I'd be able to, either. Every one of those items was a memory, and suddenly those seemed more precious than ever.

"Thanks—it does look better," said Josh, glancing around. "But, Laine . . . are you okay? That conversation at Hadley and Topper's was a lot."

"It wasn't my favorite," I agreed. Brunch itself had been quiet, bordering on terse; everyone, even my mother, seemed to be afraid to say the wrong thing, and Josh had ended up saving the day by telling everyone about his company and the investors he'd been speaking to. "And yeah, I'm fine. That went as well as it could've. Thanks again for making it easier. Everyone was really glad you were there."

"Absolutely. But are *you* glad I'm here?"

I looked around, like I'd find the answer in my mother's old clothes. Though I'd been upset that neither Josh nor Piper had thought to tell me what they'd been planning, it'd been impossible to stay mad. After all, him being there really had saved the day. Even if I *could* have handled that on my own, I wouldn't have wanted to. Really, I didn't give Josh nearly enough credit. "I am," I admitted.

He smiled shyly. "I can't tell you how good it is to hear you say that." But his face grew serious as he sat on the edge of the bed. "Are you really going to move back?"

"Looks like it." I shrugged, hoping I seemed casual about it. In reality, my mind was racing with all of the changes I'd have to make. I'd need to pack, and although I knew that splitting up with Josh would require dividing our stuff, having to actually do it—and soon—sounded heart-wrenching. I'd need to change the address on all of my accounts, and at some point talk to Josh about whether he wanted to stay on in the town house, and if so, how he was going to pay for that. And Melinda had emailed me just the day before to see when I could begin organizing her house. I knew the gig was a small matter in light of everything else that was going on, but I was dreading writing her back to say that I wasn't going to be able to do the job after all.

"But you love Ann Arbor," he said.

I did. I loved that I could step outside almost anywhere and be surrounded by trees and greenery. I loved that I didn't have to weave through crowds to go for a walk, that I could get a table at a restaurant without a reservation I'd made two weeks earlier, and that I didn't need to sell an organ on the black market (or have my sister subsidize me) to afford our rent. I supposed any one of these things wasn't a big deal, but collectively, they'd made the quality of my life so much better than it had been in New York. "That's true, but Mom needs me. And it won't be forever." It was painful to hear myself say that, because it implied that my mother would die. Of course I knew that no one lived forever. But somehow I was surprised to find my mother this close to the end.

He sighed. "Yeah, I'm definitely beginning to see what you guys mean about her. But, Laine, I meant what I said on the phone the other day. We could move her to Ann Arbor to live with us."

Us? He really seemed to believe that our marriage would survive my midlife marital crisis. And maybe that optimism was contagious, because I was starting to wonder if he was right.

"I know it wouldn't be perfect, but she'd adjust. And I could help you, so you wouldn't have to do this on your own."

"Josh . . ." I didn't want him getting too far ahead of himself, not when I still felt so uncertain.

He rose and came over to where I was standing. Then he put his arms around my waist. Even as I felt myself soften, my mother's words ricocheted through my mind: "You know it's okay to ask for what you want, don't you?"

She was right. I needed to let him know what was going through my mind. I took a deep breath, then said, "The thing is, Josh, it'll be hard to have a child and take care of my mother, too."

I waited to see how this would land. But if he was surprised, he didn't show it. "Sure, but you're the most resourceful person I know, Laine. You'd figure it out. We would," he corrected himself.

My eyes widened. Was he telling me what I thought he was telling me?

"But . . . I thought you weren't ready?" I was nearly whispering, because I was afraid to find out how he'd respond.

"I'm not yet," he said. I'd just begun to register my disappointment when he added, "But I will be soon. I'm super close to selling the app."

I threw my arms around his neck before I could think about what I was doing. "Really? That's amazing." I was talking about the app, but, of course, I meant the baby part, too. "Why didn't you mention that at brunch? Or tell me when I called the other day?"

"I didn't want to count my chickens—not in front of your family," he said sheepishly. "And I just figured with everything with your mom going on, you had enough to think about without having to worry about me."

"Josh . . ." I swallowed hard. "Do you actually want to be a dad?"

He was smiling, but I swear I saw tiny tadpoles of worry swimming in his pupils. "Of course, Laine. I always have. I've just been waiting for the right time."

See? There's nothing to worry about, I told myself. *He can be uncertain and still move forward; after all, isn't that what you're doing with Mom and moving back? Anyway, she was right. You could have saved yourself so much heartache by just telling him what you wanted in the first place.*

But if all that was true, why did I have the sinking sensation that Josh was just telling me what I wanted to hear?

We were still holding each other when the doorbell rang. "I'll get it," he said, kissing the top of my head. "To be continued."

"To be continued," I said as I watched him head for the door.

Moments later, I heard Kaia's high-pitched voice, followed by Piper's, echoing above me. I looked around one more time, almost like I was looking for evidence that our conversation had really happened, then headed upstairs. Piper was perched on the back of the sofa, with Rocco beside her.

"Hey, you two," I said, hoping I sounded more cheerful than I felt. After all, I was getting what I wanted! Well, allegedly. Still, why was I trying to look this gift horse in the mouth? What was wrong with me that I couldn't just let myself enjoy this? "What's the occasion?"

"You, silly!" said Piper, leaning in for an air-kiss. Kaia and Jae were circling the room—probably trying to figure out where it was safe to sit, as my mother had left the contents of the newspaper all over the sofa, one of her robes on the chair, and mysteriously, a houseplant in the center of the love seat. "I just picked Rocco up from Levi's, and since we weren't far, I thought I'd swing by so you could see your nephew."

"Who, for the record, is giant! Hey, big man," I greeted Rocco, who was at least two inches taller than when I'd seen him in the winter. "What's your mom feeding you these days? Steroids?"

He chuckled. "Hey, Auntie Laine," he said, giving me an awkward sideways hug. "Happy to see you."

"You, too, kiddo," I said, ruffling his hair.

"Piper Anne Francis, is that you?" My mother, who had awoken from her nap, had just come up the stairs. To my relief, she wasn't wearing anything inappropriate. Instead, she'd changed into a blouse and skirt I'd never seen before. I immediately wondered if she'd bought them online, and if so, for how much. Well, I reasoned, unlike the liquid face-lift and hangers, at least she was actually *using* these things. But was this my new role—questioner of all my mother's decisions? If so, I already hated it.

"Hi, Mom," said Piper.

"I haven't seen you in a while," said my mother, and Piper and I immediately glanced at each other.

"I saw you this morning, Mom," said Piper. "Remember?"

"Oh, that's right," my mother said with a tight smile. "I'm just groggy from my nap."

"You probably slept too long," said Josh, who'd walked over from the foyer. "Studies show twenty minutes is the sweet spot—any longer and you go into the wrong sleep cycle, which is why you feel lousy when you wake up."

"Really? I didn't know that," said Piper.

He nodded enthusiastically. "That's one of the things Power Doze will help with."

"Power Doze?" said my mother.

"That's the app I'm about to launch," he said gently, as though we hadn't already discussed that at brunch. I shot him an appreciative look, and when he smiled at me, warmth spread through my core. He said he needed me, but really—I needed *him*. No wonder our marriage hadn't been particularly rewarding lately. I'd not been appreciating him at all, not like I should have been.

"Oooh! I knew about the relaxation feature, but I didn't realize it had timing optimization, too," said Piper, who immediately began rattling off a bunch of things about circadian rhythms and "leveraging" caffeine. She seemed genuinely interested, and now I felt twice as guilty; why hadn't *I* asked those questions?

"Laine?" said Josh.

I must have been lost in thought, because my head jerked up when I heard my name. "What's that?"

"I was just saying that I was thinking of making dinner," he said. "Your mom has stuff for pasta, and I bought a loaf of bread earlier."

But Josh never cooked. "Really?" I said, unable to hide my surprise.

"I mean, I've been trying to learn a few new things," he said with a hint of pride.

And suddenly I saw it: he may not have called that therapist yet, but he *was* trying to do better; to be a better husband. And maybe, just maybe, he was getting ready to be a dad, too.

"That sounds great," I said sincerely. "Thank you."

"Course," he said.

"We're not staying for dinner, but I'll help if you want," said Piper. "I'm not half bad with a sharp knife and frying pan."

Josh laughed. "Just don't use either on me, okay?"

"Deal," she said. "Anyway, that'll give Laine a chance to spend some time with the kids."

I had actually been thinking that I wanted to spend time with Josh and check out his new culinary skills, but who was I to argue about hanging out with my niece and nephews, who I hadn't seen in nearly half a year?

"Perfect." I turned to Rocco. "I know you're pretty grown-up, but how do you feel about helping me take these two to the park?" I said, directing a thumb toward Jae and Kaia.

"I can do that," he said with a grin.

Kaia had to use the bathroom first, and then I did, too, and it was another ten minutes before I was able to hustle all three kids to the front door. We were about to leave when I heard Josh and Piper laughing in the kitchen. It was a good sound—one that reminded me of past holidays and family celebrations, when the two of them often ended up following one tangent to another, then another. And Josh—well, he looked . . . really happy.

And suddenly I had a thought that stopped me in my tracks. Here I'd been thinking about how he hadn't provided me with what I wanted.

But what if I hadn't been giving him what he wanted, either?

EIGHTEEN

Laine

After my conversation with Josh, I had half a mind to cancel on Ben—except I didn't have his number, and walking over to his apartment to tell him I wasn't going to have coffee with him seemed like the epitome of pathetic. Also, I couldn't articulate why I felt weird about our meeting. Sure, I'd been attracted to him many years ago, but I was married now—and it looked increasingly likely that I was going to stay that way. Besides, Josh hadn't even blinked an eye when I told him I was going to see Ben.

"Sure," he said, not looking up from his computer. "I'll keep an eye on Mom and get a little work done. Have a good time."

"Thanks," I mumbled, grateful that he wasn't paying close attention, because my cheeks were warm and probably pink. Josh knew I'd once had a friend named Ben, but he thought we'd just drifted apart—and that was because I'd never mentioned what had happened. I'd always told myself that I didn't want to rehash the painful past. Which was absolutely true . . . so I wasn't sure why I felt like a liar.

I tried to push these dueling thoughts out of my head as I walked to the café we'd agreed to meet at, which was a few blocks away on Hoyt

Street. Ben was sitting at a small table out back when I arrived, and he stood when he saw me.

"Hey, Laine," he said with a smile. He was wearing another linen shirt, this one green, and a pair of dark jeans. I'd almost thrown on a sundress but had settled on a clean T-shirt and a pair of shorts because I didn't want it to seem like this was a big deal.

Even if my shaking hands said it absolutely was.

I tried to smile back, but my mouth wouldn't work. I'd spent the morning cleaning the upstairs apartment with my mother—who'd mostly tried to convince me to keep her random purchases, including but not limited to the liquid face-lift—and at first I'd almost been able to distract myself. But I'd grown more and more anxious as it grew closer to the time Ben and I were supposed to meet. Which was silly—if it went badly, then we'd just end up in the same boat we were already in. And obviously I knew how to handle that.

Except I didn't want it to go badly. Maybe it was Belle's absence, but even surrounded by my family and Josh, I could not pretend that I wasn't deeply if weirdly lonely. And some part of me, however ridiculous, felt like maybe Ben would make me feel less like a stranger in my own life.

"Uh. Hi." I was in front of him now, and he looked at me for a split second, then opened his arms for a hug, which I awkwardly accepted.

But then I breathed deep and realized he still smelled exactly like himself, by which I mean decades of memories: when we teamed up against the jerky little kid who kept grabbing Piper's butt on the way to school and told him we'd give him the wedgie to end all wedgies if he did it again. (He didn't.) When we nearly burned down his kitchen trying to make brownies after school. And the time in high school when we snuck off to Limelight, the infamous Manhattan club, and danced until dawn—even though both of us were truly terrible dancers. There were few parts of my childhood and adolescence that hadn't included Ben, and I knew that, more than anything else, was why I could describe it as happy.

"Thanks for meeting me. I wasn't sure you'd come," he added as we parted.

"I almost didn't," I blurted. Then I grimaced because I hadn't meant to say that.

He leaned back in his chair and smiled even more broadly. "Don't censor yourself on my account."

Now, in spite of myself, I smiled. "I'll do my best not to."

"What can I get you to drink?" he asked.

"Whatever you're having is fine."

"Two Strawberry Hill surprises?" he said, referring to the teeth-achingly sweet wine we used to steal from Reggie, who didn't have my mother's highfalutin taste in booze. We'd pour it into Solo cups and sneak it into Ben's bedroom. Even then, we knew it was barely potable.

I must have been feeling more comfortable, because I laughed. "Please, no. How about a latte?"

"Skim milk?"

I made a horrified expression, and he laughed.

"Glad you still have good taste," he said, and I swear I could tell he had to stop himself from winking. "Be right back."

A torrent of emotions swept through me as I watched him head back inside. I'd thought about this moment for ages—dreaded it, wished for it, wondered if it would even happen before it was too late. At first, I'd just wanted to tell him all the ways he was wrong about me and my mother. Sorrow set in soon after, because I knew, deep down, that he was right—I *had* let my mother make my decision for me. By then it was too late; there was no fixing what I'd broken. And yet I couldn't help but long for everything to go back to the way it was before that awful conversation.

Before I knew it, Ben was back and handing me a mug of steaming coffee. He sat down in front of me. "So," he said. "Where do we begin?"

I wrinkled my nose. "I don't really know."

"Me, neither. But I'm glad you're here." He lifted his mug. "To old friends."

But we weren't anymore. So instead of responding, I shifted in my seat, then took a sip of my coffee. "How'd your dad doing?" I asked after a moment.

"Dad's had a couple health scares, but he's hanging in there," he said. "My mom died, though."

My jaw dropped open. Sixteen years was a long time not to be a part of someone's life, and, of course, he hadn't been there when my father died, either. Still—hearing that he'd gone through his mother's death without me only made the loss of our friendship feel greater.

"I'm so sorry," I said. "When?" His mother had claimed she'd send for the boys when she got settled in California. But she never had, and she hadn't come to visit, either. Ben hadn't talked about it a lot, but it was impossible not to notice the many ways it shaped him. It wasn't just that he hated to be in his house. He'd check the mail two, three times a day around his birthday in September. His mother would send a card, and finally in his late teens, he admitted that he'd been waiting for her to write that she wanted him to come live with him. He dated plenty, but never stayed in a relationship more than a month or two, and although he hadn't said as much, it seemed obvious to me that he didn't want to give anyone the opportunity to leave him.

No wonder he was so upset when I said goodbye. How had I never realized that before?

"Last year," he said with a shrug. I knew that shrug—at least, I used to—and it meant the opposite of what it was supposed to convey.

"Ben . . ."

He met my eyes. "I saw her a couple times when I was living out in San Francisco. She got herself a whole new family. I have two half sisters. They're okay, I guess. I don't know them all that well, and they're not super interested in changing that."

"That's—" It was awful, that's what it was. He used to tell me how abandoned he felt. How he wanted to get on a bus and show up on her doorstep, just so he could tell her how horrible she was, and how furious he was with her. I often thought about Ben's mother when my own wasn't living up to my standards. It never hurt quite as bad when she, say, forgot to wish me a happy birthday until the very end of the day, or neglected to take me bra shopping yet again. At least I *had* a mother. "That's really unfortunate," I said, hoping this was tactful enough.

"That's for sure," he said, nodding. "So, you still in Ann Arbor?"

"How'd you know that?"

"Social media," he said matter-of-factly. Unlike me, he didn't seem embarrassed that he'd looked me up. "I checked on you from time to time, just to see how you were doing. But you don't really post about anything but your dog."

I looked away. That was true. Why *hadn't* I posted more photos of me and Josh?

"Nice-looking animal," said Ben. "Spaniel?"

"Thanks," I said quietly. "She died recently. Cancer."

"Dang. I'm sorry."

"Thank you. She was my . . ." *Best friend,* I added mentally. *I needed someone after you let me go. Someone who could never say what I never wanted to hear. And she was that, and so much more.* "I loved her a whole lot." I didn't know what to say next, so I took to my latte like a woman who's just stumbled upon a water fountain in the middle of the desert. The coffee was basically a mirage, but even the illusion of relief was better than nothing.

"You still married?" Ben asked after a moment.

I glanced up at him, somewhat relieved that I'd posted at least one photo of Josh. "Let me guess—social media?"

He smiled again. "Yeah. How's that going?"

I had a decision to make: keep things light—or be real. And when I looked at him, I realized that I had no interest in keeping things light. If we were going to do this, we were really going to do it: the good, the bad, and the painfully honest. "Look," I said. "I know this is probably weird—"

"Probably not," he said, and I cracked a smile.

"Fair enough. But I want to get this out of the way before we go any further. Why did you want to get together? Like, is this about burying the hatchet and moving on, or about us being friends? I'm not trying to get you to answer one way or the other. But before I tell you about my life now, I guess I need to know what this is."

He ran a hand over his head and looked away for a moment. When he turned back, I saw that for as much as he'd changed, he was still the Ben I'd known . . . and adored. And something—I'll call it hope—began to unfurl deep within me. "I mean, I've missed you, Laine."

"Me, too," I said frankly. "A lot."

"Thanks," he said. He was still looking at me, and it made me feel kind of naked. I forced myself not to look away. "And to your question, we obviously figured out how to get on without each other."

He wasn't being mean, but it still stung to hear him say this. "There wasn't really another choice," I said.

"Looking back? Yeah, there was. But we're two incredibly stubborn and arguably stupid people," he said, leaning back in his chair. "I made lots of friends over the past sixteen years, and not one of them has been you, Laine. No one wants to find the spiciest Indian restaurant in all of Jackson Heights and burn their tongue off for a full hour."

I couldn't help but laugh, thinking about that dinner we'd had the summer before college. My stomach hadn't been the same for nearly a week after, but it had been worth it. Ben and I had loved trying new food—the spicier, the better—but it had been ages since I had anything remotely different from what Josh and I usually ate; his stomach was too sensitive. But also, I suppose I hadn't wanted to think about how fun it would've been if Ben had been there to share the meal with me. Deep down, I knew that I compared the two of them, and I hated that. There had even been a moment when Josh proposed—a fleeting moment, but all the same—when I'd thought, *No. This isn't the man you're supposed to spend the rest of your life with.* I was attracted to him. We had fun together. He loved my dog, who'd become his dog, too. He was ambitious and kind, and he wanted to stay in Ann Arbor and start a family, or so he said at the time. But for all that, a tiny voice in me said, *He doesn't get you. Not like Ben does.*

Did, I'd immediately corrected myself. And with that simple grammar shift, I was reminded that instead of comparing them, I needed to keep them in entirely different categories. When it came to Josh, close friendship was not the goal. Because a best friend? They only were until they weren't anymore. But Josh asking to stay the course with me—through sickness and health, good times and bad. *Forever.*

Yet here I was. Contemplating letting that sure thing go.

"No one likes my dumb food jokes, either." Ben smiled even more broadly. "What did one berry say to another?"

I groaned. "It's you who got us into this jam," I said, and we both grinned.

But then his face fell. "When my mom died . . . no one knew what that meant for me. Everyone around me—even my dad—thought I'd dealt with that loss a long time ago. But as you knew, I never really did. When I flew out to California to bury her, I kept thinking it would have been easier if I could've talked to you. If you'd been there with me."

If anyone else had said this to me, I would've felt incredibly guilty. Then I would've looked for ways to make it better. But now I was just . . . sad. And I let myself sit with that. "So why *didn't* you call?" I asked after a moment.

When I looked at him, I was pretty sure I saw the exact same pain he was seeing. "You left me. At least, that's what it felt like. No," he corrected himself. "That's what it *was*. You didn't come over after, or call, or do anything to tell me that you still cared. I felt rejected, and, Laine—regardless of whether we were going to stay friends or take things in a different direction, I never thought you of all people would reject me."

"I'm really sorry," I said frankly. "I never thought about how much that would hurt you. All I could think about was how hurt *I* was."

"Thank you," he said. He leaned forward and rested his elbows on the table. "And I'm sorry that I hurt you. I never should've said what I said."

"No, if you meant it, you absolutely should have. I just wish . . . well, I wished you'd brought it up some other time. Not when we were in the middle of our one-and-only argument."

"And that's why you never reached out?"

"Yes," I said. I could swear that the couple sitting at the next table was listening in. Well, let them.

He looked away briefly. When he turned back to me, sweat was forming on his brow. "I was wrong."

"Come on, Ben. You don't have to say something you don't believe."

"I'm not gonna lie—I *did* believe that for a long time. I couldn't think of a single other reason why she'd tell you not to date me. But now that I know what I know, I see that I was wrong."

"You know, it wasn't just you that I left behind," I said, crossing my arms over my chest. "I avoided her. I moved to Ann Arbor partially to prove that I could do what my mother didn't want me to." I eyed him. "But what did you mean, now that you know what you know?"

He put his head in his hands for a few seconds before looking up at me. "This is really hard for me to say."

"Okay . . ." I had no idea where he was going with this.

"Did you know your mom and my dad . . . um. That they were friends?"

That was his big reveal? "I mean, obviously," I said. "We kind of made them be, if you think about it."

"Did you ever notice that they stopped talking around the time we were in high school?" he said.

"Sure—probably because they didn't need to keep an eye on us anymore."

"But they used to sit out on the stoop and talk for hours when we were in middle school. We were totally free range at that point. And don't you think it's weird that my dad had a key to your parents' place?"

What was he getting at? "I'm not following," I admitted.

He leaned forward. "They were together, Laine."

"No way." The ground beneath me seemed to sway. "My parents . . . loved each other." Was their relationship one I wanted to emulate? No. But they had loved each other.

At least I thought they had.

"That may be true, but your mom and my dad had an affair," he said quietly.

I drew in my breath sharply. As much as I wanted to tell him he was crazy, I somehow knew he was telling the truth. In fact, it made so much sense, I almost felt like I'd already known this. "How did you find out?"

He shifted in his seat. "My dad had surgery on his heart in March, and they had to put a stent in. He doesn't do well with anesthesia, which I didn't know because he's never had surgery before. I went to see him in the recovery area afterward, and he kept calling, 'Sally, Sally,' over and over." Ben looked incredibly sheepish for someone who'd always been nearly impossible to ruffle. "So, you know. That was awkward. When he was finally with it again, I told him what he'd been doing, and he admitted that they'd been together. I don't know all the details, but . . ."

It was horrible to hear him say this. And yet I could see it all clearly—the way my mother and Reggie barely ever looked at me and Ben when they'd sat on the park bench, supposedly watching us. How Reggie would come get Ben from our house when he could have called or hollered for him or given him a curfew. *Of course* they'd been more than friends. Had my father known, though? Was that why he'd been so distant from my mother? "How long?" I asked.

"They were apparently, uh—" He looked down and cleared his throat. "*Lovers* for a long time. Like, more than a decade. And then they broke it off when we were in high school. Right around the time your mom started seeming kind of weird to me. She was probably uncomfortable about the idea of us being together because it would have meant she'd have to interact with my dad even more."

There was a lump in my throat that wouldn't go away. More than a *decade*. That meant it wasn't accidental, nor was it some sort of midlife crisis. It had been entirely intentional.

It had been . . . love.

"Would you ever have told me this if we hadn't run into each other?" I asked quietly.

"Actually, yeah. I wrote you a long email and couldn't bring myself to hit send. Then I ran into Hadley and . . ." He shot me a pained smile. "When I found out you were going to be in town, I somehow knew I'd end up seeing you. Then, sure enough—there you were, right on Smith Street, like I'd conjured you. I'm sorry, Laine. I kind of wish I'd never found out, so I'd never have to tell you. But here we are."

"I'm glad you did. All those years, I racked my brain trying to figure out why she wouldn't want me and you to be together. I . . ." I grimaced. "I kept coming back to the idea that she was secretly racist." For a few years after my fight with Ben, every time I saw my mother interact with someone who was Black—whether it was a shopkeeper, or a stranger, or her friend Mary, who'd been her confidante for five decades—I'd looked for signs of prejudice. While I was relieved that I'd come up empty, I still couldn't help but wonder *why*—if not that, then what was wrong with Ben that made her encourage me not to date him? Never once had I imagined that the real reason would make me rethink everything I thought I knew about my family.

"That crossed my mind, too, but it didn't add up—not with how nice she'd been to me all those years," said Ben.

As relieved as I was to hear him say this, I was still in pain. I must have looked it, too, because he touched my arm lightly and said, "Laine? You going to be okay?"

"I don't know," I admitted. "Probably not. But I'm glad you told me."

And I was. My parents' marriage had been a lie. My mother had lied to me. To all of us.

But what hurt even more was realizing that my mother hadn't been pulling my puppet strings to protect me. She didn't care at all about whether or not my friendship with Ben went the distance.

No, the truth was that she'd put her own needs—her own heart—before my own. And as horrible as learning that was, it was a good thing I'd found out now.

NINETEEN

Laine

As Ben and I walked back from the coffee shop, I couldn't help but notice how many of the brownstones were decorated the same as they'd been when we were kids—this one with metal patio furniture that had been rusty since before the dawn of time; that one with a yard full of garish garden gnomes. They may have been exactly like they used to be, but Ben and I weren't. I guess that's why I was surprised at how normal it felt to be walking with him. Especially in light of the conversation we'd just had.

"I never answered your question about my marriage," I said. "I asked Josh—that's my husband's name—for a divorce last week."

"Damn." He didn't say anything else for nearly a minute, and I didn't try to fill the space the way I would've with someone else. "I'm really sorry. Divorce sucks," he finally said, shaking his head. "I've been on the other side of it for six years, and it still gets to me sometimes. Feels like a big failure, even when it was absolutely the right decision. Which it was, in my case."

As I looked at him, I realized I wanted to know everything that happened. But I wasn't sure I had a right to. "If you don't want to talk about it, I totally get it," I said.

He shook his head. "No, it's okay. My ex, Celeste, she just never really got me."

Goose bumps pricked my skin, and I glanced away, embarrassed. Why should I be happy to hear that?

Without breaking his stride, Ben added, "I guess I never got her, either, and one day, we sort of looked at each other and admitted that it wasn't working for us. What's going on with you and Josh?"

"It's kind of a long story."

"I have time," he said, but then he held up a hand. "Actually, I'm sorry—I don't mean to push. If it's new, I can totally get why you wouldn't want to get into it."

The strange thing was that I actually did. "It's okay," I said. "The truth is, I want to have kids. I have for a while, and the window for that is closing. But every time I'd mention kids to Josh, he'd tell me he wasn't ready."

"Did he know how important it was to you?"

I'd last seen Ben three presidents, one dog, and a handful of gray hairs ago. And yet here he was. Calling it like he saw it—and not being wrong.

"He does now," I said. "I just told him the other day. And he says he's almost ready. So . . ."

We'd been walking more and more slowly as we approached our block, and now Ben stopped walking for a second and cocked his head. "Will you move forward with the divorce, now that you've talked and he's considering having children?"

"I don't know," I confessed. "My family loves Josh. He doesn't want a divorce. And he's willing to move here to help me care for my mother. We'd take the upstairs apartment."

"Way to bury the lede, Laine," said Ben, pretending to stumble backward. "Are you really thinking of moving back?"

"Yeah." I wrinkled my nose. "But—don't take this the wrong way—I'm not sure I want to. It seemed like the right thing to do, but now . . . I feel really unsettled."

"Because of what I told you," he said apologetically.

"Yes, and also no. I needed to hear the truth. Now I just have to figure out what to do with it." Bad enough that my mother cheated on my father. But why had she dashed my chances for happiness for her own convenience? Granted, my getting romantically involved with Ben probably would have been messy. Still, it would have been *our* own mess to deal with—not hers.

"Will you say anything to her?" he asked.

"Repeatedly hitting my thumb with a hammer sounds more fun than that, but I think I probably should," I confessed, and he chuckled. "Still, she's losing her mind, you know? So how fair is it for me to confront her about something that happened ages ago?"

"You can love her and still speak your mind." He was peering at me with concern, and yes, some affection, and maybe that's why my stomach felt kind of strange and fluttery. "I know it's been a long time, but you seem like the same Laine I used to know. And that Laine can handle this."

"Laine the people pleaser?" I said, only half-joking.

"No," he said, shaking his head. "The person who really loves her mother, but who had the courage to say she wanted a divorce. That's a big change for you, isn't it? At least from when you were younger."

"It is," I admitted. I no longer knew if I was ready to divorce, but I *was* proud of myself for telling Josh I wanted one when that had still been true. Even six months earlier, I'd never have done that.

He smiled. His top teeth were like an orthodontics ad; the bottom were like a bunch of kindergarteners trying to form a straight line. "And that person will know what to do about this, too, don't you think?"

I wasn't sure I did think that—but I wanted to. "I hope you're right," I said.

"I'm always right most of the time," he said, and I grinned back at him.

We were just about in front of my mother's brownstone. "Well. This is me," I said.

"This is you," he said. "Hey, Laine?"

"Yeah?" He had such a great face. So calm. So . . . Ben-like. In spite of our conversation, looking at him made me feel like things were going to be okay.

"Do you think we can try again? To be friends, I mean?" he said.

Yes, I immediately thought. *The answer has been yes since the second I saw you on Smith Street, and even before that.*

"I'd really like to," I said. "But how do we do that after all this time? I . . . I really don't want to screw things up again."

"I don't, either." His brown eyes held my gaze, and even though I was pretty sure glancing away was the socially acceptable action to take, I didn't do it. After not seeing him for sixteen years, he was finally here in front of me, and it was like someone had found the key to the secret part of me that had long been locked up. I was not about to cut this moment short.

Finally, Ben reached into his pocket for his phone. "Well," he said. "As for how to do this, I think it starts with us exchanging phone numbers so I can text you later to find out how your talk with your mom went."

I laughed, not because it was funny but because I didn't know what else to do with the overwhelming feelings of delight and relief that I was experiencing. "Okay," I agreed. "Let's start there."

~

My elation dissipated as I let myself inside the apartment. My mother was at the kitchen table, pencil in hand, staring down at a crossword puzzle. She didn't hear me, and I watched her for a moment, wondering whether it was worth it to discuss what I'd learned with her.

I almost expected to hear Ben's voice, but instead, it was my own that rang through my head. *You were willing to give up your life for her,* I thought angrily. *Your dream. She's asking you to put her needs first in the most significant way possible—she at least owes you an explanation.*

"Mom?" I said.

"Hello, dear."

"Is Josh here?" I asked her.

"No, he went for a run," she said, still staring at the paper.

"Mom," I said. "I need to talk to you about something."

"Anything, dear," she said. Her absentminded tone made me wonder if this was the right time to bring it up.

Stop worrying about what's right for everyone else, the voice within me argued. *It's the right time for* you, *Laine. And the longer you wait, the more likely you are to chicken out.*

"Mom, can we talk?"

She lifted her head and I examined her. Her expression didn't seem glazed over, and that was a start. "What is it, Laine?"

I had to say it quickly before I lost my nerve. "Were you and Reggie having an affair?"

The sound that came out of her sounded almost like a squawk. Then she said, "Laine Alexandra Francis, that is a very bold . . ."

Her darting eyes told me she couldn't remember the word.

"Accusation?" I supplied. I felt bad that she'd had a lapse, but I wasn't willing to let that derail this conversation. "But is it, Mom? You told me—you told *everyone*—that you and Dad loved each other. I mean, I knew your relationship wasn't perfect." Far from it, really; I'd been trying hard to remember a time when I could actually remember them being affectionate to each other, and the only thing I could think of was their fortieth-anniversary party, when they'd been posing for a photo. "But you two were married for four decades. If you weren't happy, why not ask for a divorce?" I hadn't realized how angry I was until I heard the clipped tone of my voice. "And why Reggie? Couldn't you have picked anyone other than Ben's father?"

"Laine, that is my business," she said in a hurt voice. "Not yours."

I pulled out a chair across from her and sat down. She pushed the paper away, which is when I realized she hadn't filled in a single square. *That's not what's important right now,* I reminded myself. "No, Mom. It's mine, too. Because it's why you told me not to get involved with Ben, isn't it?"

She looked like I'd slapped her. "I did no such thing," she said in a low voice.

"Yes, you did. You told me not to get into a relationship with him because it would ruin our friendship. In fact, you said that repeatedly. And even though I didn't want to, I listened to you," I said, my anger growing by the second. "But you know what really kills me?"

She stuck her bottom lip out. "You're not acting like yourself right now, Laine. It really pains me to see you of all people giving your mother a hard time."

"You're being manipulative," I said frankly. I felt as shocked as she looked, but it felt like the truth, and wasn't that what I was aiming for? "Just like you were then. You didn't care one bit about what was good for me—you just didn't want to see Reggie anymore because you'd broken up."

She stared at me.

"Ben told me everything, Mom," I said. "And Reggie told him. All of this is so stupid! Did you think somehow Ben and I would end up getting married and you'd have to look across the aisle at the guy you really wanted to be with?"

She looked down at her nails. "Well, yes. That did cross my mind."

Now I said nothing. I couldn't; I was too shocked. She'd thought that?

"Laine, I don't want to fight with you," she said quietly. "Not when you and I are going to be living under the same roof. Please, let's not speak of this again." Her eyes were pleading. "Not to your sisters—I don't want them to think terrible things about me. Not to anyone."

I rubbed my forehead. I hadn't thought through whether I'd tell Hadley and Piper, and if so, what exactly I'd tell them. "What happened to 'I want you to make the decisions that are best for you'? That's what you said to me the other day," I said, in case she'd forgotten. "Did you even mean it?" *Or are you relegating me to the sidelines again?* I added internally. Because I couldn't help but feel that we were slipping right back into our old pattern. And this time, I didn't have it in me to pretend not to feel hurt and rejected.

She jutted her chin out. "You've always been free to make any choice you want, Laine."

Now all of the pain I'd been feeling toward her boomeranged right back at me. She was right, of course. I could have dated Ben in spite of what she'd said. Or reached out to him after we fought. I had chosen not to, and that was on me.

Well, I had a choice now, too. Would I keep on trying to make my mother happy, or finally make decisions for myself for a change?

"Laine?" Josh, clad in damp running clothes, was standing just outside the kitchen. He was staring at me, which made me wonder how much of our conversation he'd overheard. "What's going on?"

"Nothing," I said. But as I heard myself, it occurred to me that I'd fallen right back into my usual pattern—sidestepping the truth to make things more palatable for everyone else. And that was no longer the way I wanted to operate. "Actually, I need to ask you for a favor."

"Anything," he said, mopping his forehead with the corner of his T-shirt.

"Thanks. I need you to stay with Mom for a few days until Piper, Hadley, and I can work something else out."

He and my mother both looked confused. "Wait—where are you going?" he asked.

"Back to Ann Arbor, Josh. I need to clear my head."

"Laine!" gasped my mother. "We had a plan!"

"I would've had to go home at some point, Mom," I said. "I don't know how long I'm going to stay. But you told me to take what I need—and what I need is space."

"Laine, should we go talk privately?" asked Josh. He looked nervous; he probably thought this was related to the divorce. And now that I was thinking about it, it was—at least a little. Having him around made it really hard to think clearly about our separation, especially in light of what he'd said about kids. So getting the heck out of Dodge would have an added benefit: I'd get to work through my thoughts about Josh, too.

"We'll talk later," I said. "Right now, I'm going to go pack my things. Don't worry—I'll call Topper's assistant and have him transfer my plane ticket to you, so you won't be stuck here indefinitely."

"Laine, please don't leave," said my mother.

I glanced at her, but only for a second; if I looked any longer, I'd want to give her what she wanted instead of what I needed. "I'm sorry, Mom, but I have to," I said.

Because there was a place for everything—and this was not my place.

TWENTY

LAINE

The skyline had just begun to disappear in the rearview mirror when Ben texted.

I'd been feeling awful—the pained look on my mother's face as I wheeled my suitcase toward the door had me thinking that empowerment might not be worth its price. And yet I'd gotten in the car and driven off anyway, because for all my guilt, my conversation with Ben—and yes, the one I'd had with my mother—had revealed the real issue. Whether I had a child or not, with or without Josh, it was time to admit that I had a choice, just as my mother had said. And to prove that when push came to shove, I could make hard choices instead of doing what was easy just to keep the peace.

If only those choices didn't make me, and everyone I loved, quite so miserable.

But then two little lines of text appeared on my phone, and my mood immediately lifted. *Jeez, Laine,* I thought. *Just how starved for companionship are you, exactly? And if that's the case, why the heck are you taking off on your own?*

Actually, I was famished for friendship, I admitted as I pulled off the highway into a truck stop so I could read the text and respond, and refuel the car, which had less than a quarter tank of gas. Or maybe it was just that I really wanted to talk to Ben.

Know it's still early(ish) in the day, but I wanted to see how things were going, he'd written. *It was good to see you again*

It was great to see you, too. Lots happening. Let me know if you have a minute to talk, I wrote back. *If you don't, no worries—will catch you up later*

Moments later, he called. "I have a minute. All the minutes, actually—I'm off until tomorrow." Over coffee, he'd mentioned that he was working as a private chef for an actor and her family who lived in a brownstone in Brooklyn Heights. They traveled frequently, but he was on retainer, making what he described as "good money for a super part-time gig."

I laughed. "Well, I'm glad. Thanks for calling." Across the parking lot, a trucker honked at a car that had nearly cut him off.

"Of course. But, uh, where exactly are you?" said Ben.

"New Jersey, actually. Getting gas."

"Does that mean things didn't go well?"

"Depends on how you define *well.* I decided to drive back to Michigan."

Silence.

"Ben?"

He cleared his throat. "Sorry, I'm here. And I'm glad you're doing what you need to do. But I'd be lying if I said I wasn't a little bummed that you just . . . took off."

Again. He didn't have to say it; I cringed as I caught the subtext.

He continued, "We just started hanging out again, and while I know you said you weren't sure about moving here, I guess I was hoping we could hang out again sometime soon while you were still in town."

Did he? Now I couldn't help but smile. "I know—I was hoping that, too."

"Too late to point out that there are thousands of hotels in New York, and you could have rented a room at any one of them?" He was being playful, but I still felt sheepish. Driving back to Michigan *was* pretty extreme. And yet . . .

"It's hard for me to think straight with my family around," I said. "And right now, I have an awful lot to think through. Josh is going to stick around in New York for a few days until I can talk to my sisters about what we're going to do with our mom. So that will buy me some time in terms of deciding whether I want to stay married."

"Gotcha," he said, and this time, I couldn't tell if he was implying anything else. "So you think you'll stay in Ann Arbor?"

"I'm not sure yet. I've got some things I need to deal with." Including calling Melinda and seeing if she still wanted me to do the organizing job for her and Ravi. I'd been really excited about that. I still was, actually. Why had I so readily dropped something that was important to me?

Oh right—because I *was* a people pleaser. Well, no more.

"So the big news is that I told my mom that I knew about her and your dad," I said.

"Whoa. And?"

"No surprise, she was upset. Said it was none of my business and denied that she'd told me not to get involved with you."

"Good for you."

"It doesn't feel good, but I'm glad I did it."

"I get it."

Somehow I knew that he did. "Thanks," I said. "And thanks for listening."

"Anytime," he said. "Keep me posted, okay? Maybe even let me know that you made it to Michigan in one piece?"

I was glad no one was around to see the smile that had surfaced on my lips. My life was kind of a wreck. My beloved dog was dead, I was contemplating divorce, and I had just yanked the rug out from beneath my mother's feet—and my sisters', really—after learning the terrible truth about her past.

And yet Ben was my friend again, and though I'd never admit it to anyone, that almost made up for everything else.

"Of course," I told him.

"Already looking forward to it," he said.

I was, too.

~

I got gas, then got back in the car and called Hadley.

"Laine!" she said as I was merging back onto the highway. "I just spoke to Mom. I can't believe you just *left*! What happened? She said you said you needed space. Did you and Josh get in a fight or something?"

I sighed. "Nothing happened, Hadley. Well, that's not true. Mom and I had an argument."

"But you and Mom never fight!"

"Well, we do now."

"What on earth were you arguing about?"

"I don't want to say. You can ask her if you want." It didn't seem right to forever alter my sisters' perception of our parents' marriage without my mother's permission. Not while she was still alive and able to tell them herself, at least.

"Really? We're not in the habit of keeping things from each other."

The highway blurred before me. "I know that, but this one's not mine to tell, Hadley."

"Fair," she said. "But you didn't even say goodbye to us."

"I'm sorry about that. But I'm sure I'll be back sooner or later."

"So you're going home to pack? Or does this mean you're not going to move back, after all? I'm really hoping it's the former, because it's not like we can just call 1-800-Home-Aid and get someone in tomorrow. We need to interview people, and probably do a test-drive of some sort, and figure out all the money stuff. And I'm going to need your help with that, Laine."

"I know," I said softly.

"I'm still looking for a new nanny, and even though Topper's picking up a ton of slack, we're both sleep deprived and at our wits' end. And I'm pretty sure Piper's supposed to be doing a shoot in London in a week or two."

"I know," I said again. "And I promise I'll come back. I just need some space first."

"When will that be?"

"I'm not sure," I admitted.

"Laine, we just decided on a plan. Now you're saying that maybe that's not the plan, after all? I'm not trying to pressure you, but this really throws a wrench in everything."

"And yet you are pressuring me," I said gently. "Hadley, I'm sorry, but yes—I *am* having second thoughts about moving to New York. I didn't put nearly enough thought into that before saying yes. And the more I think about it, the more I have to admit that I really don't want to."

"Why? What's that about?" she said, and I was willing to bet my meager savings that she asked her clients that in the exact same tone she'd just used on me.

The minivan in front of me had a "Baby on Board" sticker affixed to the back window. I couldn't help but wonder if the universe was trying to tell me to keep speaking up. "I want to have a baby," I said.

"You *do*?" squealed Hadley. "Laine, that's amazing! You're going to be the best mother. And our babies won't even be that far apart! They'll grow up together—won't that be so great?"

I'll admit, my sister's enthusiasm made me feel all warm and fuzzy inside. But that warmth still didn't fix the inherent problem. "Not so fast, cowgirl," I said. "I don't know how I can possibly take care of Mom and a baby. And given my argument with Mom, I'm not sure I want to."

"I know there's a lot to work out, but we can figure it out," said Hadley. "One second." She started cooing at the twins, and when one of them gurgled in the background, I could swear I felt a twinge in my left ovary. "The main thing is for you to be there at night, and that wouldn't be that hard, would it? Especially if Josh was there with you. Wait—so does this mean you're not going to get divorced?"

"That's the other issue," I said. "The reason I told Josh I wanted a divorce was because he still wasn't ready to have a kid. And I'd been mentioning it to him for years now."

"Why didn't you tell me this earlier, Laine? Here I was thinking you'd lost your mind."

I gripped the steering wheel and steeled myself to tell her the truth. "I didn't tell you guys because I was worried you'd tell Josh the reason, and I didn't—I *don't*—want him to say yes out of obligation. I want him to want it, you know?" After the conversation he and I had the other day, I still wasn't 100 percent sure that he did. But maybe a few days apart would bring clarity to both of us.

"Oh, Laine. You don't give me enough credit. If you told me not to say anything, I wouldn't have. And Piper . . . well, actually . . ."

"Yeah, she totally would have blabbed," I said.

Hadley laughed. "Fair enough. Laine, I'm so happy for you."

"Thank you, but don't get too excited just yet. First, I need to figure out my marriage. Second, I need to actually get pregnant, and you of all people know that can be easier said than done."

"One more reason for you to move to New York! Trust me, you do *not* want to go through this alone. I can help you. And I have the best fertility guy—I'll send you his info."

All of a sudden, I felt choked up. I should've turned to Hadley sooner, but at least she was here for me now. "Thanks, Had. That means a lot to me."

"Don't thank me," she said. "Just come home soon."

~

I pulled into my driveway hours later, worn out and woozy from driving. When I got inside, I set Belle's urn on the mantel, then peeled off my sweat-soaked clothes and got in the shower. I stood there so long that the hot water ran out and my skin turned bright pink. Afterward, I wrapped myself in a towel and wandered around the town house. Why had I agreed to paint the walls red, when it only made the tiny living and dining rooms look that much smaller? And a green plaid couch—really? Were we going for hunting lodge chic?

Oh right: I'd said yes because Josh had wanted them. I could still remember his smile at the store, and how he'd looked so pleased with his furniture find that I couldn't bring myself to admit that I hated it on sight.

But that wasn't Josh's fault—not even a little. It was mine.

My eyes landed on the spot in the corner of the living room where one of Belle's many dog beds had been. Josh had suggested putting the bed away—it was too morbid to leave it there, he claimed. I supposed I could've put a plant in its place, or maybe some kind of decorative vase to fill the void, but I'd left it empty. I went to the front closet, pulled out the dog bed, and dragged it back over to the corner. "There," I said as I stood back and admired my work. "That's more like it."

My eyes landed on the urn on the mantel—and damned if it didn't seem like that urn was staring at me with the same knowing expression Belle always used to make.

"You're right," I said to it. "Ugly couch or no ugly couch, it's going to be hard to leave this place. We had some good times here."

I could hear my phone ringing in the other room. I let it go to voicemail in case it was my mother calling to find out when I was coming back. I was hurting, but she was, too, and I knew when I heard her voice I'd want to do something to ease her pain—even if it was at my own expense. I couldn't ignore her or steer clear of her forever.

But right now, I needed a little more time to take care of myself.

TWENTY-ONE

LAINE

When I went out for coffee the following morning, I couldn't help but notice how very good it was to be back in Michigan. I could find a parking spot without circling for twenty minutes! I didn't have to put up with other people trying to cut in front of me in line! The woman at the counter took my order with a smile! It was all so pleasant. And yes—so easy to imagine having a child here.

But as I drove home, it occurred to me that maybe that had less to do with the Midwestern pace and more to do with the fact that I didn't have to interact with my mother. As I'd anticipated, being away from her had given me a chance to think. Trouble was, the more I thought, the more I had to admit that I really didn't want to move to Brooklyn, even for a year, and that was not just about when and where I wanted to start a family.

I wasn't even angry with my mother anymore; not really. I was just so very *disappointed*. I'd once heard Hadley remark that disappointment was a more palatable form of sadness, and I supposed that was true. I'd always understood that I wasn't at the top of my mother's priority list, but to find out that my heart had been at the very bottom . . . that was one thing I didn't want time to think about.

Yet moving back was what I'd agreed to do—and my sisters were counting on me. And now Hadley was saying she'd help me with the pregnancy, even if I didn't have a baby with Josh. How could I possibly say no to that, especially knowing that I was only agreeing to a temporary stay?

After I let myself inside the town house, I called Josh to see how things were going. I'd been expecting him to call—more than once—to find out how to use the coffee maker and whether to make my mother breakfast and all the other daily details that I normally would've handled. But he hadn't reached out.

"Everything's fine, Laine," he said, and he *did* sound awfully calm. "Mom seems pretty normal, to be honest. She went to bed at nine, so it's not like there was an opportunity for her to do anything strange last night. And we had a nice little chat over coffee this morning. Honestly, I know I saw her slip up while you were here, but she seems better than ever."

Hearing him say this made me feel less guilty for having flown the coop. Still . . . "Where is she now?" I asked. He hadn't lowered his voice when talking about her, so I assumed she wasn't nearby.

"She went out to get bagels."

I pictured Georgie's empty storefront. What if she was wandering around, lost and confused in her own neighborhood? "And you *let* her?"

"Of course I did. Isn't that what she'd been doing before you came to Brooklyn? She's been living alone for years now."

"True," I allowed.

"And it's not like you're going to lock her inside all day after we move in upstairs. We'd be keeping an eye on her, not babysitting her twenty-four seven."

We. I didn't point out that I hadn't made up my mind about that.

"Relax—I've got this," he told me. "By the way, I'll be home in two days. I have another meeting with that investor I was telling you about, so I can't really stay here any longer. And Topper's assistant was able to switch the name on the flight. Is that okay?"

Two days? Granted, I knew that's when my flight had been scheduled. But that was so *soon*, and I was no clearer on whether I wanted to get back together with him.

Yes, you are. You know exactly what to do.

I swatted the air, like that was enough to get rid of that pesky voice in my head. "Of course, that's fine," I said. Except what if my mother started creeping upstairs at night again, or slipped out of the house?

"Laine, she's really fine," said Josh, answering my silent questions.

"All right," I conceded. As he'd pointed out, she'd already been alone for a long time. Her memory loss *would* get worse—but not right away. I was overthinking this. "I'll talk to Hadley and Piper about having them check in on her after you leave," I told him.

"Perfect. This meeting is super important, so I appreciate that. Laine?"

"Yeah?"

"I couldn't do this without you, you know. And even if I could, I wouldn't want to."

"Thanks, Josh," I said. Hearing him voice his appreciation filled me with warmth. "I'll see you soon."

It was only after I'd hung up that I found myself wondering why, after our big talk the other day, neither Josh nor I had broached the subject of children.

~

"So . . . I've changed my mind." Melinda Mahadik was smiling at me, all bright white teeth and frenetic energy.

"No problem!" I said, making sure to sound upbeat, because this was a big gig and I did not want to mess it up.

I'd called Melinda shortly after speaking to Josh to set up a time to do a consult. "Oh no, I don't need a consult. You've got the job," she'd said. "I have seven rooms in desperate need of an organizer, and

I don't want a stranger in my house." Then she threw out a figure that was nearly as much as I'd made from all of my other jobs combined and asked me to come by that afternoon.

Now I was standing in her mudroom, which was still teeming with winter gear—coats and boots, a pair of sleds, and a set of snowshoes.

"Instead of the mudroom, I think you should tackle the game room," she said. "We're barely ever there."

It didn't really make sense to start in the room that the family used the least. But the customer was always right: that's how I'd approached my other organizing gigs, not to mention my freelancing, and wasn't that a large part of the reason I'd always kept busy? "I can start wherever you'd like," I said.

"I was hoping you'd say that." She'd started walking toward one of the many halls off her great room, but she spun around suddenly. "Are you sure this isn't weird for you?" she said with a grimace.

"I take it you heard about me and Josh, then?" I said with what I hoped was a casual smile.

"Josh told Ravi, who, of course, told me," she said, glancing out the floor-to-ceiling windows through the great room. We weren't couple friends with Melinda and Ravi, but they often invited us to parties, and I'd spent plenty of time in their meticulously landscaped yard.

"The divorce is kind of on hold right now." I was surprised to realize how good it felt to say that out loud. "We're talking things through."

Melinda's face lit up, and I felt like I'd done something good. "I am *so* happy to hear you say that!" She gestured for me to follow her down the hall. "You guys are such a great couple. I'd hate to see you split up. And dating after divorce—eek," she said, her expression turning sour. "My sister's doing that now, and she tells me it's kind of a nightmare."

Suddenly Ben's face popped into my mind, and although obviously Melinda couldn't hear what I was thinking, I found myself blushing. I wanted to be friends with him, I reminded myself; nothing more. Any hint of romance was just my brain's way of coming up with ways to quickly fill a Josh-size vacuum. Besides, it was looking increasingly unlikely that Josh and I would separate. And wouldn't staying together solve almost all of my problems? Find someone to be the father of my child? Check. Not draining our savings to pay a divorce attorney? Check. Having help with the child *and* my mother, making my sisters happy, keeping everyone one big happy family? Check, check, and check.

"Yeah," I said to Melinda. "I'd rather skip that if at all possible."

"Right?" she said, directing me into the game room.

The room was nine different types of disaster, which made my heart flutter with excitement.

"So. I definitely want to have built-ins installed," said Melinda, surveying the mountain of board games pushed against one wall. I'd never been envious of someone else's mess before, but I couldn't help but view the disarray as a sign of a happy family. Would Josh and I have a similar mess in our house one day? I was having a hard time imagining it. "What do you think?"

"I think built-in shelving is a great idea," I told her.

"Do you have a guy?" she asked in a tone that informed me she expected me to say yes.

I did not, in fact, have a guy, and I couldn't help but wonder if I'd bit off more than I could chew. But Josh was always telling me I was resourceful, and surely I could rely on that trait now. "I'm certain I can find a great contractor or carpenter. That does mean we'll have to start in another room. Are you okay with that?"

She frowned.

I felt a little flutter of panic in my gut. "How about the kitchen?" I suggested brightly, plastering a smile on my face. "There's no feeling quite like opening your cupboards and drawers and seeing every pot, pan, and utensil where it belongs. You know what they say: a place for everything, and everything in its place."

This seemed to appease Melinda, so we trotted back to the kitchen. I declined the espresso she offered me and began opening doors. *Sweet Martha Stewart,* I thought as I took in the contents of a cupboard under the marble island. Despite the kitchen's outwardly tidy appearance, the hidden bits were in total disarray. I couldn't wait to work a miracle.

"I'm going to take some measurements today; then I'll need to purchase some shelving and containers to get things in order," I told her.

"Do whatever you need to," said Melinda before taking a sip from her tiny mug. "I just want to be able to find my can opener for a change."

"I can absolutely make that happen for you," I said, and this time, my smile was genuine. Productivity was to me what sunlight was to a plant; it was so good to feel useful! Really, short of being in love, it was possibly my favorite feeling.

Then it hit me: if I moved back to help my mother, I'd be really, really useful. All I needed to do was focus on that, and then the transition wouldn't seem so bad.

"Awesome!" She threw back the rest of her coffee, then returned my smile. "I'm off to spin class, but you know how to reach me."

I waved my phone at her. "Yep! Got your number. Have a great workout."

I'd just slipped my phone back into my pocket when Melinda reappeared in the kitchen. I knew I was in trouble when she flashed her bright white teeth at me. "I was just in my closet looking for a different shirt when I realized I really need you to start in my bedroom. You don't mind, do you?"

My eyes shifted to the pots and pans I'd piled on the counter. "Not at all."

I kind of did mind, but the customer was always right. Especially when she was helping to fund my future.

TWENTY-TWO

Laine

The roads were nearly empty when I left for work the next morning, making it feel less like early June and more like mid-August, when school was out and everyone rushed to the lakeshores for one last hurrah before the temperature dropped and the leaves began to turn. The Mahadiks lived in a wooded neighborhood near the arboretum, and I had to take a winding road that looped past the river to get to their house. I drove slowly, taking in the stately old homes and the canopy of trees over the road, trying to enjoy the view while I had the chance.

Because the longer I thought about it, the harder it was to deny that I would be heading back to New York sooner or later. Returning to Michigan had been a lovely, much-needed reprieve, but it would not, could not, last. My mother was fine for now—Josh had been updating me even as I continued to avoid her—but who was to say what three months from now, or six, or a year, would bring? The only certain thing was that she would be worse, and even if I couldn't yet see past my disappointment over my mother's selfishness, the rest of my family needed my help.

It was impossible, but I couldn't help but wish I had a time machine so I could go back a year—though three to five would've been ideal—and make the choices I was now making, but at a different juncture in life. Then I'd be a younger potential parent whose mother had a sharper brain, and I wouldn't find myself having to decide between the immediate issue of my parent's care and the nebulous promise of motherhood, which might never actually materialize.

I'd just pulled up to the Mahadiks' when my phone started buzzing in the cupholder. I expected it to be my mother; she hadn't called once since I'd left, which made me think she was upset with me. I didn't feel guilty about bringing up the affair with her, even if I was beginning to wonder if storming off had been the best move. But I didn't want her to be angry with me, either.

It was Ben.

How's things in the mitten state?

Really good, I wrote back. *Working on a big organizing gig right now. There are some hiccups to work out, but I'll get there*

Want to talk?

I did, actually. *Yes,* I wrote.

A few seconds later, he was on the other end of the line. "Hey."

"Hey yourself," I said, unable to keep the smile out of my voice.

"Tell me about this gig."

I loved that he cut right to the chase. "It's seven rooms—the biggest project I've ever worked on, and the pay is amazing."

"But?" he said.

I looked through the windshield at the Mahadiks' home. The facade was stucco, painted a buttery color, and the roof was covered with terra-cotta tiles. "But the woman I'm working for keeps changing her mind about what she wants me to do."

"Don't let her."

I snorted. "You make it sound so easy."

"It is. When clients do that to me, I don't negotiate or explain. I just say, 'I'm unable to do that. Here's what I can do.' Then tell her whatever it is that works for you and see what happens."

"What if she fires me?" I asked, aghast.

"So?"

"You're crazy, Ben. What do you mean, *so*? My reputation is at stake."

"It's really not, Laine. People respect a person who doesn't let others walk all over them. And would you rather be liked or respected?"

I'd never considered that question before. "Both, please," I said, only partially joking.

"Sometimes that's doable, sure. But not always, so you have to know in advance what's important to you. Either way, boundaries are your best friend, Laine."

I didn't have a best friend anymore. So technically that position *was* open. "Thanks, I think," I said.

"Is that your way of telling me I pushed too far?" he said.

I smiled. "No, I actually mean it. I needed to hear that."

"Then you're welcome, I think. Anyway, you already knew it. Deep down, at least."

Did I?

"Any thoughts on when you're coming back?"

"Still not sure," I said. Hadley, Piper, and I were going to have a call in a couple days about finding an aide for my mother. I knew they'd want an update on my plans, too, and I didn't see how I could possibly tell them I didn't want to return. If only hiring a full-time aide wasn't so cost prohibitive. And who was to say my mother would even tolerate a stranger in her home? I remembered Diana, one of my longtime editors at the *Free Press*, telling me how her elderly mother, who'd been dealing with heart failure, had kicked out her aide. There'd been nothing Diana and her siblings could do about it. Unless they went to court to get her mother's rights revoked—which they weren't willing to do, and even if they had been, the process was expensive and complicated—she got to decide who was in her house. Her mother had died soon after.

"I hear that between Detroit and Ann Arbor, there's a pretty good food scene," said Ben. "Maybe if you end up staying put for a while, I can take a little road trip out to Michigan? If you'd be up for company, of course. I know you've got a lot going on."

Before I could think about it, I blurted out, "I'd love that."

Then neither of us said anything right away. I couldn't possibly know what he was thinking, but I suspected it was not so dissimilar from what was running through my mind.

Which was that I wanted Ben to be my friend again. And he was, actually, even if our friendship felt different and somewhat tenuous. But I'd be lying if I said that part of me didn't want something else—something more. Was that only because things with Josh hadn't been going well, or was there more to the subtle but increasingly persistent feelings I'd been picking up on?

"I should probably get to work," I said.

"Of course. Talk soon?"

"Definitely."

"Great. Bye, Laine."

"Bye, Ben."

As I hung up and got out of the car, I suddenly felt very tired. So much time had passed; and now, once again, there were many miles and multiple states between me and Ben.

What was this all for?

I did my best to clear my thoughts and look chipper as I greeted Melinda. After some small talk, she directed me down a long hall, then up a set of stairs to her daughter's bedroom. It was really a suite, with its own bathroom and a large study off of the bedroom. The walls, carpet, and furniture were all shades of lavender and violet.

"Rita's really into purple right now," explained Melinda.

Oh, I could tell. "I thought you said it was a disaster?" I said, taking in what was objectively a remarkably tidy room.

"Wait until you open her drawers and her closets. Total nightmare!" said Melinda, holding her hands up.

"Got it. Do you want to help me figure out what to keep and what to toss?"

She shook her head. "I've got a meeting for the children's foundation. Rita's an average-size eight-year-old. Get rid of anything that doesn't seem like it'd fit her anymore."

I didn't actually know the dimensions of an "average-size" eight-year-old, which only served to remind me that I was childless. But surely, I could figure that out . . . couldn't I?

"What about sentimental items?" I asked, thinking of the tiny yellow tutu that Kaia had continued to wear, even though it hadn't actually fit her in at least a year. "How will I know what she wants to hang on to?"

"Oh. Hmm. Just do your best, I guess."

I nodded, even as I pictured how Kaia would weep if she discovered her tutu was gone.

Then I thought of what Ben and I had just discussed and realized that "my best" was not acquiescing to something that I didn't feel comfortable with and wouldn't actually serve my client.

Melinda was already starting for the door when I called to her.

"What is it?" she said, spinning around.

I was too nervous to even try to smile. "I couldn't live with myself if I tossed something that Rita wanted to keep. Do you think either you or she could find a time to help me go through everything? Once we sort out what I should keep and what should go, I can put it all away."

She frowned. "She's at camp right now, and I have an appointment that I can't miss."

I could feel sweat forming near my temples. If I were, say, Hadley, this would've been a normal conversation. But I wasn't, and I was beginning to understand just how rusty I was at asserting myself.

As I thought again about what Ben had said, a solution came to me. "Then why don't I tackle the kitchen today? It's the most-used room in the average home, and that's typically the best place to start," I said. Then I held my breath, waiting for her to tell me that wouldn't work for her, and actually I could go take a long walk off a short pier and find someone else's home to organize.

But she just nodded. "Sure—I trust your judgment. I can help you tomorrow afternoon, if that might work."

I broke into a smile. "It does. Thank you."

The minute Melinda left the room, I pulled out my phone and texted Ben. *What do you know? Boundaries* are *my best friend.*

TWENTY-THREE

LAINE

I'd just made breakfast for myself the following morning when my mother called. Although it was the first time I'd heard from her since I left, I hesitated because I didn't really want to pick up when I had no idea how our conversation would go. With each day that passed, I felt less raw about what I'd learned about her and Reggie—and me and Ben. And yet the fact that she hadn't called to apologize or check in on me only served to remind me that, any way I sliced it, I *wasn't* her priority. No wonder I wasn't in a hurry to leave Ann Arbor.

But maybe I was still feeling emboldened by my conversation with Melinda the day before, because I hit the answer button. I needed to start facing my problems head-on, rather than constantly avoiding conflict.

"Laine?" said my mother. "It's Mom."

"I know, Mom."

"Well, dear, I was just wondering when you were coming back."

My heart sank. Here I was thinking she wasn't worried about me, when it was possible she didn't even remember our fight? "Do you recall what we talked about when I left?" I asked.

"Regarding Reggie?" she said. "I do."

So she did remember.

"Laine, I'd really rather not discuss that again."

My irritation immediately reared its ugly head, and I had to order myself not to pretend it wasn't there. "That makes two of us," I said frankly. "But when you ask me when I'm coming back, I'm going to remind you why I left."

"Well, you didn't say you were staying away indefinitely."

No, I hadn't.

But truth be told, I wanted to.

"It's not like you to stay angry," she continued. "Really, to get angry. And I don't like it. But I am sorry, you know." I felt myself begin to soften when she added, "For whichever part you're upset about."

Whichever part? How about cheating on Dad? Directing me away from Ben? Always putting yourself first?

"I'm upset about all of it," I said. "And I don't know how long I'll be away, but it looks like it's going to be a while. I'm in the middle of an organizing job." With the exception of the game room, I actually anticipated being finished with the job for the Mahadiks in the next week, but Melinda's friend Charlotte had emailed me last night to see if I could swing by for a consultation. I hadn't responded to her yet, but hearing my mother—cogent, capable, and yes, clinging to her belief that I had no right to be angry—made me think that I could at least delay my return to take on a new job.

But secretly it also made me wonder what would happen if we simply hired an aide and I stayed put. If I just . . . did what I wanted to. It was almost too radical to fully comprehend, and yet it was where my brain kept going.

My phone beeped. When I glanced at the screen, I saw that it was my ob-gyn's office. I swear my heart skipped an actual beat—because there was only one reason they'd be calling me right now. "Mom, I need to take this. Hold on a second." I switched calls before she could respond.

"Laine Francis?" said a woman.

"This is her."

"This is Sophia from Dr. Kim's office. I have you on our cancellation list for preconception appointments. Dr. Kim has an opening on Monday at eight thirty a.m."

Dr. Kim was my ob-gyn—the one who'd been too booked to see me anytime soon. But now she had an opening; Monday was just a few days away. So now I wouldn't have to wait any longer or talk to a stranger—even Hadley's "fertility guy," who was probably amazing, but still—about getting pregnant.

"Would you like to come in?" she said.

"Are pigs made of bacon?" I said.

"Pardon?"

It occurred to me to save that remark for someone who would understand it. By which I meant Ben. "Sorry—yes, I would love to take the appointment. Thank you so much."

"Not a problem! I'll email you a confirmation, and we'll plan on seeing you Monday at eight thirty."

"I'll be there," I said, smiling as I switched the call back to my mother. This. Was. Happening. "Mom?"

There was a fumbling sound. "I'm here," she said breathlessly. "I set my phone down for a second, and the next thing I knew, I'd misplaced it. This place is already falling to pieces without you around."

Normally I'd have taken this as a compliment. I'd always cleaned up for her, even when I was just in for Christmas; it made me feel useful. But now her comment seemed . . . manipulative, to be honest. Just like Ben had pointed out all those years ago.

"Are you having a hard time being on your own?" I said.

"I'm not on my *own*, Laine. Josh has been lovely company. Thank you for lending him to me." There was an edge to her voice—one that brought out the sharpness in my own.

"He's not a lawn mower, Mom. You're not borrowing him."

"I *know* that. All the same, you'd be a fool to leave him."

She knew just the wrong thing to say sometimes. "Mom, while I'm glad you remembered that Josh and I have separated, I'd rather not get into it right now." It would be too confusing to tell her that maybe, just maybe, we were going to get back together after all.

Because what if we didn't?

"I'm just saying."

"And I hear you," I told her.

"Well, good," she said. "So when are you coming home?"

"Do you need me to be there?"

"Not at all. As I've told you girls repeatedly, I'm a grown woman who's been on her own for some time now. While I'd love to have your company, I don't *need* you, Laine."

This was exactly what I wanted to hear. So why did it make me feel sad?

"Good," I said. "Because I'm really busy here and I'm not sure I'm going to be able to return to New York anytime soon."

I was about to tell her that I needed to go when she said, "Well, then, Laine, I guess this is goodbye."

"Mom," I began, but she was already gone.

~

I was at the Mahadiks' for most of the day—and thank goodness for that; work made it nearly impossible to feel too awful about my mother. Was she selfish? Yes. Did she know all of the right buttons to push? Of course she did. I didn't want her to be angry or to hurt her feelings—but I was going to need to learn to deal with other people's emotions if I was going to live my life on purpose. And she herself said she didn't need me.

As I drove back to the town house, I could feel fresh optimism blooming inside me. Now that Melinda was letting me concentrate on one room at a time instead of constantly asking me to move to the next thing, the work was effortless—easier than writing, even, and that had always come naturally. Not only was this new career going well, I truly loved it and could easily see it becoming my lone focus sometime soon. Back when I'd first set up the business, Josh had told me that word of mouth would always be my best marketing strategy. Apparently so, because one referral was leading to another. It was a warm day, so I rolled down the windows to my car. Van Morrison was on the radio, and I turned it up high and happily sang along. My mother was doing fine for now. I finally had a doctor's appointment that would serve as the springboard for my fertility journey. And yes, Ben was back. Life was good.

As I turned the corner onto my street, I spotted Josh sitting on the steps of our town house. I'd been so immersed in work and my thoughts about my mother that I'd forgotten he was coming home that evening. And he hadn't called me to pick him up from the airport, either, even though that's what I always did when he was traveling. Though I did feel a little guilty, it occurred to me that it was probably another element of his newfound self-sufficiency, and I couldn't exactly feel bad about that.

I parked and walked over to him. "Hi," I said as I approached him. He'd taken his suitcase inside. But instead of scrolling on his phone or working on his computer, he was just . . . sitting there. It was like seeing a horse lying down in the middle of the field; you knew they slept that way from time to time, but you still couldn't help but wonder if they'd fallen and couldn't get up.

"Everything okay?" I said, sitting down beside him. "You could've called me to pick you up, you know."

"Yeah," he said with an indecipherable smile. "But I knew you were working."

"Well, welcome back. It's nice being here after being in the city, isn't it?"

He looked around. We were surrounded by town houses, all white and beige and pale brick like our own, and the young trees on our street didn't provide the canopy of shade that so many other Ann Arbor neighborhoods were famous for. I supposed it wasn't the nicest part of town, and yet I felt comforted by its familiarity. I wondered if he did, too.

Apparently not, because he said, "I guess? New York's growing on me."

I looked at him with surprise. Having been raised in the kind of suburb where no lawn went unmanicured and parents had to make the heart-wrenching decision whether to send their children to exceptional public schools or outstanding private ones, Josh always walked around New York like he was expecting to get mugged in broad daylight. "Only took fourteen years."

He smiled sheepishly. "Something like that. There's just so much happening, though. I can't help but wonder if I'd have been successful if I'd moved to a big city instead of staying here."

"You're not *not* successful," I pointed out.

"Which isn't the same as being successful."

We looked at each other.

"Maybe that's true," I said, "but what good does it do to think about that now?"

"None, I guess." He shrugged, and I realized that his button-down wasn't wrinkled the way it normally would've been. He'd either ironed it or not left it in the laundry basket for three days after pulling it from the dryer. Either way, it was even more evidence that he really was changing. Growing up, one might even say.

"So . . . I have news," I told him.

His eyes lit up. "Good news?"

I nodded enthusiastically. "My doctor called this morning."

Now he frowned. "Wait—is everything okay?"

Um, hello? I just told you I wanted a baby the other day? "Well, yes. It was my ob-gyn."

"Huh," he said.

For someone so smart, he could be incredibly dense sometimes. But I would simply have to connect the dots for him. "I have a pre-fertility appointment for Monday."

"Oh," he said in an unreadable tone. "What does that entail?"

The helium balloon of my enthusiasm had just sprung a leak and was now zipping through the air as it deflated. And still, I grasped wildly, trying to catch it. "I'm not actually sure," I said, attempting to smile, "but it's the first step in finding out what I need to do to get ready to get pregnant."

"Got it."

"Why aren't you excited?" I said. I knew why *I* wasn't, but what was wrong with him?

"You are, and that's enough, isn't it?" he said, and now he was the one with a tight smile. "After all, I'm not the one getting poked and prodded."

"I don't know how much poking and prodding is going to happen at the first appointment, but do you want to come with me?"

"Sure," he said, but then he looked down.

My throat was getting tight. *Don't be dramatic, Laine,* I told myself. *He said himself he doesn't like to count his chickens before they've hatched. And aren't we literally talking about eggs right now?*

But that was old Laine lecturing me. Laine 2.0 said what she was thinking, even if it led to a disagreement—or worse. I took a breath to collect myself, then said, "Josh, I've been waiting for this for a long time. Years. I know it's my fault you weren't aware of that because I wasn't direct about telling you. But I want this, more than maybe anything, and I'm going to this appointment with or without you."

He'd been staring at his feet, or maybe the cement, but now he lifted his eyes. Then he touched my arm lightly and said something I never could've predicted.

"No, Laine—you *did* say so. You told me after the twins were born. And like, a bunch of other times over the past year. You weren't pushy about it, sure, but I knew. I just tried to ignore it so I didn't have to deal with it."

There was a terrible honking noise, not unlike a goose that had just been shot out of the sky. It took me a second to realize I'd been the one to make it. I tried to look at him, but my tears had turned him into a watercolor, and now my shoulders were shaking.

"Oh, Laine," he said, putting his arms around me, and the shaking stopped a little. "I'm so sorry."

"It's okay," I said, but I was still crying. "I just feel . . . stupid."

"Why?"

He was still blurry as I detached from his embrace. Then, before I could second-guess myself, the truth came spilling out. "Because I wasted all that time. If I hadn't been so busy trying not to confront you, I would've known ages ago that you didn't want to have a kid. Now I'm an 'advanced maternal age,'" I said, parroting what I'd read on a fertility website. "And for all I know, it's too late for me."

"No," he said, shaking his head fiercely. "That's not it at all. I *do* want kids."

"Just not with me," I said as the tears continued to stream down my cheeks.

"No, that's not it, either, Laine," he said quickly. "I was trying to make some money. Trying to build a future for us before you actually got pregnant."

"Money? I know we're not vacationing on yachts these days, but we're not living under a bridge, either." I gulped down a sob. "We could've made it work, Josh. Actually, I *am* making it work—I even changed careers, and I'm doing so well."

"I know you did, and I love you for that. You're so hyper-capable that it astounds me sometimes." He wiped away my tears with his thumb, then added quietly, "But *I* wanted to be successful. I didn't want our kid to see me as the guy with a million failed businesses. I wanted something to stick before I became a father. I never thought it would take this long, but I wasn't willing to leap before I knew there was a net."

The pain etched in his face told me he was telling me the truth, and it was all I could do not to wrap my arms around him and try to make it better.

But what about me? Who would make it better for me, when my husband had just admitted he'd known what I wanted, and had let me long for my dreams by myself after I'd supported his for the entire length of our relationship?

"Laine?" said Josh. He was peering at me with concern. "What do you think we should do now?"

I held his gaze for a long time. My beautiful, brilliant Josh. He hadn't meant to hurt me. He had done his best.

It was just that his best wasn't enough for me. Not anymore.

I smiled sadly at him. "Josh, I think we should get a divorce."

TWENTY-FOUR

Sally

Oh, what was I thinking? Did I really believe none of my girls would ever find out? What a fool I've been—what a fool.

I *do* need Laine. Why on earth did I say I didn't? But now she's given up on me. This isn't just about Reggie, though that's more than enough. When she stormed off, I thought it would blow over quickly. I thought she'd go for a nice drive and think through things and realize that everything I've done has been for her and her sisters.

Well, not everything. She's right about that. But I certainly never meant to hurt her. Doesn't she know that?

But then she didn't come back. And Josh left, too.

What were they fighting about? I can't remember anymore.

Then our call today . . . it wasn't good. I don't remember exactly what she said, but there was a whole lifetime of anger in her voice. All the things she kept locked up inside—they're out now. I knew from the way that she was speaking to me that she'd already made up her mind. She's not going to live with me here. She probably never was. And can I fault her? I didn't move to Florida to be with my mother at the end, even though that's what she wanted. Now Laine wants to have her own life. Her space. I understand that, even if I wish it weren't so.

But now the girls will have to send me to that terrible place. Not right away, but it's only a matter of time. Aides don't last. They don't know you the way your child knows you. They can't put up with the same things. And so they make their recommendation: it's time to take the next step. What they don't say is that it's just one short step from the grave.

You'll be with other people. You'll make friends—that's what we told my mother. But you don't know those people. Most of them don't know themselves anymore. That's not good company. They just make you lose your mind faster.

Everything will be taken care of for you. Because you can't take care of yourself—no one adds that part. And the less you can do for yourself, the meaner you become. I can still remember my mother throwing her oatmeal all over me like a toddler because she mistook me for a nurse. I could weep just thinking of it, the way she'd curse at me after a lifetime of never using those words. And then her face, childlike with sadness and confusion, whenever she caught herself. By the end, she never caught herself, and all I could hope was that I'd find her crying rather than angry. What a terrible thing to have to wish for.

You'll have the best care. That means lots of drugs—that's what they give you when you get mean. Sedatives. Sleeping pills. My mother's mouth hanging slack, a river of drool making its way down her chin. Heart beating. Dead eyes.

No. I won't go. But I don't know how to convince them to let me stay.

What did Reggie always say? "When you don't know the way, walk until you find it."

Reggie. If only he were here now, we could walk together. But I can go where we went.

Yes, that's what I'll do. I'll go for a nice long walk. I'll see our happy places and think happy thoughts.

I'll remember.

TWENTY-FIVE

Laine

After more tears and some discussion, Josh went to Ravi and Melinda's to spend the night at their guesthouse. Even if he wanted to have children—and he swore that he did and was willing to start right away—something in me had shifted profoundly. It was almost like his confession unearthed the truth, which I must've been trying to rationalize away. I loved him, and I always would. As I told him, I wanted him to stay a part of our family and would do everything I could to make that happen. But I didn't want to be married to him anymore. And—this was the truly remarkable part—now I understood that I didn't need to have a clear explanation for that, not even for myself. I simply . . . wanted something else for my future. However frightening it was to go rushing into the unknown, there was a freedom there, too—one that I must have been craving all along. Though my eyes were swollen and my heart was heavy, I fell asleep that night with a deep sense of calm.

When Piper called early the next morning, my first thought was that Josh had told her what had happened. My second was that I'd need to be okay with that. Josh was a free agent now, and it was entirely up to him how he wanted to interact with my family. If he and Piper decided to put each other on speed dial so she could support him through our divorce, so be it. As Hadley had reminded me, I could lean on her. And although I was waiting for the dust to settle before I shared my news, I had Ben, too.

"Morning, Pipes." I hadn't talked to her since I'd arrived in Michigan, but that wasn't that unusual; Hadley and I touched base at least once a week, while it was sometimes an entire month before Piper or I called each other. "I take it you heard the news. Before you try to talk me into—"

"Laine!" she interjected. "Mom's missing!"

I'd heard her just fine, but her words didn't quite compute. "What do you mean, *missing*?"

"She's gone, Laine!" She sounded frantic, but Piper had always been a mite dramatic, so I waited for her to say something that would indicate that this was just another one of my mother's shenanigans and Piper had caught a rabid case of Hadley's anxiety. Maybe my mother wasn't home, but surely she was just at Bashir's or off getting bagels or maybe even at Ben's, looking for a spare set of keys.

Instead, Piper said, "I went over there to drop off some extras from our farm share last night, and she wasn't there. The door to her apartment was unlocked, and her purse and phone were on the counter. I thought maybe she'd gone to see Mary or something, so I left a note telling her to call me when she got it. But she never did, and I called her a bunch of times last night and she never picked up. So I came over this morning as soon as the kids were awake and her stuff was exactly where it was yesterday. She's still missing, Laine. I have no idea where she is!"

I inhaled too fast and nearly choked on my own breath. "Why didn't you call me sooner?" I sputtered. "I could have asked Ben to look for her or—I don't know. Something!" Something other than sit here, six hundred miles from the woman who birthed me and clearly needed me, luxuriating in my stupid, selfish thoughts and my ridiculous so-called needs.

"You said you wanted space! Hadley and I were trying to give you what you asked for!"

Oof. That *was* what I asked for. And everyone knew what they said about that. "I'm sorry," I said miserably. "I shouldn't have left."

"That's beside the point now, isn't it?" squawked Piper.

"Stay calm," I said, as much to myself as her. "I talked to Mom yesterday morning, so she hasn't been gone that long."

"You did? Did anything weird come up?" said Piper.

"She seemed normal," I told her, but even as I said that, it struck me that normal was no longer the way to measure how bad things were. After all, she'd seemed "normal" right before I'd found her upstairs with enough inventory to start up her own personal home shopping network. "Well . . . she and I did have kind of a tough conversation."

"Another one? What is going on between you two? You never fight!"

"That's kind of what she said, and I thought I was sticking up for myself for a change," I said miserably. "I must have really upset her. Did you call the cops?"

"Hadley did. It hasn't been nearly long enough for them to do anything about it—it has to be at least forty-eight hours. We called Nettie and Mary, too, and I went over to Bashir's twice. No one's seen her."

"Did you check the upstairs apartment?"

"I don't have keys."

I slapped my forehead. "I'm an idiot. I think I still have her set in my purse." I'd left in such a huffy hurry that I hadn't remembered to return them.

"Then she's not up there, so don't worry about it," said Piper. "Anyway, I went up there—put my ear to the door but didn't hear anything. And I didn't hear footsteps from her apartment, either. I'm worried, Laine. This feels wrong."

"I know," I agreed. "It does."

I had my doctor's appointment on Monday—the big one that I wouldn't miss for the world, but would need to miss for my mother. On top of that, I was supposed to finish the Mahadiks' house and try to set up a consult with Melinda's friend.

And now none of that mattered.

I needed to be in New York, helping my sisters and my mother. That's where my *actual* life was. "I'm going to throw some stuff in a bag and hit the road," I said. "Hopefully you'll find Mom before I reach the city, but if that doesn't happen for some reason, then at least I can help." And once we found our mother, I would be staying at her side. How had I possibly thought she would be okay on her own?

"Call Josh, Laine. See if he'll go with you. It'll be easier if you two can split the driving."

"Now's not the best time to be telling you this, but we've decided to go through with the divorce. Well, I have," I clarified.

"I know that, Laine," she said.

So he had called her. At least he had someone other than me to talk to, I reasoned, even if that person happened to be related to me.

"He has an important meeting," I said, recalling why he'd flown back.

"Stop micromanaging him, Laine, and let him make his own decisions."

She was too blunt—but she wasn't wrong.

"Fine," I said. "I'll call him as soon as I hang up with you." I'd already grabbed the cooler from the cupboard and had begun filling it with snacks and drinks. "I'll leave in the next twenty minutes, even if Josh can't go."

"I was hoping you'd say that," she said with palpable relief. "If anyone can find Mom, it's you."

"I hope you're right," I said. Because I owed it to my mother—to all of them, really—to find her. I was ashamed of myself and the way I'd allowed my anger to blind me when I should've been caring for my only living parent.

I could almost hear her voice now: *Well, then, Laine, I guess this is goodbye.*

Had she been warning me—or telling me I was already too late?

TWENTY-SIX

Laine

"Obviously I'm coming with you, Laine," Josh had said when I called him to tell him about my mother. "I'll be ready in five."

And although I'd once remarked that Josh would be late to his own funeral, he was already standing outside the Mahadiks' house, duffel bag in tow, when I pulled up. My heart sank when I saw that Melinda was on the lawn beside him. I tried to put on a brave face as I got out of the car, but I had a strong suspicion that the smile I was aiming for was closer to the expression a gorilla might make after someone has stolen her pet kitten.

"Laine, I'm so sorry to hear the news," she said, holding out her arms to me. I wasn't big on hugging people I wasn't related to, but I let her embrace me anyway because it was the least I could do, given that I was about to leave her high and dry.

"No, *I'm* sorry," I said into her hair; she still had her arms, which were surprisingly strong, wrapped around me. "I feel terrible that I haven't finished up the last couple of rooms yet."

She took a step back and cocked her head. "What are you apologizing for? You can finish when you come back."

"Right," I said, swallowing the lump that had just formed in my throat. I didn't have to tell her now, I assured myself; I could do it later, after I got to Brooklyn and sorted everything out. If we found my mother—and I'd been praying to all kinds of deities and celestial bodies that we would, and fast—I would have to have Josh mail my belongings to me. Because it was abundantly clear that she could not be left alone. How had I ever thought it was okay for me to just pick up and leave?

"Safe travels, and keep me updated," said Melinda, squeezing my shoulder.

"We will," I promised as I looked over her shoulder at her house. Such a lovely place; it would have been so great to have finished the job, and not just because of how fantastic the before-and-after photos would look on my website. Melinda was all warm wishes now, but once she found out that I wasn't returning, she'd be thinking something else entirely about me. And even though we weren't friends, per se, I realized that I actually kind of liked her, and didn't want her to feel the exact opposite about me.

I asked Josh to drive the first stretch of the trip. My nerves were shot, but I also wanted to have my hands free in case my sisters called. I decided to text Ben, too, to let him know what was happening and see if he'd keep an eye out for my mother.

After I put my seat belt on, I looked over at Josh. "Is this going to be weird, us being in a car together for ten hours?"

"Why would it be?" he said, slipping on his sunglasses.

"Because of our conversation yesterday."

"What about it?" he said. "You said yourself that I'm going to stay a part of the family. And this is what family does, right? They help each other."

"What about your meeting with the investors, though?" I said. "You probably won't be back in time."

"So?" He shrugged. "If that's the thing that makes them decide whether or not to buy it, then it was never going to happen in the first place. Besides, you won't be back for your doctor's appointment, either, will you?"

I shook my head sadly.

He reached over the gear shift and squeezed my hand. "Sometimes we make tough choices for the people we love."

Sure. But sometimes we acted like selfish little children and let our elderly mothers wander around New York City sad and confused and utterly alone.

~

Hadley was on the phone with the police when Josh and I arrived. Josh had driven nearly the whole way, going so fast that it was a near miracle he hadn't gotten a speeding ticket. But we'd arrived in nine hours, including bathroom breaks, which was an all-time record. As I told him, I owed him.

"Right, right," said Hadley in what I recognized as her reasonable voice—the one she used right before she kindly informed you that you were an idiot. "I hear what you're saying, but that's simply not acceptable. No. Just because she hasn't been *diagnosed* with dementia doesn't mean she doesn't have it. I'm telling you, she's been suffering from memory loss for at least a year now."

Josh met my eyes. "It's not your fault," he mouthed. We hadn't spoken much on the drive, but at one point, I'd tearfully confessed to him that it was my fault my mother was missing and had told him about our arguments—well, except for the part about Ben and me. Just like he was now, he'd dismissed my explanation as nonsense. But I knew better. Even if I had needed space, I didn't have to imply it was permanent. What's more, I could've at least called Hadley or Piper and told them the ominous way she'd said goodbye. If Piper had checked on her earlier, or Hadley had called—or, or, or; there were so many possibilities that were better than this scenario—then she would be at home where she belonged. Because for all my frantic texting and calling with my sisters, who'd been combing Brooklyn all afternoon, she still wasn't back. With each passing hour, it seemed more possible that she wasn't going to be.

And that was because of me.

"She's elderly," said Hadley, practically spitting into the phone. "Believe me, I looked this up. You're supposed to be helping us."

Piper was leaning against the bookshelves and gnawing on a cuticle. She grimaced at me, then whispered, "She's been arguing with this guy for ten minutes now."

"That's not like her," I whispered back. Hadley didn't argue; she moved forward with her plan and expected everyone else to follow suit. Maybe because of that, they did.

"Yeah, well, it's not like Mom to pull a *Gone Girl*," said Piper.

"Thank you!" huffed Hadley. "That's only exactly what I've been asking all along. Good. Okay. Please call the minute you know anything." She sighed and tossed the phone on the sofa. "They're going to send a patrol car out to look for her."

"They don't even know what Mom looks like, do they?" I said.

Hadley plopped down beside her phone. "I dropped off a picture earlier, right after I got done pumping."

Now *that* was more like Hadley. Honestly, I wouldn't have been surprised if she'd already posted "Have You Seen This Woman?" fliers all over the city. Meanwhile, I'd taken the better part of the day to get back to where I was supposed to be all along. Daughter of the year over here. "Thanks. Hey—I need to tell you both something. Josh already knows," I said, and he nodded. "Mom and I got in an argument."

"We know," said Piper. "That's why you took off for Ann Arbor."

"No, there was another one."

"What happened?" asked Piper.

"Well, we argued about the first argument." My voice was quavering.

"Which was about . . . ?" asked Hadley. I still hadn't told them about Reggie, nor did I intend to; it wasn't my place.

"About something that happened long ago," I said. "Like I told you, you'll have to ask Mom if you want more detail." *Assuming we can find her,* I added mentally.

"That's super weird, Laine," said Piper.

"Maybe you should tell us," said Hadley. "What if your argument has something to do with where she went?"

I shook my head. She hadn't wandered off to New Jersey to look for Reggie—not when it seemed like she didn't consistently remember that he'd moved. That had nothing to do with it. This was about me implying I didn't want to take care of her.

"Why *did* you leave, Laine?" said Piper, looking at me suspiciously.

I sighed. "Without getting into the whole thing, when I saw Ben last week, I learned some things that I had to bring up with her. Which led to our argument."

"So it wasn't about you and Josh?" said Piper, looking back and forth between us.

"No," I said.

Josh cleared his throat. "There's probably no good time to tell you both that Laine and I are really getting divorced."

Piper looked like she was on the verge of tears. "You *are*?"

"Yes, but Josh will always be a part of this family," I said, looking at him.

"Which is why I'm here." When he turned to me, he didn't need to say a word for me to know what he was asking. I nodded.

"Laine wants to have a baby, and I . . . I wasn't ready," he told them. "I'm still not sure if I am." It hurt to hear him say this out loud, but it was a relief, too.

"Laine!" yelped Piper. "Why didn't you say so?"

"I didn't want you both to try to convince me to make it work with Josh," I explained. "I've decided I'm going to do this on my own." It was a shame that I wouldn't be in stirrups in another day or so, finding out whether or not my body was up for the job.

"Laine deserves to have what she wants," said Josh.

Why did he have to go and say that? Getting what I wanted was what got us into this mess in the first place. "Listen," I said, "we really need to split up and look for Mom more, before it gets dark." It was close to dinnertime, and the sun would stay high in the sky for several more hours. I wasn't sure those several hours would be enough, though. "I just wanted you both to know that I'm the reason she went missing."

"Oh, Laine," said Hadley with a heavy sigh. "I love that you're always thinking about everyone else. But believe me when I say that Mom disappearing has everything to do with her and nothing to do with you. It's time to let that idea go."

I met her eye. "With all due respect, Hadley, it's time for me to start taking responsibility for how my actions impact others." My mother hadn't done that when she'd told me not to get involved with Ben. If anything, that was a lesson for me. Maybe she'd made the wrong choices—but I still had time to make the right ones.

~

We were just about to head out when Ben rang the doorbell. I'd been texting back and forth with him on the drive to Michigan, even though it was a little weird to do so with Josh right next to me, and he knew she was still missing. All the same, I was surprised to see him standing there, holding two coffees. My head was pounding, and I felt the most terrible combination of tired and wired. But seeing him standing there made me feel a little better.

"Hey," he said. He looked kind of bashful. "Thought you might want a little fuel," he said, passing me one of the coffees. "And maybe some help finding your mom?"

"I'd love that," I said. "Thank you. Let me check with—"

Just then, Hadley, Piper, and Josh came barreling out the front door.

"Hey," said Ben.

"Ben," said Piper, hugging him. "It's been way too long. How are you?"

"Hey, Piper," he said with a smile. "Good—thanks. It's great to see you, though I wish it were for a different reason. Hey, Hadley," he added. Then his eyes landed on Josh, and he quickly extended his hand. "You must be Josh."

Josh shook it. "And you must be Ben."

My eyes flitted back and forth between them, wondering what their first impressions were, and whether this was as weird for them as it was for me. I still hadn't told Josh that Ben and I had stopped being friends because we'd nearly become more. After all, it was irrelevant to our divorce. And yet, in spite of my family's predicament, just having Ben close to me was making me feel warmer than the weather warranted. And I knew that sooner or later, I owed Josh the longer version of the story.

Ben smiled generously. "I am indeed. I was just telling Laine I'd be happy to help you all search for Sally. If you want, of course," he said, but now he was looking at me.

"The more people, the better," said Hadley. "Why don't we divide and conquer?"

"That's a good idea," I said. I looked at Piper and Josh, who were standing side by side. They were both subtly leaning toward each other. I couldn't help but think that meant something, even if they didn't realize what they were doing. I was surprised to find out that it didn't bother me all that much. "Why don't you two take the car? Had, you can make the rounds at all the places Mom might have gone. Ben and I will walk through the streets, see if we can spot her."

"Smart," said Hadley. This was the ultimate compliment from my Ivy-educated sister, and admittedly, I felt so pleased that you'd think she'd just handed me the Nobel Peace Prize. "She's on foot, so she couldn't have gone far."

"Thanks," I said. "Let's go."

"Great. Everyone have phones?" said Hadley.

We all nodded.

"Let's do this," said Hadley.

The three of them scattered immediately, leaving me and Ben standing on the stoop. He put an arm around my shoulder and squeezed me. "You going to be all right?"

"I don't know," I confessed. "Definitely not until my mom's home safe. But I'm glad you're here."

He wasn't tall like Josh, so when he turned to look at me, we were already face-to-face. And as I looked into his warm brown eyes, I felt almost exactly like I had three decades earlier when he'd ambled over to my stoop. *Seen.*

"Me, too, Laine," he said. "In times like this, you really need a friend."

TWENTY-SEVEN

Laine

I'd never been able to find my way out of a cardboard box without assistance, but Ben had a natural sense of direction, and he wove us from street to alley to underpass with efficiency. Searching on foot wasn't as fast as being in the car, but we could see more, and we were able to stop and ask shopkeepers if they'd seen my mother. But no one had, and my last conversation with my mother kept going off like a fire alarm in my brain: "I guess this is goodbye."

I desperately wanted to believe she was just trying to teach me a lesson, but that had never been her way. No, I'd hurt her—not just in leaving—and she'd fled. She may have wandered off before, but she'd never gone further than Bashir's or Ben's before returning home.

This was about me telling her I wasn't going to live with her, as I told Ben while we walked. And that made this feel twice as bad as it would've otherwise.

"You don't really think that, do you?" he said as we crossed back over the Kane Street bridge, which connected the corner of the neighborhood that was cut off by the highway. The sound of cars whooshing past filled my ears, and I had to raise my voice for him to hear me.

"Sure, I do," I said. "I mean, there's the issue with your dad, too—she didn't deny it, and I told her it was up to her to tell my sisters."

"Think she's going to?" he asked.

"I doubt it." I shaded my eyes to try to see if the older woman approaching us was my mother. My heart sank yet again when I saw that it wasn't.

"I feel terrible about telling you that," he said as we made our way down Hicks Street. "I don't know if I should've, but there didn't seem to be any other way to explain why I'd come to see things differently. Laine?"

"Yeah?"

"I'm really sorry I said those things about your mom all those years ago. I was just so mad, I couldn't see straight."

"About?"

He glanced away. "I was in love with you."

My stomach dropped, and I couldn't speak right away. "You were?"

"For the longest time," he said, meeting my gaze again. "You must have known."

"No," I said.

But then I thought about the summer between our junior and senior years of college. We'd both passed up internship opportunities elsewhere to come home—to be together, though neither of us had come out and said that. During those hot, lazy days, he'd started looking at me longer than he used to—not just once, like that night after high school graduation, but regularly. And when we touched, even if it was just our hands grazing, it felt different.

Because it was.

"I was, and you left me. And, Laine—you *knew* that was my thing. I never let anyone get close to me because of my mom taking off. But I let you, and then you just . . . ran."

It hurt so much to hear him say this, because every word was the truth. "I know," I said. "I'm so sorry, Ben. I was so upset that you'd pointed out that I worried more about other people than myself—and in this case, more than you. I always thought you accepted me for who I was. But when you said that, it made me think you looked at me like some dumb puppet, and that made me kind of hate myself," I confessed.

"I'm sorry."

"Thank you."

"I didn't *want* to develop feelings for you, you know," he added quietly. "But looking back, it was kind of inevitable—you'd been my favorite person since the day I walked up to you in front of your apartment."

I blinked back unexpected tears. "Me, too," I confessed.

"Thank you," he said. "I think I knew that, which is why I was so crushed when you said you just wanted to be friends. I needed someone to blame, and it was easier to be mad at your mom than you."

"But she *did* come between us. And she probably was racist at times, even if I couldn't see it."

"I didn't have to say the things I did, though."

"I'm not going to lie—selfishly, I do wish you hadn't. I told myself I didn't, but I resented her for years. I couldn't stop looking for evidence that you were right. That's part of the reason I stayed in Michigan after graduation."

His face fell. "I'm really sorry."

"Me, too," I said.

We'd just slowed down to peer into an alley. "Mom?" I called. "Sally Francis?" The sun was beginning to set, and I was feeling increasingly desperate. Where could she possibly be?

"Let's keep walking," said Ben, who'd sensed my mental state and had picked up his pace even more. "You never suspected anything, though?"

"I mean, my dad worked too much, but they never fought," I said. But as soon as I said this, it came rushing back to me—how she'd try to engage him in conversation, only for him to respond with one grunt after another. How she'd put on a new dress or do her hair differently and waltz around him trying to get him to notice her. And as

I thought about it, he'd never been the one to book those vacations to the Berkshires. *She* had.

I hadn't been the only one who'd felt neglected. But the pain shooting through me now had a second source. Because I'd just realized that all the things my mother should have said to my father—*please pay attention to me. I want to matter as much as your work does. I need you*—were many of the things I should've said to Josh.

I felt wretched.

"Laine," said Ben. "Having troubles doesn't make their marriage a lie. It just makes them . . . human."

Now there was no blinking it away; my face crumpled, and tears began streaming down. That might be true, but I still wished that they'd been happy and that my mother's affair had never happened. Maybe then Ben and I wouldn't have avoided each other all these years, and our relationship would be different. And I never would've had to confront my mother, which meant she wouldn't be missing right now.

Before I knew what was happening, his arms were around me. "Hey," he said into my hair. "It's okay. It's going to be okay."

"Not if I keep crying," I sniffled. It was hot—too hot, even late in the day, the city was a sauna—and I was perspiring all over him. I didn't care. It was so good to have him here with me. And as much as I was trying to push the thought down—I had far bigger fish to fry at that moment—I couldn't help but think about his confession. He didn't just have feelings for me.

He'd been *in love* with me.

But then I immediately thought of my mother. I pulled away from him. "We need to find my mom."

Ben wiped his forehead with his sleeve and surveyed Court Street. "Where haven't we been yet? Can you think of anywhere our parents used to go together?"

"Yeah—Carroll Park," I said after a moment. "But we already checked there. And our stoops, but obviously she's not there, either.

"What about Prospect Park?" I said as it started coming back to me. "Remember how they'd always sit on that bench, right near the northwest entrance off Third Street, and tell us to go get lost for a while?"

He nodded. "You've got a hunch?"

"It might be nothing . . ."

"No, we should follow it," he said. His arm was already out to hail a cab. Miraculously, one stopped right away, and in spite of this being a complete crapshoot, my hopes were rising. As we sped through Park Slope, I texted Piper and Hadley to let them know what we were doing. Five minutes later, Ben and I were standing at the edge of the park. While Prospect Park wasn't quite as large as Central Park, it was still too vast for us to cover on foot in a few hours, even a full day.

"We don't need to search the whole park," said Ben, reading my thoughts. "She couldn't have gotten that far."

"You're right," I said.

"Sally!" I called as we started along a path. *Please,* I thought. *Please be here. Please answer us.*

"Sally Francis!" said Ben. "Sally, can you hear us?"

"Did you lose your child?" asked a woman pushing a stroller in the opposite direction.

I glanced at Ben, who was already looking at me. Our child. Just the idea of it rendered me speechless for a moment. "No, my mother," I finally said. "Seventy-two-year-old white woman, five four, blondish hair." *Probably wearing way too little clothing and possibly dazed and confused,* I added mentally.

The woman made an apologetic face.

"Right," I said. "That's like one out of every twenty people who walks through here."

"Don't give up hope," said Ben, looping his arm through mine, and I was almost able to forget the despair that was coming over me. "I think I see the bench—the one they always used to sit on."

"What?" I said, but he was already pulling me in the direction of a cluster of trees at the edge of a wooded area. There, on the end of a bench that was just coming into focus, was a thin figure hunched over.

I broke into a run.

"Mom!" I yelled as I approached her. She was wearing a blouse and a pair of linen pants—both dirty now—and was slumped over a tattered cardboard box. My heart sank.

But she was speaking! "Laine?" she said faintly. "Is that you?"

"Mom," I said, kneeling beside her. I wrapped my arms around her. "I'm so relieved. Are you okay?"

"I'm fine," she said, but she didn't sound that way at all, and my relief was very quickly being replaced with a fresh wave of worry. "Just very tired."

"What are you doing here?" I was trying not to look frantic, but her eyes were glassy and unfocused, and she didn't look good. "Did you spend the night here?"

She nodded, and I took a deep breath. *She's alive, Laine. She's going to be okay, even if it doesn't feel like it.*

"Here," I said, handing her one of the water bottles we'd been carrying. "When's the last time you had some water?"

"Oh . . . I'm not sure."

Had she taken a sudden turn for the worse, or was this just the result of spending the night in the park? Either way, I realized, she needed to see a doctor.

"Sally," said Ben. "How did you end up here?"

"Why, I went for a walk," she said vaguely. "I wanted to remember some things, and sometimes walking helps."

Ben and I exchanged a quick glance.

"Then I found a gaggle of kittens," she said, motioning toward the box. "I had to find a place to put them. I thought . . ." Her voice trailed off.

I looked in the box beside her. Sure enough, the box held three tiny creatures—two long-haireds, one of them gray and one a brownish gray tabby, and another with black-and-white hair that was neither long nor short.

"Girls or boys—I can't get close enough to tell," she said as though she hadn't heard me. "I heard them mewing for food. I'm hungry, too."

"Here," I said, grabbing one of the protein bars I'd packed in my bag. I was desperate to do something—anything—to help her, to make this better. To ease the guilt I felt over finding her this way and knowing I was responsible for it. "Eat."

She took it from me, but she didn't put it to her lips, and that's when I really started to get concerned. "These poor kittens. They need their mother. I'll need to get a dropper to feed them." Then she looked up at me like I'd just arrived. "You're here, Laine. You came back."

"I did," I said, and my voice caught.

"Oh, good. You'll take care of the kittens for me, won't you? I know you're a dog person. But these little things need help, and you'll make such a wonderful mother."

I wanted to cry. I would, but she was the one who needed mothering right now.

"Does that mean you'll stay?" Then she looked at Ben. "Where's Reggie?"

"He's in Jersey, Sally," he said calmly. Then he turned to me and said in a low voice, "Laine, we need to get your mom to a hospital. Now."

"No hospital," she croaked, waving a skeletal arm in protest. "They'll lock me up with the old people. Please, Laine, you can't. Look what happened to Nana Meyers," said my mother. She was starting to slump over. "They'll never let me leave. I'll lose my mind."

It was entirely possible that a trip to the ER *would* fast-track her into a nursing home. And for all my guilt, I suddenly understood that my being here in New York—or not—was not going to be the deciding factor in what happened to her after this. Right now, she needed help. Help that I couldn't give her.

I took a deep breath. "I'm sorry," I said.

"For what?" she said, leaning on my arm. "You're here."

"Yes, I am," I said, hugging her. Then I looked up at Ben. "Please hail a cab. We need to get Mom to the hospital."

TWENTY-EIGHT

Laine

Ben and I took my mother to an emergency room not far from the park. Of course, we couldn't take the cats in, so he'd dropped us off after promising my mother he'd take the cats to a vet.

Our timing had been lucky, and my mother had been triaged right away, then put in a room and hooked up to an IV; the doctor who attended to her thought that her confusion stemmed at least partially from dehydration. This news alleviated much of the guilt I'd been having about taking her to the hospital against her wishes. Still, I had to wonder how many other decisions would put us at odds—and if she would concede quite so easily the next time.

My mother fell asleep the minute the last nurse left her room, and Hadley arrived soon after. I'm sure I wasn't winning any beauty contests myself, but I couldn't help but notice that the circles under her eyes were even darker than they'd been right after she had the twins. It reminded me of how much she'd been doing to help our mother through this—and that every second of that had taken away time she could have been spending with her family and on her business.

As I told Hadley, the doctor who'd been attending to our mother had ordered a series of tests, though not the MRI we suspected she needed; he'd asked us to schedule a separate appointment for that. She was set to be released the next morning.

"We're going to need to figure out what to do with Mom long-term," she said, her eyes flitting to our mother, who was snoring lightly.

"I know," I said, trying to ignore the thudding in my chest. As even as what had happened began to sink in, my anxiety was spreading like an oil spill. How could I possibly help her the way that she needed?

"Hello," said Josh, popping his head in the door.

"Hey," I said, waving him in. In spite of everything—or maybe because of it—I was relieved to see him. He *was* a part of this family—and knowing that he was going to stay that way was a deep comfort to me.

My mother's eyes flew open. "Come in, come in," she called to Josh, as though she hadn't been asleep at all. "I'm right as rain, you'll see. Come in!"

I looked at Hadley, who shook her head with the same incredulity I was feeling.

"Mom," said Josh, carefully kissing my mother's cheek. "So glad you're okay." He'd picked up flowers—a white and pink bouquet that he'd put in a light blue mason jar from the apartment—and set them on the table at the end of the bed.

"No need to worry—I'm fine, just fine," twittered my mother. "The flowers are lovely. Thank you, dear Josh."

"Mom?" Piper came rushing in, with Kaia trailing behind her. "I dropped the boys off with their dads, but she wanted to stay," she said to me and Hadley.

"Hi, sweetie," I said to her. It was nearly nine at night, but you wouldn't have known it watching her bounce around the room.

"Hi, Auntie!" said Kaia, who begun to clamber onto the bed.

"Kaia, get down!" said Piper, lifting her into the air and setting her down on the opposite side of the room. "We have to be careful with Grammy!"

"Don't treat me like a vase," said my mother.

Piper and I looked at each other quizzically, then at the bouquet that must have prompted my mother's word salad.

Her face flushed, which told me she'd realized we'd noticed her confusion. "I just mean I'm not so easily broken," she said quickly.

"We know, Mom," said Hadley.

"And when is Josh coming in?" my mother asked me.

"Mom—" I started.

"I'm here, Sally," said Josh from beside her.

All of the hope I'd been feeling vanished: the IV hadn't really done that much. And I still hadn't asked her why she'd spent the night in the park instead of trying to walk back—though part of me already knew the answer. She'd been too confused to make a decision.

And that was the most terrifying part of all.

I stole a glance at Piper, who was suddenly incredibly busy arranging the flowers Josh had just brought.

"That's right," said my mother. "And there's my Laine." She patted the bed beside her. "Come sit over here and tell me all about your dog." Her face fell faster than my own did, but it was too little, too late. "Oh dear." But then her eyes lit up again. "What did you do with the kittens? I hope they're all right."

"Ben has them," I reminded her. "He's going to take them to the vet for us."

"Thank you," said my mother. "Do you think we can keep one?"

"We?" I said.

"You're coming back home, aren't you? I need help, after all." She smiled tightly. "Otherwise I wouldn't be here right now, would I?"

My sisters were already staring at me when I looked over at them.

I swallowed hard. "I need to talk to Hadley and Piper, Mom."

My mother's fingers gripped my hand. "I'm so looking forward to spending more time with you, love. I really am sorry about our little kerfuffle the other day."

So she remembered that. But it didn't make me feel any better. "I am, too, Mom, but I don't think any of us should be making big decisions right now. It's been a very long day."

"Laine, love, that upstairs apartment is the best deal in Brooklyn. Why, did you know Mary is renting out her garden floor for more than three thousand a month? I'll charge you a fraction of that."

She'd forgotten Hadley's offer to cover part of the rent, though neither that nor the discount were the real draw.

If I moved in, I'd be just down the block from Ben. And I'd be lying if I said the possibility of seeing him whenever I wanted to wasn't incredibly appealing.

But the real issue was that I screwed up in leaving my mother alone without someone to watch her. She could have been mugged, or worse. She could have sat there for days without water.

She could have *died.*

Didn't I owe it to her to make sure that never happened again?

"Girls, wouldn't you love having your sister here with us in New York again?" my mother said.

"You know we would," said Piper.

"Obviously," said Hadley. "But Lainey already said she was going to stay with you for a while, Mom, so we don't need to discuss this right now. We'll take it one step at a time."

"Yes," I said slowly. "We'll talk about this later. Don't worry about it right now, okay?"

My mother smiled so broadly that it pained me to look at her.

"I'm not worried, Lainey," she said, leaning her head against my shoulder. "I know you'll do the right thing."

~

It was dim when Josh and I got back to the apartment that night. We'd just gotten to the front door when my eyes landed on the bodega.

"I need to tell Bashir we found Mom," I told him. "You head in—I'll be back in ten. Need anything?"

"Nope," he said. "I'm good."

"Great. Be right back."

A young man I'd never seen before was behind the counter when I went inside. "Is Bashir in?" I asked, and he shook his head. "Know when he'll be back?" I asked as I put the bag of chips and the sparkling water I'd just selected onto the counter.

"Nope," said the man.

I felt unduly disappointed; it wasn't like I couldn't come back later. "Thanks," I said.

"No worries. Bag?" said the man.

"Of course she needs a bag," called Bashir, emerging from the door to the stockroom. "Lainey! Hello!" he said as I spun around. Even in June, he was dressed in his usual uniform: a pastel button-down, a pair of khaki pants, and an apron with scissors, pencils, and various other tools sticking out of its pockets. His skin was as wrinkled as worn leather, and his eyes were cloudy. But his familiar smile hadn't changed, and it warmed me from deep within. "Dino's new," he said, nodding at the man behind the counter. "He doesn't know that he should never pretend I'm not here when a Francis is asking."

I laughed. "It's so great to see you, Bashir. I came by to tell you that we found my mother."

"I'm so glad! I knew you would," he said in his accented English. "How long was she gone?"

"Overnight," I said. "We found her in Prospect Park."

"Oh, Lainey. I'm sorry."

"It's okay," I said, but then I caught myself. "It's not, really."

"I know," he said. "You have a moment?"

I nodded.

"Then let's go outside," he said.

It was officially dark out, but the corner was lit up with the streetlight and Bashir's sign. There was a trio of kids on the bench in front of the store. He greeted them by name, then pulled a couple pieces of candy from his apron, handed them to the kids, and waved them off. Then he and I sat down beside each other.

"So what will you do about your mother?" he asked.

Across the street, Ben's windows were dark. I wondered where he was and what he was doing. In just a short period of time, he'd taken over much of my mental space. And though that did make me a little anxious—what if this new friendship we were embarking on didn't have legs?—I still wanted him there. "I might be moving back to help take care of her," I said to Bashir.

"No kidding!" he exclaimed.

"Someone's got to do it," I said, and now I was looking at my mother's brownstone. "How bad has she seemed to you? I know you were worried when she came over in her nightgown to buy cat food."

"Eh, Sally's always been zany," said Bashir, but I swear he was blushing a little. "Do you remember Mrs. Collins? Your friend Ben's upstairs neighbor?"

It was my turn to blush. "I do."

"She's not as bad as Mrs. Collins was when her memory started slipping away. But you girls aren't wrong to be thinking about what to do to keep her safe. You really might move back to Brooklyn, eh? I never thought I'd see the day."

I looked down. "Well, my sisters have their hands full with their kids and their careers, and my mother believes that going into a nursing home will be the death of her. And as we just learned the hard way, we can't really leave her on her own. I don't know that a home aide would be able to help the way she needs. I don't really have a choice."

"Sure you do," said Bashir. "There's always a choice."

He'd been old as long as I'd known him, and yet he was still as sharp as a tack. "Maybe I do, but I don't know the right one to make," I confessed.

He pointed across the street. "I still remember when you and Ben used to sit out on the steps reading while the world spun around you," he said with an appreciative grunt. "I see him from time to time now that he's back. Are the two of you in touch?"

"We are now," I said, and I couldn't keep the corners of my lips from curling up.

Bashir's eyes may have been cloudy, but he didn't miss my smile. "Good. It makes me happy to see you happy. Lainey?"

"Yeah, Bashir?"

"You say you don't know the right choice, but I think you do. The answer's already in you. You just have to find the courage to say it out loud."

TWENTY-NINE

Laine

Josh and I brought my mother home the following morning. On the doctor's advice, she was to rest as much as possible for the next forty-eight hours. Apparently that was just what she needed, too, because we'd barely gotten her settled into her bed when she fell fast asleep.

Once I made sure she was comfortable, I went into the next room to call Melinda. I knew she wasn't expecting me to return immediately, but I still wanted to update her so she had time to hire my replacement.

"Laine, hi! Did you find your mother?" she immediately asked.

"We did, but not until after she'd spent the night in a park," I said, cringing; even after a decent night's sleep, finding her there was entirely too fresh in my mind. "She was dehydrated, but no worse for the wear."

"Thank God."

"You can say that again. But . . ." I bit my bottom lip. "I'll probably be here for a couple months getting this sorted out. I'm really sorry, Melinda."

I steadied myself and prepared for her to tell me off. Instead, she said, "Laine, family first—always! Thank goodness you had the good sense to start with all the rooms we use the most. The kitchen looks ah-mazing, and my closet has never been better! Honestly, the mudroom and the game room can wait until you get back. There's absolutely no rush."

I was about to tell her that I probably wasn't going to come back, but something stopped me. "Thank you so much for understanding."

"Of *course*. I went through this with my mother, you know."

"Really?" I was pretty sure Melinda was younger than I was.

"Yeah, a couple of years ago—she had early-onset dementia. It was the hardest thing I've ever been through. Harder than her death, in a way. I know that sounds terrible, but it's true."

I thought of my mother sleeping in the other room and prayed I wouldn't be able to make that comparison anytime soon. "How did you help her through it?"

"Oof—not very gracefully. She wanted to live on her own, and we let her for way too long. She kept getting in her car and driving all over God's green earth. After a police officer pulled her over in the middle of Ohio and she had no idea where she was or how she got there, we had to make the call to put her in a home."

"That sounds pretty awful," I admitted. As far as my mother had gotten on foot, it would've been worse if she had a driver's license. Fortunately, she'd never had any interest in driving, and though my parents had a car for a while, they'd mostly relied on public transportation.

"It was terrible. But Ravi was my rock throughout the whole ordeal. If there's one thing that I learned through all of that, it's that you can't go it alone. Maybe Josh isn't the best person to support you right now, but do you have anyone else you can lean on?"

I had my sisters, of course. But Ben was the first person who popped into my head.

"Yeah," I said. "I do."

"Good," she said, and even through the phone, I could hear the warmth in her voice. "Hey, listen. After you get back and things calm down for your family, maybe you and I can grab a glass of wine or something?"

Rationally, I knew that would be a long time from now, if ever. And yet I still smiled and said, "I'd like that."

Josh had let Hadley in while I was still on the phone with Melinda. After I hung up, I found her in my mother's bedroom. My mother was awake again and attempting to prop herself up on her elbows.

"You sure you're okay, Mom?" asked Hadley, hovering so close you'd think that she was preparing to catch her if she fell out of bed. "You can rest, you know."

"I'm fine, dear. Better than fine!" said my mother. "You girls worry too much. I'm going to get bored out of my gourd lying here."

Josh had moved the small television in the living room to my mother's bedroom, and Hadley pressed the remote into her hands. My mother looked at it, wrinkled her nose, then tossed it near her feet. "I never watch TV in here. You know that, Hadley."

"Sure, but now might be the time to start. Or you can read or call a friend," said Hadley, gesturing to my mother's cell phone, which was beside the bed. I wasn't sure when, exactly, but Hadley had attached a cord to it so my mother could wear it around her neck when she was up and about. On the one hand, it seemed kind of infantilizing. On the other, my mother *had* come awfully close to having her face plastered on a milk carton. And if she'd had her phone on her when she wandered off, it's possible she wouldn't have spent the night in Prospect Park.

"Bring me one of those kittens, won't you, Laine?" said my mother, peering past me.

Ben had dropped the cats off that morning. I'd wanted to invite him in, but Josh had been with me, and realizing that made me uncomfortable was another reminder that the feelings I'd once had for Ben were resurfacing. And yet again, they came with a massive dose of caution. Because now I *knew* that our getting involved could definitely lead to the very thing I was afraid of: losing him.

"You're not supposed to touch them until they've had their vaccines," I reminded her. "Ben and I are taking them to the vet tomorrow afternoon. Then you'll get to cuddle them all you want."

"But I've already touched them!" she protested. "That's why I stayed in the park. I was trying to keep them warm." This had been her story since she'd regained lucidity. It wasn't her memory that was the issue, she insisted. It was just that the animal lover in her couldn't abandon a bunch of kittens, and she didn't think that she could carry the whole box back. Never mind that she couldn't tell us why she'd wandered off without her phone or purse and ended up in the park in the first place.

I pretended not to see Hadley shaking her head. "All right," I said, reaching into the large cardboard box on the other side of her room to retrieve one of the cats.

"Oh, hello there, little mew," said my mother as she took the kitten from me. It was one of the longer-haired ones, a tabby with extra toes that made its feet look like furry paddles. Why would a person opt for such a strange creature when they could have a dog?

My mother turned to me. "Maybe this one, Laine? What do you think? Is he a keeper?"

As if my opinion mattered here. But then I realized she was asking because she thought I was going to move in. "Mom, you know I'm not a fan of cats," I said.

"You're never too old to change, love," she said, putting the cat up to her face. It batted an oversized paw at her cheek, but she just laughed.

"You're really going to keep it," said Hadley, watching our mother play with the cat.

"I have no idea—but look at how happy she makes Mom," I noted.

"Right, but who will care for the cat?"

"Why, I will, of course," said our mother.

"Yes, but who will watch *her*?" Hadley whispered in my ear. More loudly, she said, "It's all fun and games until the thing gets crushed by a pile of boxes," and glanced pointedly at the stack I'd put in the corner of the bedroom. Before I'd taken off for Michigan, I'd begun the laborious process of trying to return some of my mother's impulse purchases. I planned to try to sell what couldn't be returned—but judging by how long it took me just to get through three orders, that was a ways off.

"We managed to make it out alive," I told her.

"This is as good a place as any for a kitten!" said my mother. "You know, Laine, I'd be even happier with all three. You could take your little mew here up to your apartment, and I'll keep the other two here."

My apartment wasn't, actually. But just that morning, my mother had told me I could take one of the beds and whatever else I wanted from her place—and there was certainly plenty to choose from—so I could move up there right away. Except every time I went up there, I kept having the same thought.

And that was that I just could not imagine my baby up there. There was nothing wrong with the single set of stairs, or the size of the apartment, or the view of southwest Brooklyn, which was actually pretty nice. It was just that when I imagined having a child, I pictured a grassy yard where they could play, and a cute little bungalow where you didn't have to worry about whether the upstairs or downstairs neighbors would be awoken by the sound of your baby wailing, and—well, something decidedly other than the way I'd grown up. It wasn't that my mother and father had done such an awful job, or that being a kid in New York had ruined me. But wasn't part of the point of parenthood the opportunity to do it differently than your own parents had? The more I thought about it, the more I realized that, more than anything, raising my child in Michigan would be symbolic. I loved my mother, but I was not going to be the kind of mother she'd been.

"Mom calls them all mew," I said to Hadley, but she was frowning at our mother, who was holding the tabby up to her face.

"Careful with your eyes, Mom—it could scratch your cornea! Or give you rabies," she said with a shudder. She turned back to me. "I *really* don't think this is a good idea."

"I'm sure it'll be fine, and they'll all be vaccinated by tomorrow," I said. More quietly, I whispered, "Give Mom a break. She's been through a lot."

"Yeah, well, so have I," she volleyed back. "Forgive me for wanting to spare myself from yet another trip to the hospital."

I looked at her. She was wearing the same button-down she'd been wearing the day before. I wasn't one to judge; since Belle had died, it was all I could do to put pants on each day, and if I didn't have a reason to leave the house, sometimes I simply didn't bother. But for Hadley, her outfit was a sign she was running herself ragged. And although I did still feel guilty about my role in that, I had a feeling there was more to it than whether or not I was playing caregiver.

"Hey, Mom? Hadley and I are going to go make you a snack," I said, grabbing my sister's elbow lightly. "Watch the kitten, please."

"Happy to, but I'm not really hungry," said my mother.

"That's okay," I called. "Remember the doctor told you to make sure you were getting enough calories? We'll be right back."

"What is it?" Hadley said as I pulled her into the kitchen.

I turned to face her. It was just Hadley—the sister I'd known for nearly thirty-eight years, who'd been through most of the best and worst moments of my life with me. There was no need to feel nervous.

But I was. Because beneath her tough exterior, she seemed . . . vulnerable. I wasn't used to that. And I really didn't want to make it worse.

I took a deep breath. "Had, what's going on with you?"

"What do you mean?" she said grumpily. "Mom just got back from the hospital, I don't know what we're going to do about her long-term, let alone next month, and Ainsley was up at three in the morning to nurse. Forgive me if I'm not in the best mood."

"No," I said, shaking my head slowly. "It's something else."

"I'm fine, Laine," she said, but she was looking out the window at the back patio where Josh was sweeping the pavers; the man truly didn't have an off switch.

"You're worried that I might not stay," I said.

She looked at me briefly. "Well, it wouldn't make things easier for us if you didn't."

"But? There's more to it, isn't there?"

Instead of answering me, she lowered herself to the floor. Then she leaned against the cupboard and put her head in her hands.

She looked so small and helpless and unlike her usual take-charge self that I almost wondered if I should have brought it up.

"It's okay if you don't want to talk about it right now," I said, squatting beside her. "But I know something's wrong, Hadley, and I don't want to pretend otherwise."

She didn't say anything for a long time. But when she did turn to look at me, her eyes were full of tears. "I'm not trying to make you feel guilty for going home. It's just that everything feels so hard right now," she said in a choked voice.

I wiggled closer and sat down beside her. "I know."

"But it's not *supposed* to feel hard."

"Why not?"

"Because."

"Because what?" I pressed.

"I have two beautiful children. A husband who's crazy about me. A job I love but don't actually have to do because I don't need the money."

"Yeah, you pretty much won the life lottery," I said with a small smile. I was pretty sure that the grass was still greener over on Hadley's side, but our conversation was reminding me that every yard had plenty of weeds. "But that doesn't mean you're not allowed to feel bad."

She shook her head. "I'm sorry, Laine—I know you're getting ready to try to get pregnant. I'm not trying to scare you."

"You're not," I said, and, in fact, I had half a mind to thank her. She'd reminded me of how difficult it was to raise kids—not only in New York, even if you had every resource known to womankind, but just in general. I'd been thinking about juggling raising a child and caring for my mother in the broadest possible terms. I knew tackling both was going to be hard, but I'd been telling myself it was doable. Listening to Hadley, though, made me think I'd been selling myself a fable. *Was* it even possible to be a parent and a full-time caregiver?

I wasn't sure that it was.

I swallowed hard, trying to think about how I was going to phrase what I wanted to say. After a moment, I added, "I'm sorry I haven't been here more to pitch in up until this point. I really didn't understand how bad it had gotten. To be honest, I don't know if I'm going to stay in New York. But I'm going to figure out a way to support you and Piper. And Mom, of course," I said. "You know how you told me I didn't have to do the whole mothering thing alone?"

She nodded.

"Well, you don't have to feel like you have to deal with the situation with Mom alone. I've got your back."

"Thanks, Laine," she said, resting her head on my shoulder.

"No, thank you," I said, leaning my head on hers.

"By the way," she said quietly, "I'm glad you and Ben are talking again. Maybe this sounds weird, but you look . . . younger when you're around him."

"You're such a weirdo," I said, swatting at her.

But it occurred to me that I kind of felt younger, too.

Or maybe it was just that right between the stress and grief, a sliver of light was shining through, hinting that something brighter was still up ahead.

~

On my suggestion, Hadley decided to head home to take a nap and try to recover from the chaos of the past twenty-four hours. My mother was still manhandling the kitten when I went back to her room, but the tiny beast didn't seem to mind. I wondered how old it was. Old enough to survive without a parent. I looked at it, and then at my mother, and suddenly felt incredibly sad. One day soon, I'd be surviving without a parent, too.

"You girls have a heart-to-heart?" she said, twirling one of the strings on her bathrobe in front of the cat, who batted at it wildly.

"A little," I said.

"You must have plenty to talk about, with me losing my memory," she said, waving the hand she wasn't using to bait the kitten.

This was the first time I'd heard her state it as fact, and I couldn't hide my surprise. "Yes," I said, sitting on the stool near the end of her bed.

"Laine, the thing is, I do remember most things," she said, not really looking at me. "Well, at least I think I do. It's a real brainteaser, losing your memory."

"You've been telling us you were fine, Mom," I said. "But finding you in the park . . . it tells me that maybe you're not. So I'm glad you're talking about it."

"I'd like to think I'm fine, but yes—maybe I'm not, Laine. I don't know." She looked sad as she glanced away.

"I'm sorry. That's got to be terrible."

"It's not what I'd call fun."

"Hadley made a neurology appointment for you for next month," I said. She'd called the referral from the ER doctor even before my mother had been discharged from the hospital. "The doctor might have some answers for us. Medication, maybe. A procedure."

She shook her head. "I know what the doctor will say—there's nothing to be done. You girls will have to put me into an infirmary."

I didn't correct her. "Not right away, Mom. Maybe not at all."

"Oh, Laine, let's not pretend that won't be the end. It's where the mind goes to die." Before I could respond, she added, "My mother . . ." Her voice trailed off.

"But Nana had Parkinson's," I said. "Do you think that's what you have? Have you had any tremors? Stiffness or trouble moving?"

She glanced around the room, and I wondered if she'd gotten confused. Then she said, "Laine, would you go get a pen and some paper? Maybe a notebook if you can? I'd like you to write a few things down for me while I'm fresh."

"Of course," I said, already on my feet. I had no idea what she had in mind, but if she was finally opening up to me, I was not about to question that.

I dashed to my bedroom—I hadn't packed a notebook, but I had a feeling I'd find one in one of the desk drawers. Sure enough, there were several spiral notebooks, each with just a few pages used, in the bottom drawer.

"Thank you, dear," she said when I came back. "You've always been such a good writer, and I was hoping you might help me remember a few things. This will be good for you and the girls to know, too. So, where were we? Oh yes, your grandmother. So, the thing is, Laine—are you getting this?"

"Yep," I said, holding up the pen.

"Good, good. As I was saying, it wasn't Parkinson's, Laine. Nana Meyers had Alzheimer's. And I do, too."

THIRTY

Sally

My mother asked me never to tell anyone—not even Hank, and certainly not the girls. "Take it to your grave, Sally," she'd said, and I'd sworn that I would.

But now that Laine was at the end of my bed with her notebook in hand, I knew I owed her the truth. So I took a deep breath and said what I'd kept locked inside me for decades.

"Nana and Gramps were ashamed, love. They thought what was wrong with her was some kind of shortcoming. The doctor had suggested Parkinson's as a possible diagnosis at first. For some reason, that sounded better to them, so they logged on to it."

Laine glanced away momentarily, almost like she was embarrassed, and I realized I'd used the wrong word.

"I mean latched—that's right," I corrected myself, and I saw her nod. "They planned to keep it a secret, but when your grandfather had a heart attack, I had to take over my mother's medical care for a few months while he recovered. That's when I found out everything."

Her pen was moving furiously across the page, but she barely took her eyes off me. "What happened then?" she asked.

"Well, by then, my mother was mostly too far gone to talk about it. For years, I prayed I wouldn't get the same thing. But, Laine . . . I've known I had the same problem as her for a long time."

"Mom," she said gravely. "You don't know that for sure."

"I do," I insisted. "I've known longer than I've been willing to admit to myself. As for when, exactly, it began—well, it's a tricky thing, trying to remember when you stopped remembering. There were always . . . lapses," I recalled. Why, I'd been scrambling words since I was a child; my mother even had me checked for a learning disability. My tongue just couldn't keep up with my brain, they determined. Sounded true to me. Over time, I came to notice that other people did the same thing. Not Hank—when he chose to speak, every sentence was on purpose. But my friend Nettie got her children's names confused all the time. And Mary would often use the wrong word. Even Reggie, as clever as he was, got tongue-tied with me. What bliss—there's no feeling quite like flustering the man you love. I'm sorry if it's hard for you to hear that, Laine, but it's true.

"Mom?" said Laine, and that's when I realized my thoughts had wandered off on me.

I cleared my throat. "Right. When you girls were young, I wasn't worried about my brain, but rather my heart—I knew that's what was making me so forgetful. How much space one person could take up in one's mind! Bills, appointments, meal planning—all trivial matters compared to the matter of Reggie. I thought surely after the first year or two, the rush would subside. It never did. Just to see him was to feel alive, deep in my bones, in my soul. The smell of him, the feel of his hand on my skin. His gruff laugh. His smile, which seemed to me an unexpected gift each time it appeared. All of it was a delight." I looked up suddenly and saw that Laine was blushing. "Do you want me to continue?" I asked.

"Yes and no," she admitted. "But mostly yes. What happened then?"

If I was going to tell her the truth about my mother, I figured I had to do the same about Reggie. "Well, not all of it was a delight," I admitted. "Reggie wanted me to leave Hank, for us to start afresh. Laine, you didn't know how I had to decide, again and again, to make a choice for our family and not for myself. Then, your junior year of high school, Reggie said he couldn't go on this way."

Her mouth hung open.

"Don't be so surprised—those details stay with you. He would always love me, he said. But he wouldn't carry on with the lie anymore."

"Oh, Mom," she said, reaching for my hand. I squeezed it quickly, then indicated for her to keep writing; it felt important for me to have a record, something I could read later if—no, when—things got worse with my mind.

"I couldn't see him anymore after that; it hurt too much. Even seeing Ben pained me. I knew you'd fallen for him, even if you didn't know it just yet. What was harder still was that Ben was equally besotted with you. His eyes trailed after you; he couldn't sit still when you were around."

Her cheeks were pink. "Mom . . ."

"I'm sorry, Laine. I see now that it wasn't right at all for me to tell you not to get involved with him, but I thought I was protecting you. I thought if you were romantically involved, at some point the truth would come out. And it has, although not the way I ever imagined it would."

"It's okay," she said softly.

"It isn't," I said, "but I'm glad that we're finally speaking honestly about this. How many days I avoided you and your sisters so you wouldn't see my swollen eyes and ask why I'd been crying! Unlike your father, you and Hadley, especially, never missed a thing. How many afternoons I spent walking Brooklyn by myself, in the worst possible pain, as I accepted the inevitable: Reggie and I would never be together."

"I'm so sorry," she said.

"Oh, me, too, Laine. I do wish things had been different, but there you have it. We were supposed to be talking about my memory, though."

"When did you know for sure, Mom?"

"Later, as I grew older but none the wiser, I realized some lost trains of thought never did get back on track. I remember forgetting the name of the woman who'd been with me at wine club for years; now I can't even conjure her face! Your father always dismissed my worries. 'You're overthinking it,' he said, not looking up from his paper, because, of course, he could read for hours, while I could no longer focus for more than a page at a time. 'Everyone forgets things, Sally.' But not everyone had watched their mother disappear right before her own eyes and knew that one day she might face the same fate. Not everyone knew what it was to have made the right decision at the wrong time. If I'd moved Nana Meyers up from Florida and into our home when it all began, it could have spared her some of that fast fading. That would have required telling the truth, though, and I'd promised her I wouldn't."

Laine set down the notebook and pen and sat beside me on the bed. Then she wrapped me in her arms. "Oh, Mom, you couldn't have. Don't blame yourself."

I did, but not for the reasons she was probably thinking. "I believed love and loyalty were doing whatever your mother asked of you," I said quietly. "They're not. I understand that now. And I guess I'm telling you all this now, Laine, so you have a chance to learn it before I forget."

THIRTY-ONE

Laine

I expected my mother's confession about her memory to leave me feeling gobsmacked. Instead, it brought deep relief. She already knew she had a problem; that was one hurdle I no longer needed to clear. And no wonder she'd been trying to pretend she was fine. How devastating, to carry my grandmother's secret like that—and then begin to realize that fate had dealt her the same hand. And after decades of opacity, she'd actually been willing to open up to me about her memory—and equally surprising, her relationships with my father and Reggie. To learn that, in her strange and admittedly misguided way, she'd actually been trying not to be selfish . . . well, it was such an unexpected change in the narrative that when she finally stopped telling me her story, the only words I could muster were *thank you*.

I'd just put the notebook away when Ben texted to see if I would be up for having lunch at his place. I knew Piper would be arriving around noon, so I called her to make sure she wouldn't mind if I left for a while. She didn't, and after I checked in with Josh, who was out grabbing groceries for us, I told Ben I'd love to swing by.

I'd skipped breakfast, so when I rang Ben's doorbell, I couldn't tell if the nervousness I was feeling was low blood sugar or actual anxiety. *It's no big deal,* I told myself as I tried not to fidget while I waited for him.

But when he swung open the door and smiled at me, my stomach did a weird roller-coaster move and I was forced to admit that blood sugar had bupkis to do with it. Even my mother had known he'd been in love with me. Even though it had been years ago, I still felt stunned . . . and strangely pleased.

But maybe the only strange thing about it was the realization that I wanted him to feel that way about me now, too.

"Hey," he said.

"Hey," I said back, hoping I didn't sound as awkward as I felt.

"Come on in."

"Okay," I said, following him.

"I thought I'd find out what you're in the mood for before I started cooking," he said once we were in the living room. "Omelet? Salad?"

Maybe it was the apartment—though redecorated, it was still incredibly familiar, and also seemed just so thoroughly *Ben*—but I could feel myself starting to relax. I tilted my head to one side and said, "Will I sound like a glutton if I say 'both'?"

He laughed. "Nope. That's what I was thinking, too." He motioned for me to follow him into the kitchen. I sat on one of the stools at the counter and watched him as he rolled up his sleeves and pulled an apron over his T-shirt. "Mushrooms?" he said.

"Yes, please."

"Even the weird ones?" he asked, pulling a container holding a cloud of lion's mane mushrooms from the fridge.

I nodded. "Especially the weird ones."

"Never change, Laine Francis."

I wanted to tell him that I *was* trying to change—but as I watched him float around the kitchen, his culinary moves almost balletic, I realized that some things about me probably would always stay the same. Like the fact that I couldn't help but be aware of my skin when he was around. Any other time, it was like air or gravity: just *there*, a simple part of humanity and certainly nothing to notice. But when Ben was near, there was a subtle buzz just below the surface, almost like a low electric current reminding me I was alive.

"Chives? Maybe some goat cheese?" he said, sticking his head back in the fridge.

"All that sounds perfect," I said.

He put the produce in a colander and washed it off. "You're still not picky about food, huh?" he said as he plucked out the chives and mushrooms and began to slice them on a cutting board.

"I'm very picky," I said. "Just not about food. Leave an eggshell on the counter and I'll break into hives."

He grinned. "Then you really *haven't* changed."

"Is that good or bad?"

"Good," he said. "Definitely good."

He cracked an egg into a bowl with a single hand, then another and another. It was impossible not to be mesmerized by the way he moved. He'd always had an ease to him, but in the past sixteen years, he'd developed a different sort of confidence. "I could watch that all day," I confessed.

"Cooking is kind of hypnotic, isn't it? Sometimes I just put cooking shows on in the background to relax. Like, it's impossible to think about everything that's wrong with the world when someone's chatting about salad dressing or a soufflé," he said, starting to whisk the eggs.

I nodded. That was probably why I'd barely thought about my mother since I'd gotten to Ben's. Yes, she was just a few doors down, and in light of what she'd told me, some major questions—ones that were awfully close to the life-and-death variety—were hanging over our heads. But right now, it was just me and Ben and the makings of what promised to be an amazing meal.

He sprinkled some salt in the bowl, then poured the mixture into the pan. The eggs made a sizzling sound as they spread out in the butter. "You remember when I started cooking?"

"Of course," I said. "It wasn't long after your mom left. I think I recall you saying you would die if you had to eat another one of your dad's bologna sandwiches."

He hooted as he tossed in the mushrooms and chives. "That's the absolute truth. I still won't go near the stuff."

"You remember when we almost burned this very kitchen down?" I said. The kitchen was the one room he didn't seem to loathe, so if we were at his house, we were usually here.

He shook his head, but he was already laughing again. "And how I sprayed my brother's awful body spray all over to try to cover up the smell?"

"And your dad came home, and said it smelled like someone had lit a locker room on fire."

Ben flipped the omelet with a single flick of his wrist. "But he didn't tell me to stop cooking, did he?"

I laughed, more from happiness than anything else. Recalling these old memories, the good ones, made me feel warm and safe. It made me feel like *myself*—the version I liked. "He must have known you'd go pro with it one day. Speaking of cooking, how's your new job going?"

"Fine." He sprinkled goat cheese over the eggs, which were golden brown.

I inhaled and ordered myself not to drool. "Just fine?"

He shrugged. "It's a great opportunity, but a gig is a gig is a gig. I learned a long time ago that it's easier to move on when you don't let yourself get too attached."

Our eyes met, and neither of us looked away.

My insides felt all wobbly and my heart was pounding in my chest. But I dared myself to speak anyway. "What if you want to get attached?"

"What if *you* want to?" he said, and I couldn't help but notice that his voice was an octave lower than normal.

"I do," I said quietly.

He turned off the burner, then leaned against the counter and looked at me. "I've really liked having you back in my life, Laine."

"I have, too," I admitted. But there was more to say. And though certainly there was an artful way to phrase it, I instead blurted, "Josh and I are really over. He told me he isn't ready to have kids, and we've decided we're truly going to get divorced. I know having a baby might be super complicated, and it definitely complicates things with you and me. But I *am* going to go for it, and you should probably know that. No matter what happens with my mom. And between us . . ."

Ugh, I didn't want to admit it. Saying it out loud would make it real. But now that my mother was home and the guilt and worry were clearing, I knew this was the final frontier in shedding my identity as the person who gave up her dreams to make other people's come true. "She told me she probably has Alzheimer's, and she's going to need a lot of help," I said.

"Damn."

"I know." I bit my lip. "But . . . I still don't want to move back, Ben. I love seeing you, and I want to do it all the time. Every day, to be honest," I said before I could censor myself. "And yet the truth is that I also don't want to live in New York. It feels like a place where old Laine lives. And I'm not that person anymore."

Ben was looking at me with a mix of empathy and something else, something I was afraid to make any assumptions about. And he was walking closer to me. Closer still, so near that I could smell him. But he didn't touch me, and even though I wanted to put my hands on him—really, *really* wanted to—that felt okay, too. If this was going to happen, we needed to be sure; we needed to do it right. "Laine Francis, is that your very candid way of telling me you're interested in being more than friends?"

"Yes," I whispered.

"Good," he said. "But if you go back to Michigan, what does that mean for us?"

I could feel my heart starting to flood with sadness. "You want me to stay here." Just like my sisters and my mother did. Almost everyone who really mattered to me wanted the same thing; why couldn't I bring myself to want it, too? After all, didn't everyone say that it didn't matter where you were if you had the people you loved with you? What was *wrong* with me? And now he was going to tell me that what I wanted made it impossible for us to be more than friends. I'd never wanted to slip back into my people-pleasing ways quite as much as I did then.

And yet I forced myself not to take it back.

"Actually, no," he said. "Maybe I'm getting ahead of myself, but you know I don't mind moving around, and renting this place would be a cinch. There's a nice little culinary scene happening in Detroit, and Ann Arbor isn't too bad, either. I'm not saying let's pack a U-Haul together today. But, Laine . . ."

He looked so serious that my pulse started to quicken again. Of course—why hadn't I realized that the real issue wasn't geography, but my wanting a baby? What a mess, what terrible timing! Why had I let myself feel so optimistic, when clearly the other shoe was seconds from dropping? "What is it?" I said.

He wrinkled his nose, and in spite of my panic, he looked so adorable that it was all I could do not to kiss him. "Can we worry about details later and maybe just hold each other right now?"

I had to laugh. "I thought you'd never ask."

He put his arms around me, and it felt so good and right that we stayed like that until the omelets lost their rise and went cold. I put my head on his chest at one point, and as I listened to the steady beat of his heart, I was both sated and starved; confused yet clearer than ever.

I didn't want to lose him again. The very thought of it filled me with panic and sadness.

But if I did, I would at least be grateful to have him here with me now.

THIRTY-TWO

Laine

I rose early the following morning, before Josh and my mother were awake, and went out for a walk. My heart was heavy as the sun began to rise in the sky, and my mind had barely shut off since I'd returned from Ben's; sleep had been all but impossible the night before. Because the minute I'd told Ben the truth, it was like a dam had broken. As surprising as it had been to hear myself admit it, I'd meant every word I said: I did *not* want to move back to New York. And although I did want to help my mother, I didn't want to be her full-time caregiver. I had a feeling that made me sound like a monster—or at least it would to my sisters, who were counting on me to lighten their load. As I'd promised Hadley, I would find a way to do that.

But as I paced the streets of Carroll Gardens, which were already starting to get crowded at seven in the morning, I finally understood that whatever way that was would not be what everyone else had in mind. And I was going to have to find a way to deal with whatever fallout came with it.

Josh was at the table, hunched over his computer, when I returned to the apartment. His shirt looked like he'd slept in it, and his hair was sticking up all over the place. It occurred to me that this was probably one of the last times I'd see him with bedhead.

"Morning," I said. "All good?"

He yawned, then nodded. "Just working on a few last-minute details. Launch is in two weeks."

"Wow. That was fast."

"Yeah. We're moving right along." He glanced at the computer and smiled. "I'm in talks with a health company who wants to buy it. Maybe even before it launches."

"Really? That's amazing."

"I don't want to get my hopes up, but I'm a lot closer to the goal than I've been before."

He was, and although I didn't say it, this launch did feel different; it was impossible not to feel optimistic for him. "I'm happy for you."

"Thank you," he said. "I made coffee if you want some."

"That sounds perfect," I said, pulling a mug from the cupboard. "Refill?"

"Sure," he said, and after I'd poured myself some, I refilled his and then handed him the cream.

"Mom still sleeping?"

He smiled. "I heard her snoring when I got up. How's it going with you two? Have you made any decisions?"

Where to even start? "Josh, I have a lot to tell you." I lowered my voice. "Mom told me yesterday that my grandmother had Alzheimer's, not Parkinson's. She thinks she does, too. She had me write it all down in a notebook, and she said she's getting ready to tell the rest of the family."

He was very still, and I could practically see the wheels in his mind turning as he processed this. "Wow . . . I mean, we suspected, but . . . knowing is another thing."

"I know," I said, sliding into the chair beside him. "We've got some decisions to make. Big ones. Everyone wants me to stay."

"But you want to be in Ann Arbor."

I startled. "How'd you know that?"

He leaned back in his chair and stretched his long legs out in front of him as he observed me. "Laine, I've known you for fourteen years, three months, and some-odd days. I'm pretty good at reading you. Well," he said, making an exaggerated grimace, "most of the time."

"Fair enough. And yeah. I'm just not sure I want to be Mom's caregiver." But even as I heard myself, I realized that I had to stop trying to tie the truth into pretty little bows and give it to him—and everyone else—straight. "Actually . . . that's not true. I don't want to," I admitted. "I want to help her, but not the way I said I would. I just feel really crappy about taking it back." Even what I'd learned about my mother and Reggie didn't assuage the obligation I felt toward my one living parent.

"Then don't," he said.

"You say that like it's easy."

"It could be. You already have a home, and you just stay there. That's definitely easier than moving. Um, Laine?" His right eye had started twitching. It only did that when he was super nervous.

"Whatever you have to say, you can say it, Josh. It's okay."

"Um, the town house is all yours. If you want it, I mean. I'm going to move out."

"Okay . . ." I wasn't sure why this would cause him anxiety.

He coughed. "I'm actually thinking about moving here."

"To New York?" I said, unable to hide my shock. This was how my sisters must have felt when I told them we were divorcing. It made . . . zero sense. "Really?"

He nodded. "Ever since we decided we were going to divorce, I've been thinking that it's time for me to try something new. Something different. I don't know if being here will be better for business, but if this deal goes through . . . I think I'm ready for a fresh start."

I knew exactly what he meant. I leaned over and hugged him. "I'm so happy for you," I said. "You deserve it."

"Thank you," he said, hugging me back.

"Josh?" I said, my arms still wrapped around his bony torso. "I love you. I always will, even though we're divorcing. I just wanted you to know that."

"I love you, too, Laine," he said. He was getting choked up, which made me feel teary, too.

"Thank you. I'm really sorry, you know."

"For what?" he said as we let each other go.

"For not being a better friend to you," I said softly.

"Yeah," he said. "Me, too."

The black-and-white kitten had just wandered in from the other room, and she immediately made a beeline for my foot, which she promptly began to circle as she rubbed herself on my ankle.

"Thought you didn't like cats," said Josh, eyeing her quizzically.

"I don't," I said, bending to pick her up. In fact, I'd called them furry aliens more than a few times. "But weirdly, this one kind of reminds me of Belle. It must be her coloring. Or the fact that she's the smallest."

"Laine Francis, cat lover," said Josh, shaking his head in mock surprise. "Never thought I'd see the day. Maybe you're ready for a fresh start, too."

"I guess I am," I said, as the kitten nestled against my chest, purring contentedly.

I squeezed my eyes shut, just for a moment, and thought of Belle. She hadn't done us in; we'd done that all by ourselves. And just as she'd appeared in my life at the perfect moment, she'd left it at the right time, too.

Now here I was, with an opportunity to make the most of this new chapter. I just needed to find the courage to turn the page.

THIRTY-THREE

Laine

Back when Hadley was going through her coaching certification program, she'd once remarked to me that, with few exceptions, there were no "right" choices; there was only what we made of any given decision. I found myself hoping this was true as I kissed my mother goodbye later that afternoon. Ben and I had an appointment to take the kittens to see a vet on Atlantic Avenue, and Josh was out meeting an old business school classmate of his; Hadley and Piper were both busy. So I had to choose between leaving my mom alone, and doing what she wanted, which was to take the kittens in to get their vaccinations and checkup. And yes, doing what I wanted, too; I didn't know when I was leaving town, but as long as I was here, I wanted to see Ben as much as possible.

As I was fretting, it occurred to me that maybe I was thinking in black-and-white terms. In addition to making sure the kittens were healthy, my mother wanted to enjoy her independence as much as possible, and I wasn't abandoning her for an entire day. Maybe there was a way to have everything I wanted—if only on a small scale.

After making sure my mother had her phone around her neck (that Hadley was even smarter than I gave her credit for), Ben and I walked over to the vet clinic. It was a cozy-looking place, with navy-painted trim and photos of all sorts of animals in the window. Really, it looked an awful lot like my vet back in Ann Arbor. The one I'd last walked into with Belle . . . and walked out of alone.

Ben was about to reach for the door, but he paused and stepped out of the way. "What is it?" he said.

"Nothing," I said, trying to shake off the feeling that was creeping in. But it was no use; sadness was already spreading through me like quicksilver. Grief was funny that way—just when you thought you'd made it to shore, it pulled you right back under. "I just don't like the vet. Not anymore."

"Because of Belle?"

I nodded as the back of my throat tightened.

The urn, I thought suddenly. I'd left it on the mantel back in the town house. A shameful heat rose to my face. "I forgot her," I muttered. "I can't believe I forgot her."

"Your mother?" said Ben.

"No, my dog." I shook my head. "I left Belle's urn in Michigan." In the chaos of trying to get to New York as fast as possible, it had completely slipped my mind. I wondered if this was how my mother felt when she realized she'd forgotten something important.

Ben frowned. "Were you going to scatter her ashes in New York?"

"No," I said, and now my shame and sadness were tinged with embarrassment. "I'm just . . . not ready to be without her yet, I guess."

"But here you are. Managing all the same." He set down the cat carrier he'd been holding and put his arms around me. "It's okay, Laine. It's going to be okay." He looked into my eyes. "Do you believe me?"

I nodded, because I wanted to believe him.

"Hey—do you want me to take the kittens in myself? Because I don't mind. You can go shop or something," he said, gesturing to the shops up and down Atlantic Avenue.

Through the mesh walls of the carrier, I could see the kittens climbing on top of each other like crabs in a bucket. "No, but thank you. I think I can handle it."

"Okay, but if you start to feel like you can't, say the word and I'll take over. All right?" he said.

I leaned forward and hugged him. "You're honestly the best."

"I'm not, but you can keep saying that," he said, and I laughed. "Let's go see about these tiny terrors."

The veterinary clinic smelled like it was supposed to—wet dog and cat urine and bleach. There were a couple of dogs in the waiting area, but to my relief, both were small and yippy, like Piper's dog. "Punters," Josh used to call them when we saw them at dog parks. Well, he'd have to get used to her punter if he was going to be sticking around.

"You think you'll get another dog at some point?" asked Ben, who was sitting beside me in one of the plastic seats lined along the window.

I shook my head. "Maybe one day, but not anytime soon." Everyone said a puppy was as much work as a baby, and I was focused on the latter. I'd asked Dr. Kim's office to put me back on their cancellation list, but I'd also left messages with a few other doctors—all in Michigan—to see if they might be able to see me. I'd need to tell Hadley that I wasn't going to call her "fertility guy." That wasn't the hard part. Telling her why I wasn't going to was much trickier.

Ben leaned in and whispered, "Laine? You okay? You've got a faraway look on your face."

"Oh. I, uh . . ." I sighed and met his eyes. "I was just thinking about baby stuff. Family stuff, really. I'm seeing my sisters tomorrow—we're supposed to talk about making plans for my mother."

"What do you think you'll say?"

I peered down at the kittens, who were still clambering over each other. Then I looked back at him. "I'm going to tell them that I don't want to move back. I'm just afraid of how they're going to take it."

He took my hand and squeezed it lightly. "Let them react however they want."

I frowned. "Obviously I know I can't control their reactions. They're their own people. I just don't want them to be upset."

"Yep."

"But?" I said, because I could tell he had more to say but was trying to be gentle with me.

"Well, it's just that if you're worried about their reactions, you're probably thinking that there's some way you can say or do it that will make it easier. But there likely isn't—and even if there was, wouldn't it feel better to let things unfold the way they're going to?"

I closed my eyes for a moment and tried to imagine the worst-case scenario. Piper pouting and accusing me of being selfish. Hadley going into hurricane mode—silent and eerily still, then exploding into action. Maybe they'd both run off or stop talking to me for a while.

No, that would have been my reaction, I realized suddenly. Because *I* was the one who avoided conflict at all costs.

And suddenly I saw it. As Ben had said, they were going to react however they reacted. All I had to do was leave room for them to have their own opinions and emotions while still having my own back.

I leaned over and kissed Ben's cheek. "I'm so glad you're here with me right now."

He laughed in surprise. "Go on."

"Laine Francis?" said a tech who'd just appeared in the waiting room.

"That's me," I said, rising to my feet.

"Right this way," she said, motioning for us to follow her down the hall.

The walls of the examination room were plastered with posters about cats, and there was a cat-size scale on the metal table. I let out the breath I hadn't known I was holding. This wasn't like Belle's vet, and it was going to be okay.

The tech disappeared. Then a few minutes later, she returned with the vet, who introduced herself as Dr. Patricia. Unlike my vet, who was a tall, lissome redhead, Dr. Patricia was short and curvy, with a halo of dark curly hair and a berry-stained smile. I liked her on sight.

"So, what do we have here?" she said, peering into the carrier. She pulled out the tabby. "Oh! Gorgeous."

Maybe if you like furry aliens, I thought, watching the thing squirm in her hands, but then I realized that it *was* awfully adorable.

"About eight to nine weeks old, I'd estimate." She turned to me. "You said they were abandoned?"

I nodded. "My mom found them in Prospect Park."

"They're young to be without a mother, but with the right care, they should do just fine." She handed the tabby to Ben, who was sitting beside the table. He looked surprised but put it on his lap. "Are you going to keep all three?"

"I wasn't planning on keeping any of them," I confessed.

"Not even this little one?" she said, retrieving the black-and-white one. "Oh, you're a sweet thing." She peered into the carrier. "Definitely the runt of the litter."

Unexpected tears sprang to my eyes as I remembered my vet back home saying the same thing about Belle.

I blinked hard. "My mother's dealing with some serious memory issues," I explained.

"I'm sorry to hear that," she said. "Though sometimes having a pet can be good for older adults, even if they have memory issues. I understand, though, if that's a burden for you—or whoever's the caregiver for your mother."

Caregiver. Had a word ever felt so loaded? "We're trying to figure that out," I said.

She nodded. "Cats tend to be a bit easier than dogs, on the whole, but a pet is still a responsibility, and no one would fault you if you weren't up for it. We work with a local adoption agency to help find foster homes for cats, so just let the receptionist know if that's something you're interested in. Anyway, it's good of you to bring them in."

"It's the least I can do," I said, looking at the kitten. Her legs wiggled this way and that as Dr. Patricia lifted her up. "Definitely a girl!" she announced. "Since the other two seem to be doing fine, I think I'll start with this little gal. Does she have a name?"

"Not yet," I said. Yet? What was I saying? You didn't name a pet unless you intended to keep it.

"What I like about animals is that they tell us what to call them when they're good and ready." She set the cat on the table and shone a light into her eyes, murmuring approving things. As she pried open her tiny mouth, the cat mewed in protest. Then Dr. Patricia put her stethoscope to its heart. The lines in her forehead deepened as she moved the stethoscope around. I was about to ask her what was wrong when she said brightly, "Well, I'm noticing a slight heart murmur."

"Really?" Oh no—here came the tears again.

"It's rarely a sign of a major problem," she said, misunderstanding my response. "Especially when it's this faint."

I had to clear my throat to speak. "I know," I said quietly. "My dog had one, too."

"Is that so!" she said. "Well, then you know—nothing to be too concerned with, though we'll keep an eye on it. Never a bad idea to be careful with your heart."

My eyes landed on Ben, who was already smiling at me, and I smiled back at him.

"We'll get her vaccinated today, along with the other two," said Dr. Patricia. "But that'll come at the end. Do you want to hold her while I examine the last kitten?"

I nodded and took her from the vet. For all my mother's affinity for the species, I'd always found cats aloof and frankly kind of boring. But I couldn't help but laugh as the kitten went to battle with a few stray strands of my hair. Then, just as I was wondering if I should put her back in the carrier before she ripped my flesh open with one of the tiny razors at the end of her paws, she climbed up my shirt, right over the left side of my chest, and put her head down. I felt a rumbling, then heard a faint whirring noise. Was something wrong with her? No, I realized. She was . . . purring. The way cats did when they felt safe and content.

"Hello there, you strange little thing," I whispered. "Are you going to tell me your name?"

She rumbled in response.

I thought of the way my mother had laughed delightedly that morning as the cat played in her lap. Even the memory of it made me happy now.

"Joy," I said, smiling down at the cat. "Of course your name is Joy."

THIRTY-FOUR

Laine

Hadley, Piper, and I had agreed to gather at her place the following afternoon to discuss plans for our mother. Josh offered to come with me, but I'd thanked him and said no. This was one conversation I needed to have on my own.

"Wine?" asked Hadley when she let me in. She'd just put the twins down for a nap and looked like she would've preferred to join them.

"No, thanks," I said as I wandered into the living room.

"Suit yourself. I'm ready to drink the whole bottle, pump and dump be damned."

"I'll take some," said Piper, who was sprawled across the sofa reading a magazine. She glanced at me. "You should have some, Lainey. Might make this a little less painful."

"I would, but I really don't like wine," I said.

"Since when?" my sisters said in unison.

"Since . . . always," I admitted. I usually said yes when it was offered to me because everyone else was drinking, and then I'd take the tiniest of sips to not be rude. But aside from the occasional margarita, I wasn't one for alcohol.

"Oh," said Piper, frowning. "Well, I feel dumb. Sorry—I should've picked up on that."

"Me, too," said Hadley. "Sparkling water, then?"

"Don't apologize," I said. To Hadley, I added, "That sounds perfect."

"I thought maybe you'd bring Josh," said Piper, pushing herself into a seated position as I took a seat on the sofa across from her.

"I figured it would be best if the three of us spoke first." Hadley's living room was enormous, especially by New York standards. Through the windows, the sun glinted off high-rises, and airplanes passed in the distance. "Hey—did you know Josh is thinking of moving here?"

Piper's eyes lit up, and that was when it really hit me: whether she knew it or not, she brightened at the mere mention of him. I wondered if she had any idea that her affection for him might be less familial and more romantic. Once the dust settled on our divorce, I could almost imagine them being together—and the fact that this was peculiar yet not upsetting was nothing if not a sign that I'd made the right decision to end things. "But you're divorcing," she said suddenly. "So . . . wait. Would you be moving here separately?"

"It's complicated," I said carefully, "but for now, safe to say he's ready for a fresh start."

"Wow. The kids will be thrilled," said Piper, but her smile told me she was the one who was especially excited about this development.

Hadley reappeared. "What's this about?" she said, handing us each a glass.

"Josh is thinking of moving to the city," I told her.

"Really?! That's amazing. Maybe you two can pack up a van and move together. Two birds and whatnot."

Maybe not, I thought.

"You guys, we need to talk," I told them. "About what to do about Mom, yes—but also about me."

Hadley sighed so deeply you'd think I'd just announced we needed to figure out how to repair the ozone layer. Come to think of it, that sounded less complicated to me. "There's not enough wine in all of New York to make me ready for this conversation," she said.

"That makes two of us," said Piper, who took a long gulp from her stemless glass.

"Mom knows she has dementia," I told them. "She admitted it to me the other day." She'd told me it was okay to share that part with them, but she wanted to tell them about Nana Meyers herself.

"Whoa. I can't believe she admitted it," said Piper, stretching her legs in front of her.

"Me, neither," I said. "But I'm glad she did. I feel like it's going to make it easier to approach her about a solution."

"So what *is* our solution?" asked Hadley, looking at me.

I tried to hide my surprise, because I'd assumed she'd take the lead on this one. "Well, I know we won't have the full picture until she sees the neurologist, but it's safe to assume that her dementia is going to progress."

Piper nodded, but I saw that her eyes were welling with tears.

"You okay, Pipes?" I said.

She nodded. "Yeah . . . it's just sad. Mom's not even that old."

"I know." I moved over to where she was sitting, put my arm around her, and said what I was thinking. "This is awful. Heart-wrenching, really."

And it's about to get even worse after I tell you what I'm planning, I added mentally.

But then I thought about my conversation with Ben. Maybe it would get worse. But I was prepared to handle that.

"Here's the thing, you two," I said, looking back and forth between them. "Given what just happened with Mom getting lost and spending the night in the park, I don't know that my 'keeping an eye on her,'" I said, making air quotes, "from the upstairs apartment is going to be enough. Do you?"

Hadley shook her head.

"No," Piper said quietly.

"Me, neither," I told them. "And I definitely don't want to be the reason why someone finds her floating in the Gowanus."

Piper cringed. "Jeez Louise—that's a little graphic."

"I'm sorry, but that's where my mind went when she was missing, probably because she used to say that's exactly where she'd go if we tried to put her in a nursing home. And if you'd seen her at the park . . . well, it was terrifying."

"Fair," said Hadley, eyeing me. "But are you proposing we hire a full-time home health aide?"

"We already decided that wasn't financially feasible," I pointed out. "We'll have to figure something else out."

"Actually . . . I talked to Topper the other day. We're willing to cover any extra costs."

"Whoa," said Piper.

"Seriously. Are you sure?" I asked.

"I am," said Hadley. "As Topper pointed out, the whole point of having money is to be able to help in situations like this."

"I don't even know what to say, other than thank you," I said softly.

"You're welcome," said Hadley. "The real question is, will Mom agree?"

"Given my talk with her the other day, she won't be happy, but I think she'll be open to it. And if she completely loses her memory . . ." A vision of my Nana Meyers curled onto her side beneath a thin sheet appeared in my mind. "I don't know," I admitted. "I guess I hope it never comes to that."

"We all know Mom thinks a nursing home is a one-way ticket to the grave," said Hadley frankly.

"I know," said Piper. "Maybe it is."

"Maybe we have to be okay with that," I said, and although they both looked surprised, neither of them corrected me.

"I took a look at Mom's bank accounts," said Hadley. She glanced out the window briefly before looking back at us. "The aide is expensive, but a decent nursing home is a fortune. At that point, we may need to take other measures to cover the cost. We might even need to sell the brownstone," she said sadly. "And that's provided we can talk her into giving one of us power of attorney before we have to go to court for it."

I hadn't really thought through the financial or legal implications of all this. Would we really have to sell our childhood home? As much as I didn't want to live there anymore, the thought was depressing.

And yet I was surprised to realize that it didn't change my decision.

"I can help some, too," said Piper, setting her wine on the coffee table. She'd been wise enough to sock away her income at the height of her success and had accumulated enough of a nest egg that she never had to worry about getting a "regular" job. And, apparently, to help our mother.

"I can't yet," I admitted. "My new business is going well, and I hope that will continue, but I'm serious about trying to get pregnant soon, and I don't know where that will leave me financially. Which brings me to the next thing." I swallowed hard. "I love you both so much, and I don't want to hurt you. Or Mom."

Piper was frowning, but Hadley's face had already fallen. Of course, she knew what I was about to say next. How naïve of me to assume this would be a surprise to her.

"I'm not moving to New York right now," I said. "I'll stay another month or two, but then I'm going back to Michigan. I don't know if I'm going to stay there forever, either. But I don't want to have a baby in New York. I can't even fully explain why—but it's important to me."

Hadley rose from her chair and sat beside me. I took a deep breath, waiting for her or Piper to say something more. But she just put her arms around me, and then Piper did, too. At once, I realized that I'd been worried for nothing. They might not like or even agree with my decision. But my sisters loved me, and they were going to support me anyway.

"Thank you," I said as they held me. "I'm so sorry."

"It's okay, Laine," said Hadley. She gave me a sad smile. "I never actually thought you'd move here."

"You didn't?"

She shook her head. "Nope."

"Me, neither, to be honest," said Piper. She squeezed my shoulder. "I wanted you to, obviously. And when I heard you and Ben were speaking again, I wondered if maybe that would change your mind. Especially since you and Josh decided to go through with the divorce. But . . . I don't know, Lainey. New York really isn't your place anymore, is it?"

"No, it isn't," I conceded. I looked back and forth between them. "But you really aren't upset? What about Mom?"

"I'm not upset at all," said Piper. She smiled at me. "I've mostly done what I wanted all these years. I'm not going to judge you for making the right choices for your own life."

"Same," said Hadley. "And as for what we're going to do—well, we're going to figure it out one day at a time. We'll start with hiring an aide and find some sort of solution for nighttime. I'd have preferred it if you were in the upstairs apartment overnight instead of a stranger, sure—and not just because it's cheaper. But maybe we can find someone we trust to be up there and install some kind of alarm system or something."

I was getting choked up again. They were being so generous that I didn't even know what to say or how to express my gratitude. "Thank you," I whispered. "I am so lucky to have you both."

"Oh, don't thank us yet. You're going to be involved in the decision-making process, you know."

"I do. And I'm going to do as much as I can."

"I know you are," Hadley said with a wink.

"We want you to visit more than you have been," said Piper. "But to be fair, I think we owe you a few more visits, too."

"Yeah." I laughed. "You sure do."

"So now what?" asked Hadley, leaning back against the arm of the sofa. Call me crazy, but she actually looked more relaxed than she had in days, possibly even weeks.

I took a deep breath. "Now I tell Mom."

THIRTY-FIVE

Laine

My mother was on the patio when I got home from Hadley's.

"Everything all right?" I said. She was sitting at the wrought-iron table that had been out there at least as long as I'd been alive; she brushed the rust off every few years and bought new cushions when the old ones fell apart. There was a pile of papers in front of her, held down with a large rock, and my first thought was that she was having another episode and had lost her train of thought.

But when she looked up at me, her gray eyes were clear and bright. "Everything's fine, Laine," she said. "Have a seat."

"Sure," I said, taking a chair on the other side of the table. "Are you working on bills?"

She had incredible posture, my mother, and even now, she sat with her back straight and her head held just so. I wondered if she'd do that even when her mind was long gone, or if she'd end up the way I remembered my Nana Meyers, slumped over and barely communicative. It was painful to imagine. "Actually, no. I was just reviewing some forms I filled out with George."

George was my parents' longtime friend, who also served as their attorney from time to time.

"When did you see him?" I asked.

"I can't remember, exactly. But it was sometime before you got here. The first time this summer," she clarified with a smile. "Not after you got back after our fight."

"I see. Is this about the brownstone?"

"No," she said matter-of-factly. "I granted you power of attorney and gave all three of you girls medical power of attorney. Since you have two roles, I wanted you to take a look at the paperwork and see if you were all right with it."

I almost fell right off my chair. "You did *what*?"

"Exactly what I said."

"I . . ." I didn't know what to say. How could I possibly tell her that I was leaving when she'd just put me in charge of her wishes?

"It's not too late for me to change it if you don't want the responsibility. I just needed to make a decision in that moment, and I did."

Stunned, I took the chair across from her. "Why did you pick me? I've been in Michigan." *And I'm going to stay there.* "And Hadley's the one who's good with money."

"Yes, and you're the one who's good with people," she said, shuffling the papers into a neat stack. "Good with me, at least."

"Thanks, Mom. But . . ."

"Well, what is it?" she said, watching me.

I would've rather have talked about almost anything than what I was about to tell her, but there was no way for us to have an honest conversation from here on out if I didn't tell her what I'd decided. "Do you remember telling me that you wanted me to make the choice that was best for me?"

She considered it for a moment, then said, "Yes. In fact, I do."

"Well, I don't know that moving back is what's best for me, Mom. Remember how I want to have a baby?" I said, and she nodded. I steadied myself, then said, "I don't want to raise a kid in New York. And it's going to be really tricky for me to . . . to take care of you and my child."

"What about Ben?" she said.

I looked at her with surprise.

"Oh, Laine," she said. "I'm not blind. I could tell when he dropped off you and the cats the other day that you two are so happy to be together again."

I felt flustered. "He was a good friend to me. It's especially nice to have someone like that around again."

"I'll bet it is. I'm sorry I encouraged you not to pursue him."

"Thank you," I said. "But you don't have to keep apologizing."

"I might forget that I've already done it, so I can't promise to stop," she said, and I smiled.

Then she looked down at the papers and sighed softly. "Reggie wanted me to marry him, Laine. He asked all the time at first, and then every year or two. Then one day, he stopped asking. And a while after that, he left. Said he was tired of waiting for me to tell my truth."

"Mom. I wish you'd told me this earlier."

"Well, Laine, I never wanted you to find out. Sometimes the truth is terrible for the people you love, and so you decide to keep it to yourself." She reached across the table for my hand. "I know it doesn't seem like it, but I am sorry. And I *do* want you to do what's right for yourself—after all, you still have time. Don't stay here with me unless you want to."

I was overcome with emotion. My mother really did love me, even if her love didn't look quite like what I'd always longed for. And now she was showing me that in the most generous way I could've imagined. "Mom," I said, wiping my eyes. "I . . . don't even know what to say."

"Say you'll do what's right for you, Laine. But I do have a favor to ask you. Two, in fact."

"Anything," I said. Then I laughed and added, "Well, not so fast. What is it?"

"First, I'd like you to gather everyone here," she said, nodding toward the brownstone. "I want to talk to the whole family at one time."

"Absolutely," I told her. "What's second?"

She smiled, and oh, how I wished I could memorize that moment; there was almost nothing that made me feel as good as I did when my mother was smiling at me. "Go get that notebook, Lainey. There are a few things I'd like to tell you about me and Reggie."

THIRTY-SIX

Sally

I'd already told Laine more about Reggie than I'd ever intended to. And yet she deserved the rest of the story, so she could draw her own conclusions about what I'd done.

"*Affair* isn't really the right word to describe what happened between me and Ben's father, Laine," I began, smiling sadly at her from across the table. "I know that may be hard for you to hear, but it's true. Once in a lifetime, you meet a person and know, just as sure as you know the sun and the stars will continue to appear in the sky, that everything that comes next is going to be different. And so it was when Reggie Walker appeared on my doorstep on a muggy August afternoon."

"Was this the year they moved in?" she asked, glancing up from her notebook.

"Yes, I think it must have been."

"What happened?"

"Well, he was standing there, and he said, 'Hello.'"

Laine laughed, and I couldn't help but laugh with her, if only because she wasn't upset with me.

"I know, I know. It was just a word, but what a word it was! His voice was rich and resonant, and I'd already decided I could listen to it all day. And his eyes—I'd say they were enormous, but really, it was the intensity with which he was looking at me. I wondered if he looked at everyone like that and found myself wishing that he didn't. *Don't be a fool, Sally,* I scolded myself, but I couldn't turn away. 'Hello,' I said back to him."

"And then?" asked Laine.

"Well, he said, 'I live a few doors down.' And I said, 'I know,' even though I knew no such thing."

"So this must have been right after they moved in," she murmured, her pen moving furiously across the page.

I nodded. "Then he said, 'I was wondering if you happened to own this cat. I've been feeding it for a week or so now.' And that was when it finally registered that Reggie was holding a Polaroid of a tabby perched on a fire escape. I took the photo from him, held it up to examine it."

"Did you recognize it?" said Laine.

"No, but as I told him, I would've liked to. I already had a cat—do you remember old Chino, Laine?" I asked, thinking of our scruffy gray cat, and she nodded. "But your father was forever telling me that it was one too many. Anyway, the man broke into a smile, and told me I could have the cat if I wanted it. And I thought to myself, *Can I?* But, of course, I wasn't thinking of the cat anymore."

I hadn't meant to say that part out loud, but Laine didn't so much as raise an eyebrow as she kept writing. Maybe that's why I kept going.

"'I'm Reggie. Reggie Walker,' he said, sticking out his hand. I stared at it for longer than I should have, then blushed because it had occurred to me that he probably thought I wasn't shaking it because he was Black. Carroll Gardens was still largely an Italian neighborhood then, and even Hank and I sometimes felt we didn't belong; I could only imagine that Reggie hadn't had a warm welcome from all."

"You know, I used to worry about that, Mom," she said, meeting my eye. "I thought you didn't want me to date Ben because he was Black."

"Oh, Laine, I'm sorry you thought that, and sorrier still that my actions led you there. That wasn't at all the case, but I can see why you thought that, and that must have been awful for you."

"Thank you," she said quietly.

"Don't thank me, love. At any rate, I quickly took Reggie's hand and clasped it with both of mine and said what I was thinking, which was that it was just so wonderful to meet him. Oh, and I was Sally."

Laine leaned back in the chair and looked around the patio. I saw her eyes land on the place where Hank's workshop had once been; he'd torn it down the year before he died, intending to have a new one put up, but, of course, that never happened. I thought maybe Laine would ask me about him. Instead, she said, "What was Reggie like back then, Mom? I don't remember him that well—not from that time period."

"Oh. Well . . . he was not tall, and he was dressed—well, I can't describe it now, but it wasn't the way Hank or any of our friends would have. Casually. And as of that moment on the porch, we'd exchanged but a few sentences. I was married fifteen years already with three children to show for it. And yet, in spite of all that, I could see it plain as day: here was my future, standing before me."

"Mom," said Laine in a choked voice. "That's the saddest thing I've ever heard."

"I know. It was. But also it wasn't. Later Reggie would tell me that he'd had the same thunderstruck sensation I'd had and was trying to make sense of it, to undo what was already undoable."

I stopped talking for a moment as I recalled the conversation Reggie and I had.

"Where do you live, exactly?" I finally asked Reggie as we stood on the stoop together all those years ago.

"Number 51," he said. "First floor."

I nodded. "My family and I are on the garden and first floors here."

"I know. My youngest—he talks about your daughter. Laine, right?"

"Yes. Then Ben must be your boy." I'd seen them playing on the sidewalk and the small fenced-off area beside our stoop. I wasn't going to say this to Laine, but I'd noticed she was relaxed around him, and even at six, that was unusual for her.

Reggie nodded. Then he smiled sheepishly and glanced away, and I understood that the next move was mine to make.

"Reggie Walker," I said. What a thrill just to say it out loud! He had that same intensity in his eyes again, and though I wasn't sure I was going to make it off my stoop in one piece if I kept staring back at him, I dared myself not to look away. "It's awfully hot out here. Can I bring you a glass of iced tea?"

"I'd like that," he said.

"Mom?" said Laine, and that's when I realized I'd drifted off.

"Oh, I'm sorry, dear. I was just thinking about how I invited Reggie in for tea that day."

"Was that when—" She cleared her throat. "Your affair began?"

"Oh, no," I said, shaking my head. "He came in that day, but it would be several years before we acted on what was so clearly a mutual attraction. And, oh, how I congratulated myself for my virtue during that time. In retrospect, I wish I'd dived right in—had more time with him, rather than less. But your face when you confronted me the other day, Laine! I can't tell you how terrible I felt, knowing you thought the worst of me. I wanted to tell you how hard things had been with your father, but . . ."

But I hadn't wanted to turn her against him. I still didn't. And that's why I didn't tell her what I was thinking. There was honesty, and then there were the things that forever changed a person's perception.

The truth is, I'm not sure Hank ever loved me. He certainly didn't pay attention to me the way I needed him to. That blasted newspaper he was always hiding behind, those stupid model cars and boats. What about real life? What about the wife who just wanted to have a conversation from time to time, who didn't want to have to drag him off to a cabin in the woods to get him to pay attention to her? And how was I supposed to know that the man who was *so* smitten with me that he proposed three weeks after we met would soon lose interest in me, like a child with a toy?

What was I supposed to do, year after year of being ignored? It was like slowly being starved to death.

"Well, Laine," I finally said. "What matters now is that Reggie gave me the best decade of my life, even if it was also the most painful. I'm not ashamed to say that. I chose not to tear our family apart by divorcing your father and making Ben your stepbrother. I'd be lying if I said that wasn't the hardest decision of my life, but I don't regret it. I never should have told you not to get involved with Ben, though. As though my words would be enough to keep the two of you apart."

Laine had stopped writing and appeared to be on her way to falling right off her chair.

"He's his father's son, Ben is. He never once needed to be reminded to pay attention to you, Laine. He hung on your every word—so happy just to be in your presence. After you fought—and then you took up with Josh—I was relieved to not have to interact with Reggie any more than I had to. Yet I always thought the two of you would find your way back to each other. And you have."

"What do you mean?" she said, but something in her eyes told me she knew exactly what I meant.

"Well, Laine," I said, "now it's up to you to do the thing that I didn't have the courage to."

"And what's that?"

I smiled at her. "Say yes to your heart."

THIRTY-SEVEN

Laine

My mother's words—"say yes to your heart"—were still echoing in my head the following evening. She'd been referring to Ben, of course, but I couldn't help but think her words applied to my decision to return to Michigan, and to try to have a baby on my own, too. These were hard decisions, as every *yes* required saying *no* to something or someone else—in this case, Josh and my family. Yet as I opened the door for Hadley and Topper, I felt at peace in a way that I hadn't in a very long time.

"Hi," said Hadley, hugging me. "Do you know what Mom has planned?"

"Not exactly," I said. As she'd requested, I'd asked my sisters and Josh to come over so she could talk to us all together. "But she's been pretty normal all day. Good, even."

"Glad to hear that," said Hadley. She still looked tired, but there was color in her cheeks and her worry lines had disappeared.

"Where are the twins?" I asked.

"With a sitter," said Topper, who'd just shook Josh's hand.

I smiled at Hadley, who smiled back. A sitter wasn't full-time care, but it was progress. No wonder she looked better.

"Hellooo!" said Piper, who'd just let herself in. She was wearing a red jumpsuit and had done her makeup. I wasn't used to seeing her made up, but she looked amazing, as I told her.

"You do, too," she said as she air-kissed me. "Any idea what Mom has planned?"

"She's just finishing getting ready, but we'll find out soon enough," I said.

Josh ambled over, and Piper kissed him hello, too. "I hear you're moving back," she said conspiratorially.

He smiled at her. "Good news travels fast."

"I hope you don't mind that I told Hadley and Piper," I said to him.

"You know I don't."

"Good. And while we're on the subject," I said, looking over my head, "I happen to know of a place that's up for rent. Best deal in Brooklyn, in fact." This had occurred to me just an hour earlier as I was cleaning the apartment in preparation to have everyone over.

"What?" said Piper, opening her eyes even wider than usual.

"Laine, you're a genius," said Josh. "That would be perfect."

"That's your title—but it is a pretty good idea if I say so myself," I said.

He started running a hand through his hair repeatedly, like he sometimes did when he was on the verge of a breakthrough. "Actually, I'll make it even better. What if I kept an eye on Mom? I'd be here every night, and I could be around if she needed anything during the day."

I pulled my head back. "Whoa—that's a pretty big offer. Are you sure?"

"I know it is. And yes, I'm sure. There might come a time when it doesn't work anymore. But let me do this thing for you all, Laine," he said. He leaned in and said, so only I could hear, "I can handle it. Really. It's the least I can do for your family. Our family," he corrected himself.

"Did I just hear something about Josh moving in upstairs?" said Hadley, who was all smiles.

"Yep," said Josh.

"I'll let you two discuss," I said, looping my arm through Piper's so I could pull her toward the kitchen.

"What's going on, Laine?" she said. "Please tell me it's not bad news."

"Not at all," I said. "You'll probably think I'm crazy, but I think you and Josh might end up spending more time together now that he's moving here."

She looked aghast. "Laine!"

"Listen, I know this is weird for me to say. I just wanted you to know that if you two stay close . . . I'm okay with it."

Piper hesitated, then leaned forward and wrapped me in her bony arms. "You're so weird sometimes," she said. "But thank you."

Before I had a chance to respond, my mother was hollering for us to join her in the living room.

"You're all here!" she exclaimed. She was holding Joy in her arms, and I was tempted to tell her to be careful, maybe even take the kitten from her. But then I remembered that she, of all people, knew what to do with a cat. And when she was having a good moment, like she was now, my only job was to let her enjoy it.

"What's going on, Mom?" asked Hadley.

"Please, sit," said my mother. She was in front of the fireplace, and she waved her hand at the rest of the living room. "As you can see, Laine's been working a miracle here."

I had been, actually, but the real marvel was that my mother hadn't immediately undone my efforts. Josh and Piper sat on the love seat, and Hadley and Topper took the sofa. I started for the armchair in the corner, but Hadley patted the space between her and the armrest, so I sat down beside her.

"What a treat. All of my daughters in one place. And my sons," she said, smiling at Josh and Topper. "All of my children in one place."

I glanced at Hadley, who was looking at me quizzically, then at Piper, who was frowning. What was going on?

"So, there's no easy way to say this," said my mother. She was still standing in front of us, and she didn't seem nervous in the least. "Laine and I had a talk the other day . . ."

She looked at me, almost as if for reassurance. When I nodded, she continued.

"There's something that all of you need to know." She took a deep breath, then said, "As you may have already suspected, I have Alzheimer's disease."

Hadley drew in her breath sharply. "Are you sure?"

"Mom, you haven't been to the doctor," said Piper. "You don't know just yet."

"Piper, Hadley," she said, looking at them. "I'm very sorry—as Laine recently learned, there's something I've been keeping from you. Your Nana Meyers didn't have Parkinson's disease; she had Alzheimer's. She felt ashamed and never wanted anyone to know, and so I kept her secret for her, because I felt that's what good daughters did for their mothers. But as your sister pointed out, that's not really fair to the three of you to lie about something like that, especially when it might affect you one day. I don't know all of the details, but I have to assume that having both a mother and a grandmother with memory loss means something for you girls," she said, smoothing out an invisible wrinkle in the front of her dress. "I owe you the truth."

Hadley reached for my hand. "Thank you, Mom," she said softly. "I'm so sorry."

"No, I am. But it's going to be okay," said my mother. She looked at me again. "And, Laine, that's true even though you won't be living here with me."

Piper and Hadley both looked at me, and I nodded at them, confirming that I'd told my mother.

My mother's voice quavered as she continued, "Together, we can work something out . . . something that keeps me safe. And when that doesn't work anymore, we'll find a place where I can get the care I need. Girls, I've given Laine power of attorney, but I trust you to work together to find a solution when it comes to that. All three of you will share medical power of attorney."

I wanted to thank her, like Hadley just had, but I couldn't speak. My mother had often told us she loved us over the years, and, of course, I'd always believed her. But this was a different sort of declaration of her love for us.

Piper's eyes were wet with tears, but Josh had just grabbed a tissue box from the bookshelf, and she took one and squeezed his forearm quickly. Then he spoke. "I've been thinking about making a change, too—a big one. Laine suggested I rent the upstairs apartment, and I've decided I'd like to. If you'll let me, Sally," he said, looking at my mother. "I can help you out, make sure that you're safe and have what you need."

"Joshy, you'd do that for me?" she said, fanning herself in an attempt not to cry.

He nodded. "I know things are a little different than they used to be, with Laine and me getting divorced, but you all are my family. Sally, I don't know if this will work out for us both, but I'm willing to give it a try."

"I would love that," she said, dabbing at her eyes. "Thank you, Josh. But, Laine . . ." she said, looking at me.

"I'm good with it, Mom," I said. "Josh will always be one of us—he's an honorary Francis for life. And I'm going to stay through the beginning of July to help him get everything set up. I'll be visiting a lot more often. And I'm going to help in other ways. But . . ." I glanced at Hadley, whose bottom lip was quivering. And Piper, who was dabbing at her eyes with her wrist. "Then I'll need to go."

"It's okay," said my mother, but when I put my arms around her, she started to cry. "It's just been so lovely, Lainey, having you here."

"I know." I wondered if she remembered our fight, and decided it didn't really matter. "I can't pretend it'll be the same if I'm just visiting. I'm sorry."

Then I let her cry. My decision brought her pain, and my sisters, too. I'd made things harder for them, at least in the short term.

But I was beginning to understand that the goal wasn't always to make things simple and painless. Sometimes embracing the pain, and yes, the mess, was what it took to get to where you really wanted to be.

~

Finding solutions had put everyone in a celebratory mood, and my sisters had just opened a second bottle of wine when I excused myself to go to Ben's. He and I had made plans to get together before my mother had asked me to have everyone over, and although I'd briefly considered rescheduling, I'd ultimately decided that I could do both things. After all, my mother was surrounded by her family, and although Josh had done a double-take when I told him that I was heading to Ben's, he quickly recovered and promised to keep an eye on her and call me if she started slipping into "sundowning," as the ER doctor had referred to her evening confusion.

Ben buzzed me in, and as I stepped into his apartment, I thought about how even with the white walls and the muted tones and the clean decor, the apartment still felt as familiar, as safe and welcoming, as it had to me when we were children.

"I love it here," I told Ben as I slipped off my sandals and wandered into the living room. "Always have. I hope you keep the place."

"I like that you like it," he said, looking around like he was seeing it for the first time. "I plan to hold on to it, even if my travels take me west," he said with a wink. "Speaking of which, how did it go?"

I broke into a smile. "Really well," I said, then caught him up on what had happened.

He was grinning so widely by the time I was done that you'd think I'd just solved world hunger. "And *that* is how you do it."

"I guess it is," I said, grinning back at him.

"I'm proud of you."

"Thank you. I am, too."

"Hey, Laine?"

"Yeah?" I said, pausing near the doorway between the living room and the kitchen.

He walked over to me and put his arms around my waist. I felt my breath quicken at his touch.

"Do you remember the first day we met?" he said.

"I do. But you tell me your version."

"Okay. So . . . I'm leaning against the fence and thinking about how much I hated this neighborhood and our new apartment and basically life in general," he began. "In fact, I'm sulking my face off when suddenly I see this girl in the distance, and she waves to me."

"No—you waved to *me*," I said.

"That's your version." He winked. "And I think she doesn't want to play with me, but I think to myself, *What the heck, Ben? You've got nothing to lose.* So, I walk over to her, because it's not every day a cute girl you've never met before talks to you like you're already friends. And I stand in front of her, and she looks at me with these big brown eyes."

I swear I could hear his heart thumping against his chest. Or maybe it was my own; it was impossible to tell the difference. "Go on," I said.

"So, I ask her if she wants to be friends. But what I'm really thinking is, *But only say yes if it's for the rest of our lives.*"

My pulse quickened.

"So what do you think?" he asked, pulling me closer. "I want it to be only ever us again, Laine. Do you?"

"Yes." I couldn't help it; a tear escaped, then another. But they were the most joyful tears I'd ever shed, and I didn't bother wiping them away. "Only ever us," I whispered. And then I did what I'd been thinking about doing for, oh, several decades, and planted my lips on his.

I hadn't kissed anyone other than Josh since the early aughts, so even though I technically *had* kissed Ben before, it was still kind of weird. His lips were not chapped and basically nothing like Josh's, and although my entire body was humming with desire, I didn't really know what to do with myself. Where did my hands go? What did one do with a tongue, exactly, when it came upon another tongue? I felt like I was thirteen again and not in full possession of my person.

"Laine," he said.

"Sorry," I said, though I wasn't sure if I was apologizing for kissing him or for not being great at it or for being so stupid as to have waited so long for him. All of it, I supposed.

"You should be saying *you're welcome* right now—not apologizing." He inhaled, and I thought maybe he was trying to center himself or something. Then he said, "You smell exactly the way I remember."

"And how's that?"

"I don't know," he said, shaking his head. "Just . . . really good. Like the best parts of my life."

"You do, too," I confessed. "Ben?"

"Yeah?"

It was a risk to say it aloud. But I was done playing it safe. "I love you. I always have."

"I love you, too," he said. His brown eyes held mine. "I thought it'd go away, but it never did—not even after I put years and thousands of miles between us."

I laughed with delight because the only other option was to explode with happiness. He loved me. Ben Walker loved me.

"When I saw you on Smith Street—I felt like I was a kid again and my favorite person had just appeared," he said.

"I know," I confessed. "I couldn't quite admit that to myself, but I felt that, too. Since you've been back in my life, things have been completely upside down . . . and I've never been happier."

"Me, too." And then he kissed me.

This time, it wasn't awkward, and I didn't feel strange or sorry or weird. His lips were on mine and his body was taut against my torso as he ran his hands down my back and kissed me again and again.

And it was like . . .

Well, it was like I'd been gone for a very long time, and I'd finally come home.

THIRTY-EIGHT

Sally

Six Months Later

Everyone's here—what a treat! Hadley and Topper and Ainsley and Asher. Laine and Josh. No, Piper and Josh—that's right—and Kai and Jae and Rocco. And Laine and Ben, in from Michigan. What a beautiful couple they make! The two of them light up a room when they're together.

And Reggie, my Reggie. There he was, walking across the room toward me, stirring up butterflies in my stomach. Ben brought him to dinner one night right before he and Laine moved—of course I said yes when they asked if they could—and Reggie hasn't left my side since. How funny, this family's musical chairs! First Ben moved to Ann Arbor with Laine, then Reggie moved back into his old place, just three doors down, so he could spend more time with me and help me with Joy. That was . . . two seasons ago now. And here I still get all fluttery when he's around. It's a feeling that makes me feel deeply alive, and I can think of few things better than that. What a surprise, what a delight, to be reunited with him after all this time.

In the dining room, Piper's three were clearing the table, and what a lot of dishes they had to move. But weren't the holidays already over? My eyes landed on the credenza, where a colorful stack of presents waited to be opened. Then I remembered. They were here for me. Seventy-three—a nice long life. But as Reggie put his arm around me, I could've been forty all over again, with all of the pleasure and none of the angst.

"Happy birthday, Sally," he said. "Are you having a good evening?"

It was barely evening; they'd started early for me, as I did better then. The nights had gotten harder, just as the doctor said they would. Some afternoons weren't much easier.

"Reggie," I said, nestling into his side, "I'm having the best evening I've had since the last time we were all together."

"Happy birthday, Mom!" announced Hadley. She'd just walked into the living room carrying a cake. It wasn't just the candles that were making her glow. The twins were a year old now, and just as I'd assured her, life had gotten easier as they grew. It would get harder again, yes, but in different ways. And then one day, she'd blink, and her children would have children of their own.

Piper was hovering just behind Laine, probably making sure she didn't need anything. Maybe it's Josh, or maybe it's her sister's condition, but Piper's been at her best these days. As for Laine, she was just barely showing—but a mother always knows. I'd asked her a while ago, the last time they were in town, if my suspicions were correct. She'd joyfully confessed that, yes, she and Ben were expecting, and due late in the spring. I don't need to see her with my new grandbaby to know how lucky they'll be. Why, anyone who'd seen Laine with that beloved dog of hers would agree: she's already the most wonderful mother.

They were singing to me now. *Happy birthday, dear Sally. Happy birthday to you.*

One of the children had put Joy on my lap, but she jumped down as I blew my candles out. There must have been dozens of them! As I took them all in, a memory rose to the surface of my mind like a balloon floating in the sky.

"Laine," I said. She was on the other side of the cake, watching me. "Do you remember the time you and Ben made me a birthday cake, and it was just beautiful, but you'd gotten the sugar and the salt mixed up?"

She laughed—what a lovely woman she was, my Laine—and I could tell she was happy I'd remembered. "And you insisted on eating the whole slice, smiling right through it."

"Yes, I did." I was smiling again now just thinking about it. "Write that one down for me, yes? So I can remember."

"Definitely." She stood, and I thought maybe she'd go find one of our notebooks, but instead, she came over to me. "I love you, Mom," she said as she hugged me.

"Oh, I love you, too, dear girl," I whispered to her. "Don't you ever forget that."

It's a terrifying thing, to lose your mind, even if you know that one day you won't be aware it's happening anymore. And then you'll just be . . . gone.

But as I looked around my home, my fear faded just as quickly as it had come on. There was Hadley, my gentle warrior. Piper, whose true beauty was really within. And Laine, with her generous heart. They would be with me all the way down this dark path. To go through this life and know you're not ever truly alone—this was why a woman had children. My mother was right. Three girls: what an incredible gift.

I was loved.

AUTHOR'S NOTE

This novel was inspired by my family's experience with dementia and caregiving. As with my previous novels, I also consulted physicians and reviewed research on the topic while writing this story. Even so, *Everything Must Go* is very much a work of fiction and should not be used for reference purposes.

P.S. If you enjoyed *Everything Must Go*, please take a second to write a brief review; reviews make a world of difference in a book's success. If you already did, thank you! Either way, thank you for taking the time to read my latest. You, dear reader, are why I write.

ACKNOWLEDGMENTS

My deep gratitude to Jodi Warshaw, Danielle Marshall, Mikyla Bruder, Gabriella Dumpit, and the entire team at Lake Union Publishing; it's truly a pleasure to work with you. Tiffany Yates Martin, thank you (yet again!) for your editorial guidance. Elisabeth Weed, you continue to be the absolute best. Kathleen Carter, Lucy Silag, and Suzy Leopold, thank you for helping my novels find their way to readers. Michelle Weiner and the entire team at CAA, I so appreciate your championing my work.

Writing this novel reminded me of how lucky I am to have two amazing sisters who also happen to be my closest friends. Laurel Lambert and Janette Sunadhar, thank you for always being there for me.

Lauren Bauser, Jamie Berman, Shannon Callahan, Danielle King Colby, Stefanie and Craig Galban, Katie Rose Guest Pryal, Kelly Harms, Jacob Lambert, Joe Lambert, Nicole Perrin, Stevany and Tim Peters, Alex Ralph, Sara Reistad-Long, Matt Sampson, Jane Stinson, Michelle and Mike Stone, Pam Sullivan, Suman Sunadhar, and Darci Swisher: your encouragement keeps me going.

A big shout-out to Shannon Apostle, Annie Cathryn, Heather Gaglio, Marisa Gothie, Pam Harton, Jamie Iannuzzelli, Michelle Jocson, Amy Lehmann Sklare, Annie McDonnell, Sondra Mims,

Christina Powers, and Nikki Wilhelm for being such incredibly supportive readers.

JP, Indira, and Xavi Pagán, your love means the world to me.

This story is dedicated to one of the dearest friends of my youth, Rachael Brönsink Stiles, whose light still shines bright over all who knew her.

ABOUT THE AUTHOR

Photo © 2017 Myra Klarman

Camille Pagán is the #1 Amazon Charts and *Washington Post* bestselling author of eight novels, including *Don't Make Me Turn This Life Around*, *This Won't End Well*, *I'm Fine and Neither Are You*, *Woman Last Seen in Her Thirties*, and *Life and Other Near-Death Experiences*, which has been optioned for film. Her work has also been published in the *New York Times*; *O, The Oprah Magazine*; *Real Simple*; *Time*; and many others. When Camille's not writing her next story, you'll usually find her with her family, talking shop with other writers, or at the beach—with a book in hand, of course. To learn more about her work, visit www.camillepagan.com.